PROVING A VILLAIN

A KIM BRADY NOVEL

A NOVEL BY
EDWARD J. LEAHY

Black Rose Writing | Texas

The author grants the final approval for this literary material.

First printing

This is a work of fiction. Names, characters, businesses, places, events, and incidents are either the products of the author's imagination or used in a fictitious manner. Any resemblance to actual persons, living or dead, or actual events is purely coincidental.

ISBN: 978-1-68513-036-7
PUBLISHED BY BLACK ROSE WRITING
www.blackrosewriting.com

Printed in the United States of America
Suggested Retail Price (SRP) $22.95

Proving a Villain is printed in Baskerville

*As a planet-friendly publisher, Black Rose Writing does its best to eliminate unnecessary waste to reduce paper usage and energy costs, while never compromising the reading experience. As a result, the final word count vs. page count may not meet common expectations.

PRAISE FOR
PROVING
A
VILLAIN
A KIM BRADY NOVEL

"Edward J. Leahy has done it again. The third book in his sprawling, swiftly moving police procedural series pits Brooklyn North Homicide Det. Kim Brady against a serial killer whose reign of terror spans more than five decades. Against a backdrop of divisive city politics and escalating racial tension, a very human drama unfolds. As Leahy's characters confront life-altering choices, the stakes for Kim have never been higher. This is a gripping, richly textured novel with fully realized characters we both love to hate and care deeply about."
– Debbie Babitt, author of *First Victim*

"With steady action and great characters, this novel is impossible to put down; another winner from Edward Leahy."
– A.J. McCarthy, award-winning mystery suspense author.

ALSO BY EDWARD J. LEAHY:

Past Grief

Deceived By Ornament

PROVING
A
VILLAIN

"And therefore since I cannot prove a lover
To entertain these fair well-spoken days
I am determined to prove a villain."
–Richard Gloucester in *King Richard III*, Act 1, Scene 1

CHAPTER ONE

As he lurked in the shadows of the gutted Domino Sugar processing plant, he listened with care to the youthful voices nearby on this foggy October evening. The new park on the other side of River Street was already a magnet for teens eager to explore new pleasures, and the voices and the scent of cannabis drifting on the gentle breeze held the promise of an old pleasure of his own.

He'd seen the older boy and younger girl arrive with a group, listened as the boy enticed her to try it, to join with the others. In an instant, he'd known how it would turn out. Fog rolled in, bringing a light mist with it, and the group withdrew.

But the boy and girl stayed behind.

He let the group pass before moving a little closer to the couple, now entwined on a bench facing the river.

He lurked in the shadows, cosseted by the fog.

The boy was moving too quickly.

Excellent.

"No." Her voice. A plea. "Please don't."

"Aw, come on, Lulu. You want to."

"You don't understand."

He edged a little closer, understanding perfectly. The boy was high, and he wasn't listening. But her voice was strident. She would not give in to him.

No one else in the park. Who'd want to sit by the river in the fog?

A slap. And by the sound of it, a hard one. "That hurt, Rey."

He shrank back in the shadows as the boy strode past him and turned onto the pathway that led to South Third Street. He waited for the girl to follow, but she didn't.

She'd need comforting.

He ambled across River Street into the park, searching for anyone else present and finding no one. There she was, only fourteen or fifteen, sitting on a bench facing the East River, staring at the Williamsburg Bridge, the headlights from traffic glowing in the fog and mist. He didn't lower the hood on his sweatshirt until he was almost upon her, just in case.

"Dear child, you shouldn't be here alone at night. You might… good heavens, what's the matter?"

She turned her tear-stained face toward him, ready to trust.

Perfect.

CHAPTER TWO

Seven Months Later, Wednesday, May 16, 7:42 AM
Detective Kim Brady had just paid for her coffee and bagel at the Firehouse Deli and Grill on Wilson Avenue in Brooklyn. An officer who worked at Patrol Borough Brooklyn North—PBBN in police shorthand—rushed in to tell her, "Your lieutenant wants to see you five minutes ago."

"Did he say what the problem is?" Although she'd only been assigned to Brooklyn North Homicide six weeks earlier, she'd already figured out that her lieutenant summoned no one unless there was a problem.

The officer nodded toward the television over the counter, which was blaring the morning's headline about a radical group called Come Home Ernesto charging the police with covering up an old murder case. "He didn't say, but I'd guess that may have something to do with it. Nolan's waiting with him."

She had once wrongly accused Detective Bob Nolan of obstructing an investigation of a mass murder while he was working in Narcotics. Nolan had admitted to violating department procedures while providing evidence pointing to the mastermind of the murders. They had transferred him out of Narcotics to Brooklyn North Homicide. Kim had been reunited with him on a murder case that had led to a terrorist ring, after which she had been transferred from a plum assignment in Internal Affairs to Brooklyn North. Now they were partners.

They crossed DeKalb Avenue at a brisk pace. The corner building's distinctive tower resembling a battlement caught her eye. It, and the roofline of PBBN's headquarters, made "the Castle" the obvious nickname for the home of her new unit.

Lieutenant Adam Bostwick was certain to be pissed. Anytime someone charged the police with any kind of failure, the entire department took offense, including Kim. The case in question, involving the rape and murder of a fourteen-year-old girl the previous October, had occurred in PBBN's jurisdiction.

Bob nodded a silent greeting with just the slightest hint of a smirk as she entered Bostwick's office. He'd been an outcast in Brooklyn North until their recent case together had helped resuscitate his reputation. He'd become a good friend since her transfer.

"Nice of you to join us, Brady." Bostwick, a former Marine who maintained his blondish hair in a flat top, kept his desk tidy enough to pass the most rigorous inspection, unlike Kim's previous lieutenants. "You've heard the morning's headline. I got a call at six this morning from the Chief of Detectives. He wants us to dig out the case file on the Lourdes Ramirez murder and take a fresh look at it." The case in the news. "I want you two on the case. We had a promising suspect, a boyfriend she'd met at the scene. He admitted they had a spat not long before she was killed. Sounded like a great lead to me. Kind of ironic if after all this nonsense about a coverup it turns out one of their own offed her."

"Why did the case go cold?" The question had been nagging Kim since she'd first seen the news story.

Bostwick studied her, as if sizing up a suspect. "That's neither here nor there. See what you have in the file, find what you need to put the killer away. Bob, you'll lead. If you need anything, ask."

***

Bob's desk adjoined hers in the bullpen. "Sorry about that, Kim."

She managed a weak smile. "Not your fault. Besides, you're senior. But I'm not some new kid fresh from the Academy. I've led two major investigations in the last eighteen months, both in headline cases."

He grinned at her. "Times that try the soul." Despite the impression created by his usual rumpled look, he'd been sober for a year since his fall off the wagon.

She pulled up the case file and spent the next half hour combing through it. "Lourdes Ramirez, Lulu to all who knew her, fourteen, found dead on October 4th last year. Cause of death was a massive brain trauma, and the killer left a deep bite mark on her right shoulder." That was an odd twist. "They found her body at Domino Park."

"Facing the East River. The old plant is a huge redevelopment project."

"A jogger found her around 6:30 the morning of the fifth. The medical examiner estimated the time of death around 9:30 the night before."

Bob put down his coffee cup. The killer left her in the park. Isn't it mostly open?"

"Yeah. Tox screen indicated trace amounts of marijuana. Indications of rape, DNA evidence recovered." She brought up the lab report. "Whoa. DNA evidence of two different individuals, neither of whom were in our system."

"There were two attackers?"

Kim read further. "Probably not. One sample was from the rape kit. But she had traces of saliva around her face and neck." She copied details and names into her Notes App.

"Sounds like a make-out session."

"Possibly." She read through the remaining case notes, then checked to see who had created the file. The bottom dropped out of her stomach. Not again. "Bob, let's go check out the scene of the crime."

CHAPTER THREE

Wednesday, May 16, 9:03 AM

"… A police spokesperson denied charges that the department had prematurely closed the case of last October's murder of a Brooklyn teen, affirming that the case had not gone cold, and that the investigation was ongoing. There are no additional details."

Kim turned off the car radio. "That'll help. Thanks, Mr. Commissioner."

"Sort of like a thirty-second timeout in basketball," Bob said. "Long enough for a prayer, but not long enough to do anything meaningful."

"At least in hoops it gives you a chance to stop the clock and inbound the ball at mid-court." She made the turn from Grand Street onto River Street. "Were you aware the detective originally assigned to this case was Larry Grant?" The same detective who'd first caught a murder case that had fallen to Bob when Grant had retired. It had later morphed into Kim's terrorist case.

Bob's silence suggested that he didn't like it any more than she did. "Yeah, I saw that when I was reading through the file at the same time you were."

"I'd consider that an important fact, wouldn't you?" She parked the car across from the gutted plant, now a construction site, and they got out and walked over to a structure that looked like a series of giant steps, where a line of benches faced the river. "Fibers from Lulu's clothing were found on this bench, and the boyfriend's statement identified it as where they sat."

She turned away from the structure and walked toward the Williamsburg Bridge. She came to a square of shrubs and saplings surrounding four tall, ancient storage tanks. "Right there, in that space between the two tanks nearest the river, is where they found her body."

"Out in the open. And didn't worry about leaving DNA evidence."

Good. Bob was on the same wavelength. "Why do I always catch cases where the killer fucks with us?"

"'Cause you have a talent for solving them?"

She started walking along River Street toward the bridge. "The Crime Scene Unit also found maroon fibers on Lulu's clothing. Grant found private security video from the camera on that construction trailer of someone wearing a maroon hoodie walking this way at 9:42. Video cameras at several points along South Fifth Street caught the same guy until he turned left on Driggs Avenue."

They followed the same route. Once on Driggs, Bob pointed to a bus stop in the middle of the block. "A video camera on that house caught the kid getting onto the B62 bus at 9:47. Grant interviewed the bus driver, who only remembered someone getting on here and getting off at one of the stops at Metro-Tech."

"So, could be Jay Street and Tillary, or Jay and Willoughby. Which means he could have entered the station from any of the entrances," Bob said.

"Right. But Grant examined video from every camera in the station and never saw a kid in a hoodie." She stared at the house.

Bob followed her gaze. "What?"

She didn't break her gaze. "There are two cameras mounted. One should have caught his face."

"They're fixed-focus. He probably turned his face away."

Right. She returned to the car. Time to bring up the eight-hundred-pound gorilla in the room. "Why wouldn't Bostwick tell us this had been Grant's case?"

"That's been bugging me, too. The timing sucks. This was the case he was working on when he caught the Simmons case."

The first of five murders connected with the terror plot. Bostwick had told Bob to let it go cold, after Grant had retired and then died a few weeks later. "Why did Bostwick dump the Simmons case on Grant while he was neck deep in this one?"

Bob shook his head. "Beats me. It screwed up both cases. At least we solved Simmons."

No wonder Bostwick was so frosty. "Which made the lieu look bad. Makes me wonder if catching this case is an invitation to fail."

Bob fell silent until they reached the car. "So, where the hell do we turn now?"

"Larry Grant was a good cop, and he was on to something. We retrace his steps, starting with the boyfriend."

***

Reinaldo Torres was a senior at James J. Walker High School. The principal was cooperative, pulling Torres out of class and allowing them to question him in her office. Grant had looked long and hard at Torres, Bostwick's only suspect, but hadn't liked him for the murder. Nothing in the file even hinted why.

"Reinaldo," Kim began.

At five-seven and thin, Torres was anything but menacing. A handsome boy with a pleasant face, his manner when meeting Kim and Bob was respectful. "My friends call me Rey, ma'am."

"Okay. Rey, what was your relationship with Lulu like?"

"She was my lady. We liked each other a lot."

"Did she ever make you angry?"

"No. And I wasn't angry that night."

"But you fought."

He heaved an enormous sigh. "We argued. We went to the park and made out."

"Before or after you sparked the blunt?" Bob asked.

Rey rolled his eyes. "Yeah, okay, after."

"Did you always smoke weed with Lulu?" Kim asked.

"No, that was the only time. When I met her that night, she seemed tense, so I offered it to her to help her relax. She didn't like it much, so we stopped, and I kissed her instead."

"How far did you get?" Kim asked.

Rey blushed. "Not very. We frenched a lot, and I kissed her neck…"

Bob interrupted. "And nibbled it a little?"

Rey screwed up his face. "No, man, I don't do weird shit. And besides, I really liked Lulu a lot. She was a sweet girl."

Kim took back the lead. "So, from her neck, you headed, um, a little further south?"

Another blush. "Yeah. And that's what caused the problem."

"Too much too fast?"

"No. I knew she liked it. Only this time, she pushed me away and told me to stop. She said it hurt. I couldn't understand what the problem was, but when I asked, she got super mad. So, I walked away."

"And left her there alone?" Bob asked.

No, Bob, wrong thing to say. "When you walked away, which way did you go? Retrace your steps for me."

"We were sitting facing the river, right by the big steps. I walked back toward the street and along the path leading to South Third Street. I live on Third, between Havemayer and the Expressway."

No wonder Grant didn't like him for the murder. Unless he'd taken a long way home. With luck, Grant had kept a copy of the video in the evidence file. "And what were you wearing that night?"

"A Mets tee-shirt."

"Describe it for me." She made an entry in her app.

"All blue, with 'Mets' in orange across the front."

One more thing. "Rey, you can help us to rule you out as a suspect. Someone left saliva on Lulu's neck. You kissed her there, so it is probably yours. We found other DNA evidence on her, different DNA." A water cooler stood in the corner. She filled a paper cup halfway. "If you drink this water, you'll leave your saliva on the rim, and we can use that to get a DNA analysis. If what you've told me is true—and I believe it is—then this sample will match what we found on Lulu's neck and not the other DNA."

The principal intervened. "Rey, I think you should consult with a lawyer first."

Kim turned to the principal. "If I were in your position, I'd probably advise the same thing, and it's his right. But Rey knows the truth of what happened that night." Back to Rey. "This will permanently clear you as a suspect. Ironclad."

He took the cup. "Okay."

"Great. Now, did you have any rivals for Lulu's affections? Anyone else who liked her?"

Rey considered it. "I don't think so. She was too young for most of my friends. But you should ask Martha Perez. She might know. She was Lulu's best friend."

CHAPTER FOUR

Wednesday, May 16, 9:56 AM

Kim suggested Bob return to South Third Street to see how many buildings had video cameras between the old Domino plant and Rey's building, and how many still had video files from last September. In the meantime, she would stay at the school and interview Martha Perez.

Martha entered the principal's office looking nervous. A year older than Lulu, she looked like a J-Lo wannabe.

Kim introduced herself and explained why she was there.

Martha immediately lost her swagger. "Lulu was like a sister to me. We been friends since grade school."

"I take it you're popular with the boys?"

"Well, yeah."

"Was Lulu?"

"She only had eyes for Rey. It was so cool when they hooked up. Like love at first sight."

"Was anyone else interested in her?"

"Rey took some shit about hanging with her because she had, like, this total innocence thing. There mighta been some younger guys had a thing for her, but they never woulda tried nothin' because Rey would've pounded 'em."

"So, she never talked about attention from another boy? Even to laugh at it?"

Martha shook her head. "No way. And I never saw anyone, like, staring at her, you know, with that look guys get?"

"You mean when they're hot for a girl? Yeah. One last question. To your knowledge, was Lulu ever intimate with Rey?"

"Funny you should ask. She told me he wanted to, and that she kinda liked the idea. In fact, the day she… you know… we had talked about it. He had asked her to meet him that night at the park, and she realized he'd want to make out."

"But she didn't want to?" Kim wondered about the water cup in the evidence bag.

"That's just it. She usually loved making out, but she'd gotten her period that morning, and to make it worse, she had terrible cramps and felt shitty."

Which explained why she shrank back when he touched her breast. "So, why did she keep the date?"

Martha shrugged. "She loved him. She didn't want to hurt his feelings."

"Okay, thanks. If I have questions, I'll reach out to you." Grant hadn't mentioned Lulu menstruating in the file. Maybe he just never got around to it.

"One last question, Martha. To your knowledge, did Lulu smoke weed?"

"Once or twice. She didn't like it."

***

Kim didn't have to wait long in front of the school for Bob to return. She slid into the front seat. "You go first."

"I only found one place on South Third with video surveillance." He nodded to an evidence bag between their two seats. "Villain, a music venue, is right on the corner of Kent. Their camera caught our boy walking by at 9:12 on the night in question. Clear image, no question it's him, complete with a blue Mets tee shirt."

"But…?"

12

"I'd feel a lot better about it if we had an image of him passing another point closer to home. But there wasn't another building with video surveillance along his route."

"Any shot of him doubling back later?"

"No. Then again, that doesn't mean he didn't double back along another route."

"But the timeline, Bob. He would have had to sprint back." She patted her own evidence bag with the water cup. "The DNA will tell the tale." She recapped her interview with Martha.

"Sounds like this Lulu was a sweet kid." He started the car and headed for the Castle. "She didn't like to smoke, but her tox screen showed trace amounts of cannabis. Sounds like he might have pressured her. Which makes me think he could have done it, shirt or no shirt."

CHAPTER FIVE

Wednesday, May 16, 10:15 AM

Every time State Senator Raymond Brandt visited his patron, he all but panted with envy at the comely young assistant who showed him into the office. A good forty years younger than her boss, Brandt knew she did much more than secretarial work. As they entered, he wondered if he'd be greeted with "Good morning, Senator", which would be a good omen, or "Come in," which would portend a problem.

"Come in, Senator." Kyle Emory, the CEO of Emory Equities, sat up straight behind his antique desk, his white shirt crisp, his tie perfectly placed at his neck. He waited until his secretary had closed the door. "What's this about a police coverup?"

"The looney left at it again. They won't be happy until the hammer and sickle flies over city hall."

"Spare me the rhetoric. The group making the noise, Come Home Ernesto. They were behind the riots two months ago that were tied up with that murder case."

"Yes." The case Brandt had tried to forget. Five murders, including a Latino immigration lawyer; a kidnapping; and a plot to firebomb a church. The case had nearly cratered by the actions of Emory's secretary's brother, whom Emory had ordered Brandt to have placed in the Internal Affairs unit investigating the murders.

"I think you should see something I recorded this morning. Felipe Prinz, the leader of Come Home Ernesto." Emory pressed a button on his desk, and the sixty-five-inch screen on the wall sprang to life. Another button, and the recording played.

"It's time we recognize that what many in this city call 'gentrification' is nothing short of internal imperialism, a concerted effort to force Latinos out of the neighborhoods that have been their homes for generations. And there can be no better example than those here in Williamsburg, whose grandparents fled their homes in Puerto Rico because of poverty wrought by unchecked capitalism, and who now are forced out by the rising rents and prices from gentrification. So, let's call it what it really is: ethnic cleansing by economic means. Walk-ups are replaced by hi-rises, bodegas by boutiques, factories that once provided employment for our people by office buildings, and social clubs by hipster concert venues. And when our people still don't take the hint and 'go back to where they came from', why not drag out the old trope of how crime-ridden we are with the murder of a Latina schoolgirl?"

Emory pressed a button, and the screen went dark. "Pure Marxism."

Brandt shifted in his seat. "Lenin. He said imperialism was the final stage of capitalism."

Emory scowled. "Which side are you on?"

"I find it best to understand who and what I'm up against. Prinz is more a problem for you than for me, so I'd suggest you understand where he's coming from."

"He's a communist."

Brandt nodded. "I recall when the sons of wealthy capitalists studied the writings of Marx, so they'd understand what to avoid. Their fathers decided that resulted in too many uncomfortable questions and put an end to the practice. Amazing what targeted donations to universities can do. But your expression tells me you understand the problem. You just don't grasp the solution."

"You fascinate me, Senator. Please elaborate."

Brandt relaxed a bit. "Prinz is stirring up local anger over the latest step in Williamsburg's gentrification, in which you have a considerable investment. He's also gained sympathy from several city politicians, including the acting mayor…"

"Sabrina Dunn, the former Public Advocate who's held the office less than a month following the mayor's resignation for health reasons, and whom you hope to defeat in the special election next month."

Brandt allowed himself a grin. He'd never heard Emory bark before. "Yes. Another effort in which you've made a significant investment. And until now, you've assumed that your funding gives you the power to dictate all my actions. But—not to put too fine a point on it—that didn't work out so well last time." He nodded toward the closed door leading to the outer office. "I realize—ahem, other considerations—may have affected your judgment. And she is lovely. But we need to be thinking with our heads, not another part of the anatomy."

Emory said nothing, and Brandt held his breath. He'd been waiting for this moment for a long time, the chance to regain control of his career.

"So," Emory said at last. "What do you propose?"

Bingo. "There are two opposing narratives about this girl's killing. The Prinz version is that police are trying to blame the killing on the boyfriend to promote the criminal stereotype, but that some capitalist dupe, almost certainly white, killed the girl. Your press friends' version is that the boyfriend really killed her. Only you haven't been able to get the cops to back it up."

Emory leaned forward, resting his arms on the desk. "And what's your version, Senator?"

Time to play his ace. "I don't have one. But if the department had enough evidence, they'd have collared the boyfriend months ago. Bostwick has put Nolan and Brady on the case."

"Brady. How the hell did she get into the picture?"

"After the disaster with your lovely secretary's brother, which also made me persona non grata over at One Police Plaza, the Internal Affairs Bureau did a little housecleaning. They transferred Brady to Brooklyn North Homicide, even though she still had more than a year left on her tour, and her captain in IAB retired."

"Brady and Nolan. A loose cannon and a drunk. That the best Bostwick could do?"

"Apparently. But Brady has made some enemies in the Brooklyn DA's office, so she'll have to do this one by the book, or she'll be running the Property Clerk's office. The best thing to do now is give the police department all the support we can. Assuming, of course, that Prinz is wrong about the motive behind the killing."

CHAPTER SIX

Wednesday, May 16, Noon

"A police spokesperson this morning reiterated that the department is doing all it can to solve the murder of a high school student in Williamsburg last September and assured the public that the investigation will go wherever the evidence leads. The commissioner has flatly denied that the department knows the identity of the killer. Felipe Prinz, leader of the group known as Come Home Ernesto, has accused the NYPD of covering up the murder, giving rise to fears that the group might stir up civil unrest."

***

Kim tried to ignore the TV set at the Castle as she packaged the cup with Rey Torres' saliva sample for shipment to the crime lab. It might take as long as four weeks to get the results. As she noted the shipment in the case file, the reference to the bite mark found on Lulu's shoulder caught her eye. She brought up the photo taken by the medical examiner's office.

It made her cringe. This wasn't a nibble. It was deep.

Bob came by. "Lunch?"

"No, I was just… Oh. Funny." She pointed to the photo. "That's a signature."

"A very sick signature."

"Not my point. Killers who leave signatures have usually killed before."

"Unless it's their first kill." Bostwick's voice from behind made her jump. "Let's talk." Which Kim had already learned was his version of, "In my office, now."

Kim put her laptop into sleep mode and followed Bob into Bostwick's office.

The lieu took command. "Bob, I don't want you two getting sidetracked on this case. What do we have on the boyfriend?"

Kim resisted the urge to answer the question. Bostwick was a member in good standing of the Old Boys' Club. She'd need to bide her time.

"We interviewed him this morning," Bob said. "Kim got him to volunteer a DNA sample." He turned to her. "Did you send that in, yet?"

Nice one, Bob. I owe you. "Yes, I did. I also re-interviewed Lulu's best friend, who gave me some background." She recapped the interview.

Bostwick scowled. "Proving what, exactly?"

Bob stepped in. "I'm not sure it proves anything, but it suggests that Lulu and her boyfriend were genuinely close. It's a reason to think he might not be the guy."

Bostwick's scowl deepened. "I don't see that."

Bob turned to Kim but said nothing. Her turn. "It's highly unlikely a boy would brutally rape a girl he loved and who loved him and then kill her." She described the bite mark.

"She was high, wasn't she?" Bostwick asked. "He probably was, too."

She didn't want to argue over every piece of evidence. "Not necessarily. Her tox screen showed only trace amounts."

"For her, not for him."

"Lieu," Bob said, "there are other factors, too." He explained about the Mets shirt being caught on camera.

Kim saw her moment. "I'm going to the property clerk's office to retrieve some items from the evidence file, the drives with the clips we got of the killer on Fifth Street wearing the maroon hoodie. I want to compare the timelines of the two. DNA analysis will rule Torres in or out on the rape. I also suggest we ask for a subpoena for Torres' dental records."

"What the fuck for? It's like you're starting this investigation all over again."

Bob intervened. "Sorry, Lieu, but isn't that the best way to handle this? We sure don't want to miss anything. The dental records will show if Torres left the bite mark."

"Okay, okay. Get on the horn to Rick Conti over at the DA's office and have him get on it."

***

While Bob returned to his desk to contact Assistant District Attorney Conti, Kim headed for the property clerk's office. She stopped at Millie's Cuban Café on Wilson for a quick lunch. As she sat at a table near the window, her thoughts turned to Conti, whom she'd last seen while testifying that the coerced confession obtained by an ill-prepared officer had not informed her actions in tracking down a murderer and terrorist. Conti had stood by and done nothing while the defendant's attorney had tried to drag Dad's misdeeds and suicide into the case. Bob had done her another solid by volunteering to contact him.

"Hi, there." The voice from behind belonged to Joanna Dunbar, a local TV news reporter and sometimes an ally of Kim's. "May I join you?"

"Hi, yourself. Sure." Kim had to chuckle. Joanna had a keen instinct for digging out big stories. She also knew when to break the unwritten rules. "What brings you to Brooklyn?"

"Same thing that brings you, Detective."

"The department transferred me here from IAB." Not that she held a grudge.

"Still pissed, huh? Can't say I blame you. But sometimes misfortune ends up playing in your favor. I heard a rumor you caught the new and improved Ramirez murder case. Can you make it stick on the boyfriend this time?"

Kim had to laugh. The walls had ears. "Yes, I'm on the Ramirez case, and we'll make it stick on whoever did it."

Joanna turned serious. "You don't believe the boyfriend did it. So, that Prinz guy might be right?"

Kim held up a hand. "Slow down, girl. First, I don't know who did it. We haven't ruled anyone in or out, yet."

"This is me, Kim. Don't hand me the DCPI party line." The Deputy Commissioner for Public Information was the official mouthpiece of the NYPD. "You doubt the boyfriend did it?"

"Innocent until proven guilty." A handy dodge that was true. Joanna's smile suggested she got it. Now, it was Kim's turn. "But, let's say, hypothetically, that the boyfriend didn't do it. Why would that mean Prinz was right? It was connected with gentrification?"

Joanna took a sip of her coffee. The pause suggested she had something big. "Ever hear of mortgage-backed securities?"

"Sure. Somebody forms an LLC—a limited liability company—that buys up a pool of mortgages, using the proceeds from sale of interests in the LLC, with different classes of payouts called tranches. Why?"

"Guess which local investment firm with whom we've both had some experience has a significant amount of its assets invested in them."

"Judging by the shit-eating grin on your face, I'd say Emory Equities. How significant?"

"Over a billion. And the largest is the Williamsburg Redevelopment Group, with six hundred million."

Kim made the connection. "So, the theory is that someone killed Lulu Ramirez as part of a plot to expedite an exodus of Latinos from Williamsburg? With Kyle Emory as the bad guy? Sorry, Joanna, that doesn't pass the laugh test."

"Makes you wonder, though."

First things first. "Right now, we need to learn who killed her. After that, I can start considering possible conspiracies. Or Bob can."

"Bob?"

"Detective Bob Nolan. He's lead on this case."

Joanna's face reddened. "Not you? Are they nuts?"

Kim shot her a grin. "Haven't you heard? I can't be trusted. I talk to the press." She stood to leave.

"Our usual deal?" Joanna asked, meaning she would keep her apprised of any information she uncovered while Kim would keep Joanna informed of the progress of the investigation on the condition Joanna wouldn't use it until Kim said so.

It had worked before. Joanna was an excellent ally to have. "Our usual deal."

CHAPTER SEVEN

Wednesday, May 16, 12:28 PM

He returned from his late morning walk, carrying the sausage and pepper hero he'd bought at Luliano's, his favorite local Italian eatery. Since childhood, he'd loved all Italian food, a preference that had pleased his mother, whose favorite child he had never ceased to be. That had enraged his older brother, who'd exacted his revenge in several ways.

He turned on the television in the kitchen as he sat down to eat, savoring each bite as he listened to the latest reports of the police flailing with utter ineffectiveness in their hunt for the vicious killer of the poor Puerto Rican girl.

Sweet little thing.

He finished his hero and sucked his teeth in satisfaction. The same teeth that had left their mark, just as with his first victim all those years ago. Another sweet little thing.

Seven months later, and not a single police officer had rung his bell or asked a question. They had no clues other than the ones he'd left. And he intended to keep it that way.

As he turned off the set, he experienced a sense of discomfort, the first stirrings of need. It was too soon—only seven months.

He'd need to decide what to do about that.

CHAPTER EIGHT

Wednesday, May 16, 3:52 PM

By the time Kim returned from the property clerk's office, it was almost end of tour for her and Bob. "We have an appointment at the video lab at One-PP at eight tomorrow morning. Let's meet here and take the subway in." It would save Bob the hassle of driving from Staten Island to Manhattan, where parking at One-PP was anything but assured.

"Yeah, thanks. In the meantime, Conti got the subpoena for Torres' dental records. With luck we might have them as early as tomorrow."

"Good. According to the file, Dr. Shelton handled Lulu's autopsy."

A grin made its way across Bob's face. "An old acquaintance."

Dr. Lloyd Shelton had been a tremendous help in the big murder case when she was at IAB. "Once we get the records, I'll take them to him for an opinion. Also, I'd like to talk to Phil Vitello." Sergeant Vitello was the best man the Brooklyn North Crime Scene Unit had.

"Another old acquaintance. Why him?"

"I want to be sure we've gotten everything CSU had from the night of the murder."

"Makes sense." Bob cast a wary glance toward Bostwick's office. It was empty. "Kim, I realize the lieu made me the lead on this investigation, but we're equal partners. He's always had a thing against women cops..."

"Ya think?"

"But he's what we have to work with. Let's let him have his fiction for the moment. If we need to confront him, we'll do it together. In the meantime, please tell me what's on your mind."

That was fair enough.

***

The NBA playoffs were well underway, and with the Brooklyn Nets out of it, Kim might have expected her husband, Jake, to be available for a relaxing evening. But she knew better. As the Nets' new Director of Analytics, he would camp in front of the TV most evenings watching players the team might want to acquire, making notes on which ones he should make a point of studying on the league's spatial tracking system.

"Wow," Jake said as she walked in. "Working a big case and still home for dinner."

Which he'd already made and for which he had the table set. She kissed him. "Don't get used to it. I think this might be a bad one."

"So, I gather." He gestured toward the TV.

Senator Brandt was on screen. "With the threat of civil unrest, and the inevitable rioting and looting that goes with it, I call upon the acting mayor to authorize a full deployment of the city's police force to protect lives and property around the city and particularly in Williamsburg, where a known terrorist group has threatened several projects that the city has approved, and which will make Williamsburg an even better place to live."

"Unless you're a Puerto Rican who already lives there," Jake said.

"Jake, please." She'd noticed lately that his political views were drifting further left. At least they could agree to disagree.

"Sorry, I forgot. I guess this teeters on the edge of your investigation."

"Bob's investigation." It was out before she could stop it.

"Bob? The guy you once accused of obstruction? He's leading, not you?"

"He's senior to me by nearly two decades." She didn't want to discuss it.

"So was Mike Resnick back at Manhattan South, but you were lead on that mass shooting case."

The Cove Case. That seemed like eons ago, now. "Special situation. He was going through a rough stretch and couldn't focus." She hoped her tone conveyed the subject was not to be opened.

"You were just back after your dad's death, and you still managed."

God damn it. "I don't want to discuss it."

He gave her the look, the one that said, "Gotcha. Now, you must."

Maybe he was right. "Bostwick has him leading, but Bob wants it to be more like we're sharing the lead."

"Which," Jake put in, "will work perfectly well until the first major disagreement."

She didn't answer.

He let the silence hang for a minute or two. "Okay, Kim. What aren't you telling me?"

"Bob won't be the problem. We agree on the basics of the case. Neither of us suspects the boyfriend. The problem is Bostwick does, and it's going to take a mountain of irrefutable evidence to change his mind."

"I take it he approves of gentrification?"

There was her central problem. "This case isn't about gentrification. That's a false narrative that the media and the pols and CHE are all trying to force on the public. It's a murder case. And a rape. Not just any rape, but one committed on a girl having her period. What's more, the killer left a signature, a bite mark. This case has about as much to do with gentrification as the NBA has to do with climate change."

Jake's eyebrows arched. "Bite mark? No one has said anything about a bite mark."

"No, the department has clamped down hard to make sure the gory details don't get out. But the bite mark and the girl's condition when she was raped tells me the boyfriend couldn't have done it."

Jake considered it. "Doesn't a signature suggest a serial crime?"

"Yes, they often do." And serial criminals rarely stay in one place for long.

CHAPTER NINE

Thursday, May 17, 8:10 AM

"Okay," the technician said. "I'll make a separate file with clips from the five camera feeds that caught our hooded friend on his trek up South Fifth Street. My problem is that the image quality varies significantly by camera. I'll try to enhance the images, but it will take some time before I have it completed."

"What about the views from the two cameras on the house by the bus stop?" Kim asked.

"Give me a day or so, and I'll have them for you."

Bob threw up his hands. "Jesus Christ."

A good rule of thumb: never piss off someone whose help you need. "It's okay, Bob. We have plenty to keep us busy." She turned back to the technician. "Call me when you have something. But I need it as soon as you can get it."

"Thanks, Detective. Sorry."

Back outside One-PP, it was drizzling.

"So, I guess we return to Brooklyn," Bob said.

"Let's take a detour, first."

They followed Police Plaza Path past St. Andrew's Church and the federal courthouse and crossed Centre Street onto Reade.

"Want to give me a clue where we're going?"

"Federal Plaza. I want to run something by Ken Taylor."

Bob nodded with recognition. "The FBI agent you worked with on the domestic terrorist case."

***

Unlike the last time she'd seen Taylor, he looked fresh and alert, his white shirt crisply starched, his red striped tie snug at the neck. "Oh, no. Kim Brady. This can't be good news. The last time you paid me a surprise visit, I didn't sleep for a week."

She introduced Ken to Bob. "I hope we won't keep you up past your bedtime this time around, Ken. I'm just here to run some things by you to see if you can help us out. It's about the Williamsburg murder."

Taylor's smile vanished. "Kim, I'm always glad to help. But if we get into anything official, you'll have to go through channels. IAB usually handles interactions between the department and us."

Not what she expected. "When I left IAB, you said the FBI would always have my back."

"And I meant it. I'll help you however I can. Let's start with this: what's up?"

She explained the details of the case and produced a photo of the bite mark. "Is there any way you could check and see if you've got someone in your files who left this kind of signature on his victims?"

Taylor studied the photo. "Shit, that looks deep. Nothing that rings a bell right now, but I'll check into it. Anything else?"

Why not go for it? "How about DNA?"

Taylor's frown returned. "That's getting close to the line. Tell you what. Send me a copy of the DNA report, and I'll check to see if we have anything. If something turns up, I'll alert you and you can go through channels to request everything we've got."

"Awesome. Thanks, Ken."

They stood and shook hands.

Taylor gestured to Kim. "Her grandfather led the first case involving FBI-NYPD cooperation in the early 1940s. A serial rapist who murdered one of his victims."

Dad had said the same thing when she was a young girl. It was nice to hear it verified.

"I worked with Kim's dad in my early years on the job," Bob said. "She comes from excellent police stock."

Bob waited until they were in the elevator headed down before asking, "What made you suddenly want to talk to the G about this case?"

"Serial criminals usually move around a lot. It helps them evade detection. I figured it was worth a shot."

***

Next stop was the Medical Examiner's Office back in Brooklyn. When they'd met up that morning at the Castle, it had thrilled Kim to see Bob already had gotten Rey Torres' dental records.

Dr. Shelton reminded Kim of Ichabod Crane, but he was the most thorough coroner she'd ever met. He studied the photo of Lulu's shoulder anew. "This bothered me when I first saw it. The killer bit down hard." He brought up a similar photo on his computer screen. "This was the shot taken at the scene. As you can see, the wound bled."

Kim didn't gasp. "So, she was still alive when he…"

Dr. Shelton nodded. "Yes."

"Sick fuck," Bob said under his breath.

"Without question." The doctor never lost his tone of calm objectivity. "I've printed out a report from our forensic dental expert. It's an analysis of the condition of the attacker's mouth. The mark suggests that his teeth were significantly misaligned…"

"He needed braces?" Kim asked.

"Or would have as a child. He also appears to have two front teeth that are large and pronounced."

"Bucktoothed," Bob said.

"Yes."

"We have a suspect whose dental records we subpoenaed. Bob has the file."

Dr. Shelton took the file. "I'm not a dental expert, but I'll look." He took his time, turning from the autopsy photo to Torres' dental file and back. After a minute of study, he put the reports back in the file. "I'll give this to our expert for an official report, but there is no way the person in this dental file made that bite mark. The bite radius is smaller and the teeth are better aligned."

"And he's not bucktoothed?" Bob asked.

"No, he isn't."

"Thanks, doctor," Kim said.

The first leg of proof was in place.

CHAPTER TEN

Thursday, May 17, 10:38 AM
Kim found Sergeant Phil Vitello of the Crime Scene Unit at his desk at the Castle, pounding away on his laptop. At least she could now chat up Vitello whenever she wanted. The lean middle-aged sergeant with a bushy moustache and black hair graying at the temples had been a good friend since her days as a rookie on the streets of Brownsville. He was also the best crime scene man in the department.

His greeting was cheerful. "I heard about your new assignment. I've been expecting you." He gestured to a side chair. "Do tell."

"I was hoping you'd join me for a walk-through of the crime scene."

Vitello looked askance. "Seven months after the fact?"

She took the chair and lowered her voice. "The boyfriend didn't do it. I'd stake my badge on it."

"I, for one, never thought he had."

"No one reads crime scenes like you do. I need whatever you can tell me."

"And not just about the scene." He nodded. "Okay."

On the ride to Williamsburg, he only wanted to talk about the Mets.

"Come on, Phil," she said at last. "Can't we at least talk basketball?"

"It's been nearly a half-century since the Knicks won a title. The Garden might as well be a landfill. And your husband's crew here in

Brooklyn doesn't offer much better. At least the Mets have made it to the Series within the past decade." He lapsed into silence.

"What am I missing, Phil?"

"About the crime scene?"

Time to put her cards on the table. "No. About the handling of this case. I never met him, but Larry Grant was known as a damned good detective. And his case file on this murder suggests he was making good progress. Then, crickets."

"You may recall he caught a second case, one that was fouled up in the extreme by two precinct detectives."

"We all handle multiple cases. I realize Grant wasn't well but it still doesn't add up."

He parked the car on River Street. It was cloudy and drizzling, and the park was empty. "Let's go see."

He walked with her to the bench facing the river where Lulu had sat with Rey. "No question, this is where they met. There was half of a joint on the ground, so something was amiss if he just tossed it. We picked up fibers from her top and his tee shirt from the back support of the bench."

"What color?"

"White for hers, blue for his. Some blue fibers got on her shirt, too. Ain't young love grand? More to the point, there was no forensic evidence suggesting a struggle or injury near here. No other fibers, either."

"So, you would conclude the attack did not occur here."

"Correct, counselor." With the slightest of grins, he led her toward the bench next to where they'd found Lulu's body. "We picked up more of her shirt fibers here, as well as some maroon fibers. There were traces of blood—her blood—on the seat of the bench." He pointed down. "Right here. There were also spots of seminal fluid, presumably from her attacker."

"Her tee shirt was torn, correct?"

"Yes, at the collar."

"From when he bit her, which Dr. Shelton thinks occurred while she was still alive."

Vitello stared at her. "Yes. We found traces of her blood and strands of her hair along this sharp edge, here. They were consistent with the wound to her skull."

"Meaning he killed her by striking her head against the sharp edge of the bench."

"Correct. We found no other trace evidence that we could tie to the rape and murder."

She stared out at a passing barge and tug on the river for several minutes. "I can't get the bite mark out of my mind, Phil. This wasn't momentary rage at rejection, or a lover's quarrel gone wrong. The bite was a signature, and I'll bet money she wasn't his first."

"So, what are you missing?" He was grinning at her.

Further down, near the bridge, where River Street turned and became South Fifth Street, she saw someone studying the park and its surroundings. He looked familiar.

"Kim?" Vitello prodded her.

"Why was Bostwick so eager to let two murders—Lulu and Joey Simmons—go cold after so little time?" As she opened the car door, she made the connection on the identity of the stranger studying his surroundings.

It was Felipe Prinz.

CHAPTER ELEVEN

Thursday, May 17, 5:11 PM

As Kim was preparing to leave the Castle, she got a call from Dr. Shelton. "Our dental expert will have a written report to you in a few days, but he confirms your boy suspect could not have made the bite mark made by your killer. Also, he says the alignment and position of the teeth, the presence of all four wisdom teeth, and the absence of a molar, all suggest that the killer was a much older man."

No sooner had she ended the call than Bostwick called her and Bob into his office. "Where are we, Bob?"

Not having had time to brief Bob, she relayed the news from Dr. Shelton.

Bostwick answered with an icy glare. "I asked Detective Nolan."

Never give up the ball without a fight. "I just got off the phone with the ME's office. I didn't have time to tell Bob."

"So, we only have your word for it?"

Bob jumped in. "I trust Kim to get it right. We've also gone over all the forensic evidence. The lab will have the video evidence analyzed by tomorrow or the next day, and then we might have something more concrete to go on. But everything we have right now points to the boyfriend not being our guy. Especially the dental report."

Bostwick locked solely onto Bob. "Which we don't have, yet. Mistakes happen. The boyfriend is our guy until we have proof that he isn't. And remember, Nolan, you are leading this investigation, not Detective Brady."

***

Traffic along the B38 route was crawling because of an accident at DeKalb and Broadway, so Kim opted for the subway instead. By the time she reached the Clark Street station on the Two train, her blood temperature had eased from a boil to a simmer. Bostwick had made it clear from the outset that he didn't care for her "bulldog" reputation. She'd put it down to another chapter in the saga of the Old Boys Club, but this was more direct.

When the elevator door opened in the lobby of what had once been the Hotel St. George, Joanna Dunbar was waiting for her.

"I suppose it's way too much to hope you have good news to share," Kim said.

"Sorry, no. The bad news, if you're interested, is that CHE is reportedly planning some shenanigans tonight. Someone in the NYPD should know, since whoever told us isn't likely to tell you guys."

"Care to tell me who?" She'd gotten sources from Joanna in the past.

"They didn't identify themselves, just their signature quote about 'trembling with indignation at every injustice'. No question it's them. And they named the place: Domino Park."

"I'd have guessed that even without you telling me. I saw Prinz there this morning."

"Anything further on the murder case?"

Kim would have two problems if she told Joanna what they had: news of the findings on the boyfriend would legitimize the CHE protests and make Prinz's claims more plausible; and its appearance in the press would alert the department to a leak. Bostwick had learned of Kim's friendship with the reporter, and he would immediately suspect her. If she tipped the department about the planned protest, the department would have a leg up on getting resources to the site, but Bostwick would ask where she got her information.

"Nothing definitive yet," she said.

Joanna's eyes narrowed. "You're holding back on me. We have a deal."

Kim made her way to the exit with Joanna. No need to let a bunch of law students overhear their conversation. "We do. But speculation on this case has already stirred up the crazies."

Joanna stopped at the corner of Monroe Place. "Don't tell me you're getting departmental shit already."

"Okay, I won't. But there are lots of hidden landmines, and if I'm not careful, I'll step on one. I really can't go into it right now."

"Sorry, Kim. Let's just stay in touch, then. I have a strong suspicion we might need each other before this is over."

Kim watched as Joanna walked back toward the St. George and the subway station. As she turned for home, she punched up a number from her cell.

"Taylor."

"It's Kim. I need you to do something for me. I have learned from a reliable source that our friends who tremble with indignation are planning a gathering tonight. If I alert the department, they'll ask how I got it, so…"

"Understood. I'll alert the department and say we got it from a confidential source. Anything else?"

"Yes. That bite mark photo I showed you? The ME's office says it's an older guy. I need whatever you can find on the mark or the DNA as quickly as possible. My lieutenant still likes the boyfriend, even with the dental evidence."

"Copy that, Kim. I'll contact you if we turn up anything.

CHAPTER TWELVE

Friday, May 18, 6:15 AM
The first thing Kim did once she was up was to turn on the local news station.

"Violence broke out in Williamsburg last night as a protest against gentrification collided with a massive contingent of police. When protesters responded to police efforts to move them away from a construction site by hurling rocks and bricks at them, police responded with tear gas to disperse the crowd. Police arrested over fifty protesters, including Felipe Prinz, the leader of the group."

"More cheerful news this morning, I see." Jake rubbed his eyes as he stared at the screen. "Jesus, what a mess."

The reporter continued. "Acting Mayor Dunn called for calm, but also called into question the tactics used by police, which she deemed 'confrontational'. She also urged the City Council to consider possible limits for massive real estate projects in what she called 'neighborhoods of color' and urged calm in the coming days."

"Nice of her, after pouring gasoline on the fire," Kim said.

"They do have a point, Kim. Why the legions of police? Why the tear gas? Gentrification is pushing out people who've lived in those neighborhoods for decades. Where are they going to go?"

"You don't get it. Prinz wanted that confrontation. His people notified the media hours before the demonstration began. I was in that park yesterday. There are no bricks lying around. They brought them with them. And a thrown brick might have killed a police officer."

"Who told you they contacted the media? The right is always saying shit like that. And, what, you're saying the media called the police? How did they know to show up with an entire division?"

She recited the sequence of events.

Senator Brandt appeared on the screen. "I want to applaud the swift response by the NYPD, which prevented this riot from spreading to the surrounding neighborhood. We cannot and will not tolerate wanton violence and destruction of property in our city."

"He's right," Kim said. "If they hadn't gotten their confrontation with police in the park, they'd have moved beyond it. You saw what they did last time."

"Oh, so now you're a Brandt supporter?"

"I just said he was right about this. Remember, I have way more to hold against him than you do. How would you have felt if I had been facing that angry mob? A brick to the head can kill someone."

"Come on, Kim. You don't do riot duty."

"No, but I assure you every cop who does has someone, somewhere who cares about them and worries about them. I can't give you the answer to the gentrification dilemma. But people like Prinz are exploiting it for their own ends."

The video technician at One-PP texted her. *I don't have the full sequence, yet, as you requested, but I spotted something you need to see. Can you come down this morning?*

She texted Bob, who replied, *Sorry, I'm off to see a dentist today. Looks like an abscessed tooth. Will check in later.*

***

It didn't surprise Senator Brandt when Emory's assistant, Loretta, answered the door of his Fifth Avenue apartment dressed for the office.

Emory dismissed her with a perfunctory, "Thank you, Miss Cadman." He waited until she'd gone before greeting the senator. "Good clips of you this morning. Very mayoral."

"Did they do much damage last night?"

"Almost none. Looks like they intended the bricks for the police from the beginning. I was glad to learn there weren't any police casualties. Has there been any progress in the murder investigation?"

"DCPI says only that the investigation is, in their words, 'active and ongoing'. No other details."

Emory scowled. "I did not mean via official means."

Brandt allowed himself a small smile. "As I've mentioned before, my unofficial sources have dried up owing to previous overreach on our part."

"You mean your part."

The line he wouldn't concede. "No, ours. I acted on your instructions, and I should have been more forceful in resisting a demand that you should never have made. One should learn from one's mistakes, so I've decided never again to commit to something that's doomed to fail, and to give you my unvarnished opinion of your suggestions."

"In that case, apply whatever pressure is needed to move the case against the boyfriend forward. If not from the police side, then from the prosecution side."

That made no sense. "Forgive me, but if the police don't have a case, the DA won't be able to force them to create one."

Emory opened a cedar box and extracted a cigar. "You'd be surprised. If memory serves, Detective Brady does not enjoy a friendly relationship with ADA Richard Conti, owing to a recent encounter in court in which she got the better of him. I'm sure the good prosecutor would welcome the chance to turn some heat on her."

CHAPTER THIRTEEN

Friday, May 18, 8:35 AM

The video technician had Kim sit in front of a thirty-four-inch monitor. "Here's the video from the second camera on the house at the bus stop. I'll play it in real time."

Kim watched as someone in a maroon hoodie approached, his face turned away from the camera—so he'd known it was there. He twisted his back to face the street. "Can't see anything from that."

"Right. Now, let's see it frame by frame." He played it again.

Approach, turn head, turn body. "What am I looking for?"

He played it again.

Approach, turn head... "Stop."

The technician froze the image. "You see it."

Just a flicker. "That patch of light color at the edge of the hood."

"Yep. Caught my eye, too. I clipped this and refined the image as much as I could." He hit a button, and the improved image appeared.

She still couldn't see his face—he'd turned too quickly for that. But it was clear what the light patch was. "That's a tuft of hair. Gray hair. Our killer is an older man."

***

As ADA Rick Conti strode past the bullpen without a nod to Kim and entered Bostwick's office, she braced herself. Members of the DA staff only visited patrol borough headquarters to interview suspects or prod the police to work faster. With nary a suspect in sight, Conti's mission was obvious.

Moments later, Bostwick materialized in the doorway. "Brady, where's Bob?"

"Dentist's office. Abscessed tooth."

"Fuck. All right, you'll have to do. Let's talk."

Just before she'd left Internal Affairs, her lieutenant there, Steve Colangelo, had suggested that sometimes, there was an invisible hand at work in people's lives. Kim wondered if that hand was now giving her the finger.

By the time she entered his office, Bostwick had returned to his seat. "Detective Brady, ADA Conti."

She took the empty visitor's chair. "We've met."

Bostwick stared at a printout, avoiding eye contact. "ADA Conti has been telling me of the DA's concern that our investigation of the Ramirez murder isn't moving fast enough, given this latest outbreak of civil unrest."

Kim faced the attorney. "And just what does District Attorney Mitchell think we should do that we haven't already been doing?"

Conti squirmed in his seat. "Seven months ago, we had a firm suspect in the boyfriend. What happened?"

"I told you, Brady, when I assigned you and Bob Nolan to this case, that we needed to move quickly. All I've seen you do is retrace seven-month-old steps."

So, Bostwick had been looking at the online case file. "Considering that Detective Grant, whose case this was, has departed this life, and there's no money in the departmental budget for a séance, Bob and I decided this was the most prudent course."

He tossed the printout aside. "Well, how about this? Go out and pick up the boyfriend and bring him in for serious questioning rather than a friendly chat in the principal's office. Maybe then we'll get what we need."

She faced Conti. "May I have it, please?"

Conti appeared taken aback. "Have what?"

"The arrest warrant for Reinaldo Torres. You brought it, didn't you?"

Conti only responded with a blank stare.

"No? No warrant?" She turned back to Bostwick. "Could that be because we don't have probable cause?"

The office door opened, and Bob Nolan walked in. "Sorry I'm late. Had to stop at the dentist to get stabbed in the mouth with an ice pick." He slurred his esses, so the Novocain had not yet worn off. He glanced at each one of them. "I take it we're discussing the Ramirez case? Good. Where are we?"

Kim answered before Bostwick could say anything. "We were just discussing the boyfriend and probable cause."

Bob's expression turned to surprise. "On Torres? What probable cause? Didn't you tell them about..."

"I was just getting to that when you joined us." Back to Conti. "We got Torres' dental records. The Medical Examiner's Office says there is no way Torres made the bite mark on the girl's shoulder, that it had to be an older man, someone who has his wisdom teeth, which show in the bite mark but which Torres has not yet gotten, and is missing a second molar, which Torres is not."

Conti shook his head. "Shit."

She shouldn't be enjoying this so much, but what the hell. "Also, based on video evidence and from the fibers recovered from Lulu's clothing at the scene, we know the killer wore a maroon hoodie. I just came from One-PP, where a video technician froze and enhanced a clip showing a tuft of gray hair on a man leaving the scene wearing a maroon hoodie. Finally, Torres volunteered a DNA sample so that we can check him against the DNA recovered from the rape kit, which should be dispositive." She turned to Conti. "That is the correct legal term, isn't it, Counselor?"

Conti nodded.

"So, will we be getting that arrest warrant soon?" She turned to Bostwick. "Because I wouldn't want to risk a charge of a false arrest."

Bostwick's voice turned to ice. "You may both return to your duties. We'll discuss this later."

***

She walked to the break room with Bob.

He studied the vending machines. "Nothing in here really appeals to me at the moment."

"You look a little swollen."

He laughed. "You should have seen me when I woke up this morning." He turned serious. "I understand you have a history with Conti, but do you really think pissing off Bostwick was the best option?"

"Why did he pull Grant off this case just when Grant was making progress? Why did he let the Simmons case go cold so easily?"

Bob gestured to a pair of seats at a table and they both sat. "I had only been here a few months, so I didn't know Grant too well. I still can't figure out Bostwick. But it seems to me he's nervous around you, probably because you came from IAB. I'd guess he's afraid you'll start asking questions like that one."

"It would be nice to have an…"

A knock on the door stopped her. It was Conti. "Kim, can we talk?"

"Recent history doesn't suggest it."

Bob stood. "I'll step out."

"No, I need to talk to both of you, but primarily Kim. I came over here because my boss wanted an update on where we are. In case you haven't heard, we had a riot last night…"

"Yes," she said. "Curiously, it began at the scene of the Ramirez murder. Which I visited yesterday with Sergeant Vitello of CSU, doing a walkthrough. And guess who I spotted there just before we left. Felipe Prinz. Perhaps I should have asked for his opinion on the case."

Conti took a seat at the table. "Prinz? You sure? What was he doing there?"

"I'm positive. I can't say for certain what he was doing, but I suspect he was sizing up its potential for a battleground with police."

"That why you had the FBI call the borough chief?"

She snorted. "What makes you think I did that?"

Conti leaned forward. "I didn't until you said you saw Prinz there yesterday. The FBI said they received it from a confidential informant."

"When I saw Prinz, I didn't know what he might have had in mind or when he might have planned it. My observation was of the hindsight variety."

Conti was contrite. "Okay, sorry. And I'm sorry for Bostwick landing on you. That wasn't my goal when I came over here. My instructions were to learn where we are in the investigation, and yes, last night's violence was a consideration. But my office wants the right guy, even if it takes longer. I just need to report you've got a direction. Like this older guy."

Oh, no. She would not let him put that out there for a public free-for-all. But Bob was lead, and she looked to him.

"You're in front of me by several lengths, Kim."

"All right, Mr. Conti." Best to stick to formalities. "But for the sake of the integrity of this investigation, I will only tell you what we have if you promise you will not record it or repeat it to anyone else, not even the District Attorney himself, without further word from me."

"Jesus, Kim, we're on the same side. Why all the secrecy?"

She resisted the urge to throw their last conflict in his face. "Your coming here to press my lieutenant on a stalled investigation the morning after a riot, pushing for an arrest of a suspect we can't convict, smells to me like week-old fish."

"I didn't push for anyone's arrest. I just asked what the problem was."

She shrugged. "Lack of evidence. It was true seven months ago, and it's true now."

"And the older guy?"

She decided. "We don't know who he is. No basis for a sketch, can't even determine his race or guess at his ethnicity. But we're certain he isn't Torres."

"All I asked was your direction."

"I'll tell you when I hear from the lab. When they report that Torres' DNA doesn't match the rape kit, you can say we've eliminated him as a suspect."

CHAPTER FOURTEEN

Friday, May 18, 2:46 PM

Kim had just given Bob more ibuprofen when Bostwick called them in. "You two want to tell me what the hell is going on?" He glared at Bob.

"Kim did a good job of outlining where we are. The kid didn't do it. Some older guy did."

"A geezer wearing a hoodie." Bostwick all but spat the words.

"It happens," Bob said. "Hell, I wear hoodies sometimes." He closed his eyes for a moment. "Never before have I looked forward to root canal. Anyway, Lieu, why don't you just let us follow the evidence? This fucker has a seven-month lead on us. We won't collar him tomorrow. Kim's got some good ideas."

Aw, hell, Bob. Why did you have to spill it before we had something? But she got it. He was eager to assure Bostwick that they weren't just making shit up.

"Such as?" Bostwick's tone suggested he considered that a possibility.

She told him what she'd given to Ken Taylor.

Bostwick pounded his desk. "You went to the FBI on your own? You know goddamned well that's not procedure."

"I didn't ask for anything official, only if anything showed up in their records. I didn't want to waste your time with going through channels unless there was something there. Ken's a friend, and right now we need all the friends we can get."

Bob spoke up. "I encouraged Kim to check it out. She had good reason to cast a wider net."

In for a penny… "It's possible—and I emphasize, only possible—that we're dealing with a serial offender." She summarized the evidence. "Those guys often move around a lot—Ted Bundy committed his crimes as far apart as Washington State and Florida. If he's bitten or raped other victims, the FBI database might show it and Ken will alert me, and I'll alert the appropriate unit in Internal Affairs to start cooperation with the feds."

After several moments passed in silence, Bostwick heaved a deep sigh. "Very well, Brady, but if it comes to that, you will do all of your communicating through channels."

***

Joanna Dunbar was waiting as Kim got off the B38 at Cadman Plaza. "You look like you could use a drink." She nodded toward a college student walking by with a lit joint. "Or one of those."

Kim started walking. "I try never to take a drink when I 'really need a drink', and I never touch the other shit at all."

"I hear you had a visit from your favorite ADA today, and that whatever you told him wasn't favorably received when he returned to base." The reporter patted Kim's arm. "No, I will not ask what you told him. Did you two kiss and make up?"

"He tried, but I wasn't interested. He can go fuck himself. I told him only what I was confident he would keep to himself while preventing him from digging further."

"So, Emory's attempt to blame it all on the Puerto Rican kid blew up in his face?"

Kim chuckled. "You said you wouldn't ask what I told Conti."

"Can't blame me for trying. Everyone is itching to find out if Prinz is right on this one."

"You mean his conspiracy theory? Not a chance." Too direct, but then Prinz had pissed her off, too.

Joanna caught it. "Then what? Come on, Kim, give me something, will ya?"

"I wish I could, but if I do, you may not be able to resist running with it, and I can't afford that. This case is hard enough as it is."

"Fair enough. But try to remember that until someone disproves Prinz's conspiracy theory and replaces it with something viable, it's going to drive a lot of shit in this city. And he's already back out on the street."

CHAPTER FIFTEEN

Saturday, May 19, 7:05 AM

"Good morning. The release from custody yesterday of Felipe Prinz prompted cries of outrage from some political leaders. State Senator Raymond Brandt called it 'irrational, illogical, and irresponsible' and called for Prinz's immediate re-incarceration. Acting Mayor Sabrina Dunn responded by criticizing what she called, 'a massive overreaction by the police department' and called for greater restraint by police in the future."

***

Jake killed the television as Kim emerged from the bedroom ready for work.

"Thank you." Enough of that shit. Maybe Dunn should have to walk a foot tour in a hostile neighborhood at two in the morning. "What's the weather?"

"Cloudy, low sixties, chance of showers. No game tonight, so any chance we could…"

She let him turn her to face him. "I hope so. I could use a break." Her cell pinged with a text. She tried to ignore it and melted into a deep kiss.

When they finally parted, he grinned and said, "Now, that sounds promising."

"I didn't promise. I said I…"

Another ping.

"Go ahead," he said. "Otherwise, you'll be struggling to read it while walking to the bus stop." But his eyes flashed momentary resentment.

She shoved the offending phone into her hip pocket. "Nope. Whatever it is can wait till I'm on the bus."

Mirth crept back into his expression. "Until tonight, then."

She kept her promise as she walked from Monroe Place to Clark Street and across Cadman Plaza West. But as she waited for the light, she fished the cell from her pocket.

The text was from Ken Taylor. *We got something.*

***

This time Senator Brandt arrived at Emory's apartment an hour earlier, fearing the press might tail him. Loretta Cadman answered the door dressed for work as she had the previous day, but in her stocking feet.

"Good morning, Loretta. He up, yet?" He didn't hide his smirk.

"I'll check. Please wait in the living room."

He walked to the window, which provided a panoramic view of Central Park below. Oh, the joys one could purchase with what capital provided.

The click of high heels on hardwood floors alerted him to Loretta's approach, and that she'd finished dressing. "He'll be with you in a moment."

"Thank you. Glad you found your shoes."

The usually sunny secretary shot him a scowl before walking out. He was still chuckling when Kyle Emory entered wearing a robe and slippers.

"A little early for social calls, isn't it?"

"Sorry if I interrupted your morning, um, exercises."

"Don't be crude."

The senator had crossed a line, but he didn't care. "Can't blame a guy for being jealous."

"What's the news?"

"Mr. Conti visited our friends at Brooklyn North Homicide yesterday."

Emory relaxed. "Fine. Was he able to move them forward?"

"Upon his return, he reported to his section chief, who told me only that the investigation is ongoing."

"What, exactly, does that mean?"

"Either the police aren't talking to the district attorney, or the district attorney isn't talking to us. Either suggests that the police have decided the horny boyfriend didn't do it."

Emory extracted a cigar from the breast pocket of his robe and lit it. "They're still answerable to a state senate committee chair, aren't they?"

He was hinting for the senator to micromanage the investigation from Albany. But his previous attempt to micromanage the department had blown up in his face. "In terms of general policy, yes. On the conduct of ongoing cases, no. Anything that smacks of interference will generate a massive amount of ill will against me and against you."

"Me? How would you asking questions generate ill will toward me?"

"Two ways. First, it's already out there that you're invested in gentrification projects in Brooklyn. My media guy tells me that Dunbar woman has been doing a lot of digging."

"Let her dig."

"As if we could stop her. But the second way involves Prinz's group."

"You're afraid of some communist terrorists?"

"Afraid? No. But I want to avoid doing anything that will lend their claims any credibility. And if we come off as trying to pin a murder on a horny but innocent teenager, it won't look good for either of us. The most recent polling data shows I'm now trailing Dunn by a mere four percent. That's less than the margin of error."

"Then I suggest you fight back. Start by supporting our men in blue."

CHAPTER SIXTEEN

Saturday, May 19, 7:42 AM

Kim got off the F train at Delancey Street and took the J train to Chambers Street. Ten minutes later, she made her way through the security checkpoint at 26 Federal Plaza.

Ken Taylor brought her to his office. "I have two things for you. The first is on the DNA." He handed her a report.

She took her time. The saliva sample from Lulu's neck had generated no hits on the FBI's system. But the sample from the rape kit had generated eight hits. "Eight, besides Lulu."

Ken pointed to the report. "The following pages are lists of the cases, from the most recent to the oldest. All rape/murders, all of them remain open."

She continued reading. The most recent was in Pennsylvania, near Wilkes-Barre two years earlier. Prior to that, Verona, New Jersey in 2014. Next was in 2012, in Wheeling, West Virginia. Flint, Michigan in 2010. Lexington, Kentucky in 2007. Gary, Indiana in 2005. Columbus, Ohio in 2003. Buffalo, New York in 2001. "All rape/murders of teens, no witnesses, no description."

"Correct. And in each of them, the killer left a bite mark in the victim's right shoulder." He let her absorb that before handing her another report. "Dental records only turned up one other case. A much older case."

She read the summary. A rape/murder of a girl named Angelina Farina, age fourteen, in the Bronx in... "1963? That can't be right. The attacker would be an old man by now." She recalled the video clip from the bus stop. "Gray hair."

"What's that, Kim?"

"Surveillance video caught Lulu's killer on the street. Not the face. But under the hoodie, you could see he had gray hair." She did the math. "If he was in his late teens in 1963, he'd be in his seventies, now."

"Yes."

She finished reading the report. 1963.

The Bronx.

Forty-fourth precinct.

Where her grandfather had been working when he died.

In 1963.

CHAPTER SEVENTEEN

Saturday, May 19, 11:07 AM

Senator Raymond Brandt stepped to the portable podium in his district office facing a phalanx of reporters and television cameras. "Good morning. There has been a great deal of speculation and accusation in the past few days regarding the NYPD's investigation of the brutal rape and murder of a sweet, young high school student in Williamsburg. Wild conspiracy theories have been circulating, and are treated as rational in the city press, fueled by the acting mayor, and some have resorted to violence in the streets, again, cheered on by Ms. Dunn."

He let that sink in. "I'll make my position clear: the members of the NYPD deserve our respect and support. The killer, whoever he is and wherever he is hiding, is clever and cunning. He is evil. Apprehending him will take skill, determination, and time. As a concerned public, we don't like to hear that. We want it solved in an hour, like some TV police show. But it's a long, hard slog. We should also regard with the most bitter revulsion anyone who tries to use this or any other case as an excuse to commit violence."

"Senator," a reporter in front called out, "do you deny the people's right to engage in peaceful protest?"

"Of course not. But when 'protesters' come together armed with bricks to hurl at the police, that's no peaceful protest."

Another reporter called out, "So, you deny that protesters have experienced genuine outrage?"

He laughed. "An outrage easily quelled by smashing a store window and grabbing a new pair of big-name sneakers? Yes, I do."

"Senator!"

The crowd parted, and he saw who'd called out. It was that Dunbar woman, probably looking to drag Kyle Emory into it. He'd take care of her. "Yes?"

"How do you respond to Mr. Prinz of CHE, who charges that the murder is part of a plot to destabilize Williamsburg and force the residents to flee?"

"Utter nonsense. Mr. Prinz does not want this case solved. If he did, he wouldn't be organizing violent protests and attacking the very people who are investigating it. Every act of violence committed by this Marxist-Leninist group impedes the investigation. I could just as easily charge Mr. Prinz with a similar theory."

Dunbar pressed him. "Are you?"

Good. He had her. "I only said I could. After all, his group is making hay on all this controversy. Maybe they know more about the murder than they let on. They clearly have no respect for the law."

CHAPTER EIGHTEEN

Saturday, May 19, 2:29 PM

Kim retrieved the Farina case file from the department archives.

The detective's room at the Castle was nearly empty when she returned. Bob was in the break room having a late lunch. "Where have you been? You missed another Brandt show."

She showed him the DNA reports and placed the ancient accordion file on the table.

He read the reports through, twice. "Congratulations. You nailed it. We're looking at a serial killer. Bostwick's gonna have a cow."

"That's not all." She handed him the report on the dental records.

Bob nodded as he read. "Whoa. 1963. He's gotta be ancient by now."

"Serial killers sometimes start when they're in their teens or early twenties. That would put our guy in his seventies, now."

"The gray-haired guy in the hoodie." He nodded to the accordion file. "Is that the case file from '63?"

She nodded. "I wanted to wait until I returned here to open it. Part of me wants to and part of me is afraid to look."

"Afraid of what might crawl out of a file that old?"

She managed a wan smile. "The least of my concerns. Angelina Farina was murdered in the Bronx, in my grandfather's precinct in the year he was killed."

"Only one way to find out," Bob said.

She untied the cord that had held the file together for over fifty years. And there it was.

Lead Detective: Daniel P. Brady.

"Shit." She packed up the file. "Now, Bostwick has a perfect excuse to take me off this case. You can't tell him anything about this until I've gone through this and figured out what to do."

***

Jake wasn't at the apartment when she arrived. She checked her phone. Sure enough, there was a text she'd received while on the bus. *Meetings with the general manager and scouting staff. Will be home in time for dinner.*

She spread a plastic covering over the dining area table just in case anything crawled out of the file, but nothing did. Then she texted back. *Just got home and have work to do, myself.*

She shivered, reading Granddad's handwritten report. Police had found Angelina's body in Claremont Park on Teller Avenue in the Bronx. There was clear evidence of rape. Cause of death was a fractured skull, most likely from being slammed against the concrete steps at the entrance to the park. There was a pronounced bite wound on the right shoulder.

"Suspect identified. Known only as Paul." It was the last entry in his report.

She glanced back at the date of the crime.

May 24, 1963.

She pored through the file, looking for the notepad he would have kept with him to make notes in the field. There was the Medical Examiner's report, and a crime scene report. They had found no prints.

But no notepad.

Perhaps whoever retrieved it hadn't remembered to return it to the department.

On the top shelf in her closet was a large plastic container holding a handful of Dad's old keepsakes that she'd taken when he died. In it was the religious card from Granddad's wake. "Daniel Patrick Brady, born May 18, 1910, died June 19, 1963."

The register from the wake was there. Two volumes.

There was the framed photo that had held the place of honor on Kim's family's mantel until her parents divorced. Granddad in his dress uniform, with ribbons from three medals on his chest.

She found a photo of Granddad and Gram, their wedding photo. Taken at City Hall. No church wedding because Gram had been divorced.

But no notepad. That was odd, because if anyone would have kept it, Dad would. Unless Gram had thrown it away, not wanting to be reminded. No, that wasn't like Gram, whom Kim remembered as the strongest woman she'd ever known.

She turned to the register from Dad's wake. Not nearly so many attendees, but nearly all who came were from the department, except for Jake's family and some people from the Brooklyn Nets. Distracted, she paged through the list of names.

Mr. and Mrs. James Brady.

Cousin Jim. The cousin she'd never met until that night. His father had been Dad's older brother, Patrick, whom she had also never met. Uncle Pat had been fourteen years older than Dad, and something had driven them apart long before Kim was born. But Jim had read of Dad's death and decided that the two tiny strands of family that remained should stick together. She'd sent him a thank-you card after the funeral, but nothing else had come of it.

She did the math. Uncle Pat would have been twenty when Granddad died, while Dad would have been six.

She called the phone number Jim had left in the registry.

***

"So," Jake said as he headed east on the Long Island Expressway, "he asked you to meet him at a skating rink?"

"Not him, his wife. He plays hockey every Thursday night, but the rink had a problem this week and they got bounced to tonight from ten to midnight." She glanced at the dashboard clock. It was 11:15.

"I'm still stunned you never knew you had a cousin until your dad passed. What are you hoping to find?"

Good question. She'd started out looking for Granddad's notepad, but that was long since gone. "Dad told me lots of stories about his father, but none had ever dealt with his death. Uncle Pat was a lot older. With luck, he passed some onto Cousin Jim."

"Sounds thin. You expect to stumble across some gold mine of evidence?"

"I do not." She smiled, having said it with the same lilt in her voice Gram had often used. "You're getting off at Roslyn Road."

"Thank you, Ms. GPS. I can't believe you're chasing the same killer your grandfather was chasing over fifty years ago."

Neither could she. And if she couldn't believe it, neither would Bostwick,

***

"I don't see him," Kim said as she stood at the boards watching the hodgepodge of players scrambling up and down the rink. "The helmets don't help."

A middle-aged woman in jeans and an Islanders sweatshirt turned to her. "Who you looking for?"

"Jim Brady."

The woman laughed. "Right. The Henrik Lundquist wannabe." She pointed at the far goal. "That's him."

Just then, a woman charged up the ice, her skates leaving deep cuts, and cut in on Cousin Jim. She shot, and he deflected the puck to the corner.

"Poor Patty," the woman said. "She couldn't buy a goal off Jim."

When the game ended, Jim pulled off his helmet and skated over. "See much?"

"Just your great save," Kim replied.

The woman snorted. "Against Patty? Doesn't count as great. Nice meeting you." She walked away chuckling.

"Give me about fifteen minutes to shower and get human, and we can grab a coffee and talk."

He made it out in ten and led them to a nearby diner. They ordered burgers and coffee, and Kim told him about the case.

"Wow," Jim said. "They could make a movie out of that." He stopped. "Kim, I have an entire box of my dad's stuff in the attic. There may be some things of Granddad's in with it. Tell you what. Tomorrow's Sunday. Why don't you come out to the house for dinner? We can go through the box together."

CHAPTER NINETEEN

Sunday, May 20, 9:33 AM

"Let me understand this." Bostwick never raised his eyes from the tattered, musty file that he still hadn't opened. "You think the kid in the hoodie is a septuagenarian. Next, you'll be trying to sell me a bridge."

Bob's knee pressed against hers, just as Mike Resnick used to do, before he spoke. "If you look at the photos…"

Bostwick blew past him. "And, apparently, you go outside the chain of command any time it suits you. What fucking swamp do you think I crawled out of?"

Kim reached across the desk and snatched the file. "Since you don't need this, I'll take it back. I'll return it to the archives. But I'll leave you with the DNA report, which shows a one-hundred percent match with eight other murders committed over a twenty-year period. And I'll leave you with the dental analysis which shows the match to the same mark left on Angelina Farina over fifty years ago. Because, when I attended the Academy, they taught us that dental records are even better than fingerprints as evidence. Unless we're under the dictate that if the facts do not support the belief, we must ignore them."

Bostwick's face reddened. "Get out of my office and get something we can use on that kid." He turned to Bob. "You, too."

Kim snatched the copies of the reports before she left. Outside the office, she grabbed her jacket and her purse.

"Where are you going?" Bob asked.

"To catch a serial killer."

60

***

Kim had called her old lieutenant from Internal Affairs, Steve Colangelo. She sat across from him now at a table at the Sprout Deli, across the street from IAB's offices on Hudson Street, and recapped what had happened.

"Sounds like outstanding work, Kim, even by your standards. Not sure what I can do to help."

"Bostwick refused to drop his fixation on the boyfriend, even in the face of proof he didn't do it. Makes me wonder…"

"Don't wonder. Do what you need to do: get right with Conti, like I predicted you would when you left IAB."

"You mean the one who's been pressuring us to come up with something and then not listening to what we have?"

"Yeah, him. Tell him everything you've told me, including going to the FBI and what they found."

Unbelievable. "And he can join the Bostwick rant of going outside channels?"

But Colangelo only laughed. "You've been going outside channels since I first met you. It's often the only way to get things done. While you were with us, channels didn't matter too much because most of them come through us, anyway. But you won't change. And that means you must get Bostwick and Conti to accept how you do things. Bostwick might take a while, but it shouldn't surprise you if Conti is ready, especially when you show him what you've got."

"Why should I care if he's ready? I'm the one with the beef against him."

"Ancient history, Kim. You need him on your side, and there's only one way to do it."

Her cell buzzed. It was from Bob. *DNA analysis came back early on Rey Torres' sample. No match with the rape kit, but it matched the sample from the girl's neck. Want me to tell the lieu?*

Decision made. She tapped out her answer. *Yes, thanks. Tell him I'm relaying the news to Conti.*

CHAPTER TWENTY

Sunday, May 20, 11:16 AM

Conti was waiting for her at a table in Junior's on the corner of Flatbush Avenue and DeKalb. "Alone, as you requested."

A server appeared, and she ordered a coffee and cheesecake. One couldn't come to Juniors and not order their famous cheesecake.

She waited for the server to leave. "And you didn't tell anyone?"

"Again, as you requested. Am I about to be abducted?"

"You doing stand-up, now?"

He turned serious. "Just trying to ease the tension. I realize you're still pissed at me…"

"And I have every right to be." She needed him on her side, but they had to have this out, first. "You should have jumped all over that lawyer for bringing up my father."

"I warned you beforehand. My instructions were to make you fight him off on your own, with as little interference as possible."

"Great. The Nuremburg defense. 'I was only following orders.' Is that your excuse for Friday, too? When you pressed for an arrest we can't make stick?"

Conti paused while the server brought her coffee and cheesecake. When he answered, it was with a lowered voice. "I was not pushing for you to arrest the kid. But my section chief is getting political heat on this case and asked me to get you… Bostwick off the dime."

"Who from?"

"Don't go there, Kim. You stepped in political shit last time. Don't make that mistake again. And just for background when the Ramirez girl was murdered, everyone suspected the boyfriend, even Grant. Just before he caught the Simmons case, he told me he had something big. But then the Simmons case came along—you know all about that—and then he retired."

She glared at him.

"What, you don't believe me?"

"I've been through the entire case file," she replied. "There's nothing in there to suggest Torres was the guy. Not even as a person of interest. It just lists all the forensic evidence he had, including references to the video of the guy wearing the maroon hoodie."

"I don't understand."

"I gave the DNA sample from the rape kit to the FBI." She pulled out the FBI report. "Here's what came back."

"You went outside channels. No way Bostwick would have approved this without informing us."

"Sue me. Read the fucking report."

His jaw dropped. "Eight?"

"Yeah, all rape/murders with the bite-mark signature, and some of which occurred before Torres was born." She showed him the dental report. "And one other which occurred a quarter-century before I was born."

"The geezer in the hoodie." He took a moment to digest it. "Can you give me copies of these? My section chief will be..."

"No. This is a test, Conti, to see if you and I can work together. You tell no one about this until I give you the word. You tell your chief, he tells the DA, word gets out to Brandt and other interested parties, gets leaked to the press, and a serial killer who's gone his merry way for over fifty years gets out of Dodge." She snatched back the reports.

"What the hell do I say the next time I'm asked for an update?"

"Tell them Torres' DNA result proves he didn't rape her, and we're looking for the guy in the hoodie. Nothing else. And if a single word leaks, that will confirm that I can't trust you."

"I promise I won't tell a soul. But what about Bostwick? Seems to me he's your real problem. And it won't get any better when he finds out you went outside channels to go to the FBI."

"Bostwick is my headache. I'll deal with him."

CHAPTER TWENTY-ONE

Sunday, May 20, 7:20 PM

The moment Jim's wife opened the door wearing tailored slacks, a pink rayon blouse, and dress flats, Kim was glad she'd resisted Jake's urgings to dress to the nines.

"Do you have any children?" she asked as Jim served cocktails.

"No."

"Not yet," Jake added.

Conversation flowed through cocktails and dinner, and by the time they were sipping coffee, Kim wondered if her cousin had forgotten the reason for the invitation. "We got to see Jim's hockey skills last night."

Jim placed his cup on its saucer. "A brilliant performance, you must admit."

"We're basketball people." Kim's expression made Jim's wife choke for a moment on her coffee.

But Jim remained unfazed. "There's always hope. Anyway, Kim, I promised you something."

Kim followed her cousin to his study.

"My home office." He gestured to a box on the desk. "I found several of Granddad's things related to his police work and I put them in this box."

She opened it slowly, as if in a shrine. On top was a small plastic case containing three citation medals. She picked up one, a bar with wide stripes of green, white, and blue with a silver star in the middle. "Meritorious Police Duty, Honorable Mention."

"Sounds like a consolation prize."

"It does to those outside the department," she said, "but it's the highest honor of the Meritorious Duty medals, given for 'an act of extraordinary bravery intelligently performed in the line of duty at imminent and personal danger to life'. Not a consolation prize at all." She stared at it for several moments, feeling a connection to her grandfather she'd never felt before. "I have one."

"Wow. You really are your granddad's granddaughter."

"That's what my dad always said." She placed the medal back in the case. The next one was similar, but without a star. "Meritorious Police Duty. Granddad led the first ever combined investigation between the department and the FBI. I wonder if that's what this was for."

"Sorry, Kim. My dad never talked about this stuff."

She picked up the last medal and held it with awe. It was a pale green bar speckled with little stars of gold. "The Medal of Honor, the highest award given by the department. The department awarded him this after he died."

"Hey, you okay?"

"Yeah. Only now, I wish more than ever that I'd known him." She brushed the thought away. There were photos of other men and their wives, including a group photo taken at a nightclub. "Oh, wow. That's Granddad and Gram. She was so lovely."

"Yeah. Looks like it was taken at the Copacabana. That was in 1942, around the time they were married."

"Gram sure rocked that forties look. Almost makes me wish it'd come back. Not that it would work for me on the job at all." She made a note on her cell of the men in the photos, whose names were written on the back in Gram's lovely script—Frank Larkin and Sean McHugh. Then she found a photo of a much younger man and his wife, with her grandparents. "Phil Boland. Looks like they were at a party."

"St. Paddy's Day, by the look of it. He may have been Granddad's last partner."

"He looks like he's about thirty." She noted the name. Another lead to follow.

Jim frowned. "His gun isn't in there. Sorry."

"I have it. My dad gave it to me when I graduated from the Police Academy." She dug further into the box, finding several more photos and mementos. And then she saw it.

A pocket notebook yellowed with age and its pages brittle to the touch. But she turned them with great care, until she came to the page that told her she'd found what she was looking for: "Murder/rape of A. Farina, 44th Pct. 5/24/63." She was desperate to harvest its secrets, but she needed time and solitude to do it right. "Jim, may I keep this?"

"I put this whole box together for you. I expect everything in it will mean much more to you than to me."

She laid the notebook down with great care and then embraced him. "Thank you."

CHAPTER TWENTY-TWO

Monday, May 21, 6:31 AM

"Violence again erupted last night as demonstrators protesting the handling of the murder case of a high school student clashed with police in Williamsburg, charging them with a coverup. Businesses along Brooklyn's Fulton Street Mall were looted as windows were smashed and fires were set. The Fire Department quickly got the blazes under control despite dodging bricks and bottles hurled by angry demonstrators. In a prepared statement, Acting Mayor Sabrina Dunn called for calm and assured the public the police are proceeding with their investigation.

"This morning, State Senator Raymond Brandt accused Dunn of coddling rioters and betraying the city."

Brandt appeared on the screen. "A terrorist group is now cowing this administration into abrogating its most fundamental obligation, protecting the people of this city and their property. Thanks to sweeping changes to the criminal justice system championed by Ms. Dunn and her predecessor, the Marxist-Leninist leader of this group walks free, able to spout his ridiculous theories. I have every confidence the police are making headway in the investigation Mr. Prinz claims to care so much about. But any idiot knows not to conduct murder investigations in the press."

***

So, Brandt was back in their corner. Perhaps Conti had put in a good word to his section chief and the word had filtered to the senator.

Martha Perez lost her bravado as she entered the principal's office and saw Kim there.

Kim tried her most reassuring smile. "It's okay, Martha. I just need to review what you know about that night. Were you at the park?"

The girl didn't relax, and she didn't answer.

"I'll take that as a yes."

"Rey didn't do it. He couldn't have."

"I believe you. I'm trying to find whoever did. Tell me what happened."

But Martha grew more nervous. "We got to the park, and there were a few other kids there, hanging out." She froze.

Kim turned to the principal. "Could you leave us alone for a few minutes?"

The principal stiffened. "No. There should be a responsible adult here while you're interrogating this child."

"I'm not interrogating her, I'm interviewing her. She isn't a suspect or anything, and I promise that nothing she says will be held against her."

The principal held firm. "Sorry, I'm staying. Anything she has to say to you, she can say with me here."

But the look on Martha's face suggested otherwise.

"Martha, would you be willing to meet with me later to talk?"

"Sure. We get out at two-thirty."

Kim pulled out one of her cards and wrote her cell number on the back. "Meet me at Domino Park at three. Bring any friends who were with you that night if they're willing to talk to me understanding that I am not after anything anyone might have done that night. I just want to find Lulu's killer. Call or text me if for any reason you can't make it. Okay?"

Martha took the card and grinned with relief. "Okay. Thanks." She left the office.

69

"Tell me, Detective, do you always flaunt school authority, or is this a special day?"

"Only when that authority seeks to obstruct a murder investigation."

"You realize those kids were probably smoking pot that night."

"If you expect me to let their fear of you finding out for certain prevent me from getting the information I need, you're nuts."

***

Martha had texted she would have a friend with her. They were waiting when Kim arrived at the park.

"This is Rosalie," Martha said.

"Hi." Rosalie was taller than Martha, and heavier. Tight jeans didn't help her look, but her low-cut top gave the boys a good reason to forget the unflattering jeans.

"Thanks for talking to me. I realize it's difficult. I'm still trying to understand what happened that night. How did it all start?"

"First," Martha said, "you promised nothing we say gets back to…"

"Absolutely." Kim turned to Rosalie. "My only concern here is what happened to Lulu and finding her killer."

Rosalie gave a tight nod but said nothing.

Martha relaxed. "It was a super warm day, so a bunch of us came here that night to hang. One guy brought a few blunts, so…"

"Party time." Kids. "Did Lulu smoke, too?" She'd already asked, but it was always good to check for consistency.

"Only had once before," Martha replied. "She didn't like it. But she was totally stressed because she couldn't do what Rey wanted. So, when he offered her a toke, I encouraged her, figuring it would help her relax. The rest of us were feeling pretty good. But it got much cooler, and there was, like, this fog. Misty and damp. One guy invited us all back to his place, so we went, except Rey and Lulu. They walked over to that bench by the river." A sad sigh. "That was the last time I ever saw her."

Not much help. "Did you see anyone hanging around nearby who didn't belong?"

"That's why I brought Rosalie along. I didn't, but she might help you."

Rosalie shifted her stance. "We walked back along River Street, past the old factory, toward First Street. But just before we got to Tacocino, which was closed by then, I saw this guy sitting at one table. He was wearing a hoodie…"

"What color?"

Rosalie frowned. "Looked like a dark red. Anyway, as we got closer, he pulled up the hood, and he got up and walked toward the river."

"Did you see his face?"

"Not really. He turned away too fast. But he had gray hair, almost white, and real thick gray bushy eyebrows. And a funny nose."

"Funny, how?" Kim asked.

"Thick at the back, and it had a bump on top and hooked down. Kinda reminded me of Cyrano de Bergerac."

Kim wondered if she might have enough for a police artist. "What was the shape of his face? Round? Oval? Squarish?"

Rosalie looked helpless. "I don't remember."

"What about his eyes? Were they close together? Far apart?"

The girl only shook her head.

"What about his ears?"

"Sorry. He had the hood up before I could tell."

Not enough. But at least she had three elements of a description—hair, eyebrows, nose.

"One last question, Rosalie. Did you notice which way he walked after he turned toward the river?"

"Not really. I looked back as we turned up First Street, but all I saw was his back. He was walking the other way on River Street."

***

"The lieu left fifteen minutes ago," Bob said when she came back to the Castle. "And in what I would call an ugly mood."

Just what she needed. "How ugly?"

"He got a complaint about you from that high school principal in Williamsburg. Talked about going to the Chief of Detectives about your insubordination and asking to have you reassigned."

"Great. Maybe they'll let me go back to Internal Affairs."

Bob turned serious. "You don't mean that."

"No." She couldn't bullshit Bob. This was her kind of case, even more because of the connection to Granddad. But how to regain her footing? She'd checked the Duty Roster, and both she and Bostwick were off the next two days. Like a halftime that comes just as a team is getting hot and hitting baskets.

"You should use the break to relax." Bob said it in little more than a whisper.

The sign of a true partnership—he was learning to read her moods. "I should, but it's not in my DNA. I'll steer clear of this place, though."

"How did your meeting with Conti go?"

Good. He'd accepted her answer. "Too early to tell." She told him about Martha and Rosalie.

"Great. Leaves no question that the guy with the hoodie is an older man. Not a stretch that he might be in his seventies. Now, all that remains is figuring out who he is and collaring the son of a bitch."

Yep. That's all there is to it.

CHAPTER TWENTY-THREE

Tuesday, May 22, 7:57 AM

She had spent all night going through the notepad and had arrived at the Castle before seven this morning to photocopy everything in it with painstaking care. The pages wouldn't stand much more turning. She'd also laid out all her accumulated documentation and had a plan of action.

"Morning, Kim." Another good omen—Bob was here before eight and looking far less rumpled than had been his habit of late.

She'd called him Monday night and told him everything she had, all except the one item that was still a hunch, although the evidence supported it. She only had one shot at this. "Help me move this stuff into the conference room, please?"

As he laid the last file on the table he said, "You've got that old fire in your belly this morning, Glad to see it."

"Thanks. Just back me up."

Bostwick blew in ten minutes later. She almost smiled, seeing that no one was taking their time off. "Brady, let's talk."

She gestured for Bob to wait and followed the lieutenant into his office. "May I suggest we use the conference room instead? I have a lot of material to show you."

Bostwick only stared.

"Lieutenant, we haven't gotten off to the best start. But I'm a damned good detective, and I've finally gotten a solid line on this case. However, that won't matter unless I can convince you with facts. All I'm asking for is a chance to do that."

After a minute of silent staring, he said, "All right. Convince me."

"In the conference room, if you please."

Bob closed the door as they entered.

Bostwick sat at the head of the table, arms crossed against his chest. "Proceed."

"I would appreciate you uncrossing your arms and relaxing. The defensive body language is not helpful."

Bostwick cast a sidelong glance at Bob.

"You need to hear this, Lieu," Bob said at last.

Bostwick uncrossed his arms and took a moment to calm himself. "Very well, Detective. Proceed."

"Thank you." She handed him the FBI's DNA and dental records reports.

"You got these by going outside channels."

"Yes. And you might as well accept I do it anytime it will save time and get us the information we need. In my year at Internal Affairs, I made a lot of useful connections. People in this department pull favors all the time to get what they need. But I've never gone outside the chain of command to undermine my commanding officer." Even the one time she probably should have. "And I wouldn't."

That cooled the lieutenant's jets. He read over the reports. "This shows the man who attacked Lourdes Ramirez also raped and killed eight other women over a period of more than twenty years. The DNA is a hundred percent match." He turned to the dental records report. "And according to this, the bite mark on Ms. Ramirez's shoulder matches the bite mark on all eight victims, plus the Bronx victim in 1963."

"Yes. Do we have any evidence that would refute those conclusions?"

"No."

"Thank you. Now, I must ask you, not for the sake of argument, but so I fully understand the history, why were you so certain Rey Torres was the killer?"

"Because Larry Grant was so sure at first. We all agreed Torres was the best bet."

Kim handed him Grant's notes from the case file. "He doesn't say that here. Just the opposite."

Bostwick studied the notes. "Larry never told me any of this. He told me he liked the kid for the murder and never told me he'd changed his mind."

She pulled out another printout. "Another favor I pulled from a friend in our IT department. This shows the original notes and subsequent additions and deletions. You can see the original notations suspecting Torres are in strike-through type, and the new comments appear as underlined."

"Why the fuck didn't he ever tell me?" It was a cry.

"He may have wanted to wait until he had all the evidence lined up."

Bob spoke up. "And then other events intervened, and he couldn't."

Kim pulled yet out another printout. "I also spoke to two friends of Lulu's yesterday."

Bostwick frowned. "Yes, I got a complaint from their principal."

"I guess she won't be signing up for my fan club. I tried to question one of the girls in her presence, but she was disruptive. So, I spoke with the girl and her friend after school. The friend saw the killer, an older man with gray hair wearing what she described as a dark red hoodie. She last saw him walking toward the spot where Lulu and Rey had gone."

She'd caught Bostwick's interest. "You get a description?"

"Nothing a sketch artist could use. But we're filling in some blanks. We've established the geezer in the hoodie was there before the attack and appeared on camera leaving the attack. Also, why the other kids left and which way they'd gone." She pointed to the rough map she'd drawn on the marker board of the crime scene.

"So, we're dealing with a serial killer. One with over fifty years' experience." Bostwick shook his head. "Ten murders."

"Possibly eleven." Kim pointed to the photocopy of Granddad's notes. "He didn't know the full name of the killer he was hunting, just that his first name was Paul and that he was a teenager. His last note says he was going to tail his suspect that night alone."

"Meaning the killer likely killed him, too." Bostwick's voice was soft with gravity.

"That would be my conclusion. With your permission, I'll request the case file and evidence for the case of the murder of Detective Daniel Brady. And if the evidence supports it, I'd like your permission to link it to these other cases."

"Yes, of course, but…"

"I'd also like permission to engage the FBI for this investigation, since our killer has clearly crossed state lines."

Bostwick interrupted her. "Detective, you need to slow down, here. I can't allow you to remain on an investigation of your own grandfather's death. You'd become too emotionally involved."

She couldn't snap back at him. They were finally having a calm, rational conversation. She drew a deep breath to tamp down any snarky tone. "To begin with, I never met my grandfather…"

"You carry his weapon, a 1950 Smith and Wesson Chief's Special." He smiled in admiration. "A fine piece."

"A gift from my father. Furthermore, and I'm sure Bob will confirm it, I get emotionally involved in all my cases, but I never lose my objectivity because my goal is always to nail the fucking criminal."

"I'll drink to that," Bob said,

She shot him a quick smile before turning back to their lieutenant. "Will I be more heavily motivated here? Yes. Because the killer snuffed ten girls' lives for no good reason; and, yes, for my grandfather, because he was a fine police officer with a loving wife and they both deserved a long life together. But I won't lose objectivity on the suspect because I've never met him."

"Lieu," Bob said, "I would go even further. Given the nature and direction of this investigation, I recommend you make Kim the lead on this case."

Bostwick looked as stunned as Kim felt. "That's generous of you, Bob, but I'm sure Detective Brady is content to keep everything as is. Besides, you can impose some modicum of restraint if she goes too far over the line. Detective Brady, I am granting your requests. What do you expect to get from the FBI?"

"Everything they've got on those other cases, including any descriptions of the killer they might have."

Bostwick exhaled. "That's reasonable. But how…"

Out in the squad room, an alarm sounded. The door burst open and the desk sergeant, Miguel Ramos, burst in. "Everybody out. Bomb scare."

CHAPTER TWENTY-FOUR

Tuesday, May 22, 9:06 AM

"Kim, leave all that," Bob said. "We need to get out, now."

She was packing the FBI reports and the copy of Granddad's notepad in a new accordion file. "In a minute."

"God damn it, we don't have time…"

Done. She dashed past Bob to her desk, grabbing her laptop off the docking station.

"Detective." It was Ramos.

"Coming." She wasn't leaving anything she might need for this case. The place was almost empty. "Bob, let's grab a car."

"Forget it, Detective," Ramos said. "Just get out, now."

"We'll take mine, Kim," Bob said.

"Okay."

Outside, vehicles from the Emergency Services Unit, the Strategic Resource Group, and the FDNY jammed the street. They had blocked traffic along both DeKalb and Wilson Avenues off, and an NYPD helicopter circled overhead.

"Where are you parked?" Kim asked.

"Suydam Street, over by Maria Hernandez Park. At least we won't be caught up in traffic. Perhaps we should stick around."

"We can't help if we do. Besides, I'm going to see Ken Taylor over at Federal Plaza. I also need to find someone, assuming he's still alive."

They reached Bob's car. Once inside, Kim popped open her laptop and inserted a cell service wireless adapter. "Hope this thing works. Sometimes it's so slow, it reminds me of the old dial-up services when I was a kid."

Bob started the car.

"Please not yet," she said as she typed.

"You get car sick?"

"A little if I'm reading while riding. But that's not why. I don't want to take a chance on losing this signal."

"Should've grabbed a patrol car."

"Shit. Can't get in. Let's stop in at One-PP, first." She shut down the laptop and punched up a number on her cell.

"Internal Affairs, Colangelo speaking."

"Hi, Lieu. I'm officially going through channels to call you."

"Will wonders never cease. What can I do for you?"

"I've received authorization to work with the FBI on the Ramirez case and any related cases. Since you guys coordinate activities with the feds, can you please alert them?"

Colangelo paused. "You mean you want me to have Hal Adams alert the FBI people you've already been working with on this case that you'll be working with them on this case?"

"Yes. Anything wrong with that?"

He chuckled. "No, not at all. Just what I would have expected. Everybody okay over in your neck of the woods? I understand you've had some excitement this morning."

"Yes, something else I'll be discussing with Agent Taylor."

Colangelo turned serious. "Don't get distracted, Kim. This isn't like the last time, where the crazies are tied to the case you're investigating."

"Wrong, Lieu. It's exactly like last time. Only the players have changed."

A long pause. "Okay. Keep me posted. Working with Bob Nolan on this one?"

"I am." She shot Bob a grin. "He kind of grows on you."

Bob mouthed a silent "Fuck you."

***

She had two stops to make at One-PP. The first was police sketch artist Sheila Gregg.

"Hey, Kim. Good to see you. Are you guys okay? I heard about…"

"Everything was okay when I left. My partner is checking in with our lieu right now. Could you make a sketch based on limited information?"

Sheila frowned. "Depends on how limited. What do you have?"

"Gray hair, bushy eyebrows, and a long nose that's thick near the face with a bump and hooks down."

"Sounds like an Aquiline nose. What else?"

"That's it."

Sheila scoffed. "No face shape? Nothing about the eyes or chin or mouth?"

"Sorry. The witness is a fifteen-year-old girl. She only saw him for a moment and didn't have reason at the time to commit it to memory."

"This is the Williamsburg murder, isn't it?"

"It is, but keep that under your hat."

"In this department? Lots of luck."

Bob interrupted, cell in hand. "Just heard from the lieu. ESU found no bomb."

"I didn't think they would." She turned to the artist. "Thanks anyway, Sheila."

"Sorry I couldn't help. Good luck."

***

Vera Koshkin, an IT technician extraordinaire who could pass as a Russian model, stared at the laptop tucked under Kim's arm. "Brilliant American lady detective, we don't do repairs here."

"Nice to see you, too, Vera. I don't need to repair it. I just need a place to dock it so I can do some digging."

"Is spare cubicle next to mine." Vera scowled as she eyed the wireless adapter still sticking out of the USB port. "Don't waste time with those. They outdated junk."

"That's why I need the docking station."

Vera turned to Bob, her manner suddenly coy. "And good morning to you, Detective Nolan. Nice to see you again."

Kim stifled a laugh at the sight of Bob melting under Vera's flirting. "Careful, Vera. I'll tell Cord on you." Cordell Washington, a member of the IAB unit to which Kim had belonged, had finally worked up the courage to ask Vera out shortly before Kim left for Brooklyn North. They were now an item.

"Cord knows I just like to be friendly. How can I help?"

By now, Kim had logged into the department's network. "I'm trying to find someone who may or may not still be living. He was my grandfather's partner in 1963."

Vera returned to her own cube. "I can access our HR records. Name, please."

"Detective Philip Boland."

A quick riff of keystrokes. "I have. Born in 1936, joined department in 1957, made detective in 1962, assigned to the 44th Precinct in the Bronx the same year."

"Bingo," Bob said.

"Is what, this bingo?" Vera asked.

"He means you got the right man. Is there a date of death?"

Vera returned to the screen. "*Nyet*. Still collecting a pension. Current address is Chapin Home for the Aging in Jamaica, Queens."

Kim made a note of the address in her cell. "Okay. Next. Frank Larkin."

"Is here. Born 1908, joined department 1928, made detective in 1933, died 2001. Sorry."

"It would've surprised me if he had still been with us. One more. Sean McHugh."

"Is also here. Born 1917, joined department 1938, made detective 1943, died 2011."

Kim couldn't hide her disappointment on this one. "I was hoping he'd have been a little younger."

"You think he could have helped?" Bob asked.

"Perhaps not. But just to talk to someone who worked with my granddad." She disconnected her laptop. "Okay, thanks Vera."

CHAPTER TWENTY-FIVE

Tuesday, May 22, 12:22 PM

"Not a good day, Kim."

It wasn't quite the greeting she was expecting from Ken Taylor, but she understood. "Not for me, either, but time, tide and terrorist groups wait for no one. It was CHE, wasn't it?"

"That was our first thought. If we're right, even with no device, it puts us in a whole new ballgame. Anyway, I got the word from Hal Adams that we're going legit. Good. Anything new on your end?"

"I got a partial description of the killer, but it's too incomplete to be useful right now." She showed him the copy of Granddad's notes. "He may also have killed my grandfather. Did any of the departments who caught those eight other murders gather any forensic evidence other than the bite marks?"

"You mean like fingerprints?"

"Yeah."

"No. And death in all cases resulted either from a blow to the head or strangulation. What about your grandfather?"

"They shot him. I realize the method isn't consistent with the other murders. But he was tailing a suspect in the Angelina Farina murder, a seventeen-year-old boy named Paul whose habits he had discovered. If those two killings aren't linked, I'll eat my hat."

Taylor's grin only lasted a few seconds. "Okay. Then tell me this. Why would CHE target your building for a bomb scare?"

That had been bothering her, too. "If one wanted to spur the police to complete an investigation, why hinder them? Good question. But an even better one is what would make them target the Castle? Most people think the precincts handle all crimes. Williamsburg is the Ninetieth Precinct. Wouldn't they target the Nine-Oh, which is only about a half mile from the murder scene?"

"No, these guys are serious, so they know the structure of the department." Taylor consulted a notepad. "You mentioned having seen Felipe Prinz in Domino Park the afternoon of the disturbance. That's another reason this may be connected. Any chance he would've recognized you?"

"I doubt it. But Phil Vitello from the CSU was with me, and he might well have recognized him. Why?"

"Before you started on the case, CHE was making a lot of noise about how the cops don't care about Latino lives. Maybe seeing the police getting serious again about this investigation makes them nervous, like someone might take away the drum they've been beating for seven months."

She laughed without humor. "That's just sick enough to be true. Makes me wonder how much information they have about the murder to begin with."

"Probably not much. What else do you have?"

"I've located my granddad's partner at the time. He lives in a nursing home in Queens. We're on our way to interview him now."

"Call first. Trust me."

***

Bob made the turn off 164th Street onto a steep uphill side street. "Christ, this is some hill."

"I guess that's why they call this area Jamaica Hills. That's it up on the left. Looks like parking might be a challenge."

Bob parked by a fire hydrant. Before they entered, she locked her laptop in the trunk. Good thing she'd called ahead. Once Kim explained the purpose of her visit, the head nurse on the floor promised to prepare Phil Boland.

She showed her badge at the front desk, and a member of the staff came out to escort them up to his room. He was sitting in a wheelchair, dozing. A woman in her fifties sat next to him in a visitor's chair.

The woman stood. "I'm Denise, his daughter."

Kim introduced herself and Bob. "My grandfather and your father were partners."

"You're Dan Brady's granddaughter?"

Phil Boland popped awake. "Brady? Dan Brady? He's dead."

Denise rushed to his side. "It's okay, Dad. This is his granddaughter, Kim."

The old man scowled. "I don't know any Kim."

"Dan Brady was her grandfather, Dad."

He stared up at Kim, finally making eye contact. "Oh." His eyes narrowed. "Pat had a son."

Kim signaled Bob to wait by the door. "He did. My dad was Joe, Dan's younger son."

He looked befuddled. "Joe? He's just a little guy."

"He grew up, just like I did. Do you remember Dan?" It felt strange to use her granddad's first name.

A smile broke out on the old man's face. "Dan? Sure. Best cop I ever worked with. Good man. Tough as nails, and as brave as they come." His smile faded. "He got killed. Chased after that punk kid and never told nobody." He heaved a huge sigh. "He should've trusted me."

"I'm sure he had other reasons. It wouldn't have been lack of trust." Not that she could guess.

He nodded slowly, as if considering it. "Yeah. Dan was a fine man."

"You were telling me about what he was doing just before he died."

After a momentary scowl, the fog cleared. "Angelina. I forget her last name."

"Farina."

"Yeah. Pretty girl. Nice family. They were so crushed by it. Pretty girl. Long dark hair, friendly smile, brown eyes. School portrait on the mantel." He paused, as if looking back. "Found her body in the park, after the dance. Must've questioned every kid in the school. Talked to the boy who walked her home. Kevin something. Nice kid. Irish, carrot top."

Kim grinned at that.

He turned serious again. "But it wasn't him. The neighbor'd said he looked Italian."

Kim's heart jumped. "What neighbor? Someone saw him?" Granddad's notes hadn't mentioned an eyewitness.

"Crossing Teller Avenue," he said. His expression turned dark. "What'd he bite her for? Guy was a psycho."

A look of alarm flickered in his daughter's eyes. "Dad, are you okay?"

"Who saw him?" Kim wanted to go easy, but the window was closing.

"Punk kid. Dan was sure of where he lived, Little Italy, and where he'd gone to school. Taft, just like the girl. Went to lie in wait for him. Then got shot. Shot. Damned punk."

Denise rubbed his arm. "It's okay, Dad."

"Wait," Kim said. "The kid was Italian?"

"Dan was sure. Followed some lead he'd gotten. From Little Italy." He shook his head. "He never should've gone alone."

"Was the suspect's name Paul?"

The old detective dwelled on it. "Yeah. Paul. Didn't know his last name." He gazed at her. "You're Dan Brady's granddaughter? Why are you asking?"

"I'm a detective. I'm working on a related case."

"Detective, huh? Got a badge?"

She pulled out her leather badge holder and opened it.

He stared at it and ran his fingers over the badge. "That gold badge. You carry that with pride, young lady." His eyes snagged on the medals. "Honorable Mention. Purple Shield. What's this one?"

"Community Service."

He sighed. "Don't remember that one. Dan won Honorable Mention, too. Back in '42, long before I was on the job." He stared a while longer. "Purple Shield. You've been shot?"

"Just below the shoulder. Over a year ago."

He chuckled. "You got Dan's moxie."

An aide rolled in a cart of medications. "Mr. Boland, time for your pills."

Kim patted his arm. "Thanks, Detective."

He faced her, his expression clouded. "What was your name again?"

"Kim. Detective Kim Brady."

He brightened. "I had a partner named Brady, once. Best man I ever worked with."

CHAPTER TWENTY-SIX

Tuesday, May 22, 3:07 PM

"Where the hell have you two been?" Bostwick's greeting when they walked in was loud enough to shake the walls of the Castle.

"Glad to see the place is still in one piece," Bob said with a grin.

"You'd better have something good on this case to be cracking jokes."

"We tracked down my grandfather's partner on the Farina murder, now in a nursing home in Queens."

Bostwick snorted. "Great. A senile eyewitness. I assume it was a complete waste of time."

Kim pulled her Notes app, not because she needed it, but to show Bostick she considered it significant enough to record. "No. He didn't give us a lot, but he provided a couple of pieces we didn't have before. Angelina attended a dance that night at Taft High School, and she met a boy who walked her home. According to my granddad's notes, he only walked her to the corner of 172nd and Teller Avenue because she didn't want her parents to see her with him."

"Why not?" Bostwick asked.

"Because he was Irish, of course."

"And that's important, why?"

"Let her finish, Lieu," Bob said.

Kim resumed. "Her father and older brother went out looking for her when she wasn't home by midnight. They first walked to the school and back before checking Claremont Park across Teller Avenue. The older brother found her body close to the 172nd Street entrance. He called it in to the department at 1:10 Saturday morning. The coroner estimated the time of death between 11:00 and midnight."

"I'm not hearing anything new, here," Bostwick said.

Kim took a deep breath. "There were two things. One, Boland mentioned an eyewitness, a neighbor. When he talked about the boy Angelina had met, he added it couldn't have been him because his red hair didn't match what the neighbor had said."

"But there's no mention in the notes or the case file of a witness." Bostwick was growing agitated.

"No, but Boland was firm on it. He didn't say what the neighbor saw, other than the unknown boy was Italian, or at least looked Italian. He got agitated and referred to him as a psycho."

Bostwick stifled a laugh. "That's the big breakthrough? Can we be sure it's real? We're talking about a senile old guy, right?"

"He's got a tenuous grasp on current reality, but he was clear as a bell on the past. He even recognized two of the three citations on my badge holder." She shook her head. "It bothers me that my granddad never mentioned the neighbor in his notes."

"Could be it was something Boland knew but your grandfather didn't," Bob said.

She considered that. "Could be. In everything, Granddad was meticulous in recording the most minute details."

"Like his granddaughter." Bob turned thoughtful. "Can you think of any facts about a case that you'd be reluctant to put in a case file or Notes app?"

"Not really. I tend to be all-inclusive." But that wasn't true. She'd hesitated to make a note about Lulu trying weed and had only included it because it was in the tox report. "But if Granddad came across something cringeworthy, who knows?"

"At any rate," Bostwick said, "it's not a lead you can use. Anything else?"

"Yes," Bob replied. "We talked to Ken Taylor. They don't have any other forensic evidence for us, but they'll help us with whatever we need. He also thinks CHE was behind this morning's scare."

"Another headline." Bostwick walked to the door. "Brogan."

Detective Tim Brogan rolled another chair into the office. "Present."

"Tim has now fully recovered from his appendectomy and is ready to return to the fray. I'm placing him at your disposal. Since you were among the missing this morning, I had him retrieve the evidence and case file for Daniel Brady's murder. Any luck, Brogan?"

Brogan chuckled. "Fancy that. A team investigating the murder of an Irish cop and ten females, and we've names like Brady, Brogan and Nolan. Ha. Sounds like an Oirish law firm." He turned to Kim. "You'll probably want to go through all this stuff yourself, so for now I'll give you the star of the show." He pulled out a plastic bag holding a slug.

Kim looked it over. "Looks like a thirty-two caliber."

"Give the lady the prize teddy bear. Now for the special bonus, can you guess what they also found that goes with this little baby?"

She tried not to cry out. "The casing?"

Brogan laughed. "Recovered from the gutter. She goes two for two. Care to try for the trifecta?"

"Don't tell me there's a print on the casing."

"Three for three. Detective Brady, you are as brilliant as advertised."

She waved away the compliment. "Get it to Ken Taylor at the FBI at Federal Plaza."

Brogan turned to the lieutenant. "You said Bob was lead."

Bob spoke up first. "Kim and I are sort of co-leading."

Kim waited for the explosion from Bostwick, but he only said, "I thought the FBI didn't have any prints on the murders."

"They don't. They will, now." She repeated for Brogan what they'd learned.

"So," Brogan said, "we've got the fucker's DNA, but we can't match it to anything. He's just an old Italian-looking guy with a hooked nose and bushy eyebrows. That doesn't exactly narrow it down."

She'd been stewing about it since the nursing home. "He started this spree in New York and, after moving around for years, has come back."

"So, you're ready to ask for an arrest warrant?" Bostwick probably couldn't help himself. "I just saw an old 'Law and Order' episode where they got the DNA and wrapped up the case."

Neither Bob nor Tim laughed.

She let the silence hang.

"Kim?" Bob asked at last. "Any ideas?"

"We have the killer's DNA. He killed eleven people and raped ten of his victims. We have to work backward."

"What the hell does that mean?" Bostwick asked.

Only one answer. "How do people find their ancestral roots these days? They spit into a tube or swab the inside of their mouth and submit a DNA sample to a company that traces the DNA back through existing databases, and the company then adds their DNA to its database. There are also firms that police departments hire to use criminals' DNA to track their family roots, and then construct a family tree from what they call a Most Common Recent Ancestor. From that tree, they develop a list of close DNA matches to the unknown criminal and generate a list of possible suspects. It's called Investigative Genetic Genealogy or IGG."

"I read something about that recently," Brogan said. "It's how they nailed the Green River killer in Washington State."

She liked him already. "That's right. The FBI has these firms they work with."

"Must cost a fortune," Bostwick said. "No way the department would pay for it."

"Remember, the FBI is now officially working with us on this case. When we give Taylor the prints from the slug, we can ask him to submit the DNA data they already have."

Bostwick shook his head. "Not yet. Let me discuss it first with the Chief."

Great. So he could torpedo the idea.

CHAPTER TWENTY-SEVEN

Tuesday, May 22, 3:40 PM

Kim and Bob examined the entire case file on Granddad's murder while Brogan delivered the prints to Ken Taylor,

He'd been shot in the head sitting in his car on East 181st Street between Washington and Bathgate Avenues, next to the Bathgate Playground, on the evening of June 19th. Time of death was between 9:00 and 11:00. Based on the slug removed from his skull, the weapon was a .32 caliber Baretta. Prints on the slug matched nothing in NYPD's records.

"And they still don't," she muttered.

Bob glanced up. "Hmm?"

"Just reading. They came up empty on the prints. I wonder if anything will show up on a new search. An extensive search of the playground, the surrounding neighborhood, and several locations throughout the Bronx failed to turn up the Baretta. There were no reports of a stolen .32 Baretta. Let's go check out the two Bronx crime scenes."

***

They parked the car on Teller Avenue, but Kim suggested they return to the high school, first. "Stanley Kubrick graduated from the original Taft High School. So did Luther Vandross."

"This isn't the original school?" Bob asked.

"Original building, but the city closed the school itself because it was failing. It's now the Taft High School campus, and houses several small, specialty schools."

Bob stared up at the main entrance. "They sure built majestic-looking schools back in the day."

"Angelina probably came down these steps with the boy she'd met. Kevin Something. She was pretty but shy. Granddad's notes mentioned Kevin was beside himself at her death, and a nice guy."

"People thought Ted Bundy was a nice guy."

"I doubt Kevin was a serial killer. Or is. He walked her most of the way home." She started walking along East 172nd Street. "A short walk from here to Teller."

"Which may be why her dad wasn't here to pick her up. Then again, things were a lot different in those days. No one worried about kids walking alone or with their friends."

She couldn't resist. "So they say." She was pleased when the needle sank home.

"Hey. I was a seventies kid."

"Only just."

"Wiseass. Okay, so what happened next with our bedazzled young couple?"

Excellent question. "Probably not much. If they were both on the quiet side, I doubt they did more than hold hands." She turned serious as they approached Teller. "She said goodbye to him about here. Kevin turned back right away because he was so tempted to follow her but didn't want to ruin things. He doubled back past the school to the 170th Street station to catch the IRT up to his home in Kingsbridge Heights."

"While Angelina would have proceeded along Teller Avenue..."

She followed as Bob strode along the sidewalk, past the apartment building on the corner. "Stop. She must have been right about here because it's a clear line of sight from the windows of several apartments in the building, and someone saw her with the killer."

"But whoever it was," Bob said, "they didn't get a good enough look to give a detailed description. So, he might not have been waiting here on the sidewalk, because by then someone would have gotten a good look at him."

Kim pointed to the other side of the street. "He would've waited over there, shadowed from streetlights, and able to turn away if anyone came too close. If someone had accosted her on the sidewalk and dragged her across the street, a neighbor would have heard. Phil Boland said nothing like that. Her attacker lured her over to the park."

Bob followed her gaze. "So, it was someone she knew?"

"It's possible." They crossed Teller Avenue to the park, climbed the concrete steps, and stopped at the bench behind which Angelina's body had been found. "It's hard to guess what the tree growth was like here back then, but I can't imagine anyone being able to see this far in at eleven o'clock at night."

***

They drove to Bathgate Playground and walked around it twice, East 181st Street to Washington Avenue to 182nd to Bathgate Avenue, and back to 181st. The area was a hodgepodge of single-family homes, apartment buildings, two schools, and a park called "A Farm in the Bronx".

She stopped on East 181st outside the playground. "According to a rough map in the file, he had parked right here, opposite that apartment building, waiting. Why here?"

"He must've followed him to the playground. Or heard he'd be here." Bob considered it. "Maybe he had reason to believe he lived around here."

She recalled her conversation with Boland. "Granddad's partner said two things that, together, make no sense. On the one hand, Granddad thought the killer had gone to Taft. But he also was convinced he lived in Little Italy."

"So?"

"Little Italy is in Lower Manhattan."

Bob chuckled. "You're still sketchy on Bronx geography." He gestured to the surrounding area. "This area—Belmont—used to be known as Little Italy. Italian immigrants clustered here in the early

1900s. Did your granddad mention anything about interviews with students?"

"Pages and pages. That's another reason Boland's comment about Taft concerned me. If he'd suspected a kid he interviewed, he'd have mentioned it." Then it hit her. "He was a dropout. Bob, he didn't just know the first name, he knew which dropout and where to look." She glanced skyward. "Granddad, why the hell didn't you write his surname in the notepad?"

"I half expected to hear an answer just now." Bob surveyed the open spaces. "A gunshot would have been pretty loud here. It would have echoed off those walls."

"But the relatively confined spaces would have bounced the sound waves around. They would have echoed across the open space, north and west. If he lived around here, he could have retreated to his place before people had time to react." She fell silent and stared at the surroundings.

"So, our next move is what? Get a hold of the 1963 Bronx phone book and look for all the Italian names in this neighborhood?"

She resisted the temptation to laugh. "A teenaged kid wouldn't appear. Let's get Tim started on researching old Taft yearbooks..." She stopped. "Shit. Over fifty years later? Not a chance."

"And if he was a dropout, there probably wouldn't be any photos of him, anyway."

"But there might be sites for alumni. Someone might have remembered him. Also, let's see if we can track down any of Angelina's relatives who knew her."

CHAPTER TWENTY-EIGHT

Tuesday, May 22, 6:01 PM

"State Senator Raymond Brandt today hurled his most strident criticism to date at Acting Mayor Sabrina Dunn, charging her with creating 'an atmosphere of insurgency' and citing this morning's bomb scare at a police headquarters in the Bushwick section of Brooklyn. Although no group has claimed responsibility for the incident, some have speculated that the radical group Come Home Ernesto, or CHE, was behind it. The leader of the group has been vocal in his criticism of the police, claiming that they are basing their investigation of the infamous Williamsburg murder case on the same racial stereotypes that are driving widespread gentrification of the city."

***

Ordinarily, the TV nattering away while he did his ongoing weight training—important in keeping up his strength—irritated him. But, as he finished his sets of bicep curls, he could only smirk. Here was this radical group obstructing the work that could bring about the very thing they wanted—the apprehension of a white criminal.

At first, he'd feared that his little escapade in the fog might have been just a tad too brazen. But here it was, seven months later, and he'd stumped the police.

It had been so nice to return home at long last after being away for so long. And the ease with which he'd subdued his prey had confirmed that his weight training was having the desired effect.

The trainer he'd worked with when he first came to the gym greeted him as he dried off in front of his locker after his shower. "Your arms are toning up just fine. Quads, too. You taking any supplements?"

"Heavy on the vitamin D."

The trainer laughed. "You're stronger and more fit than most guys half your age."

***

He got off the R train at 77th Street. His workout had left him hungry, so he stopped at Luliano's on his way home. The hostess was a lovely young thing, triggering a hunger of another kind. "On second thought, honey, I'm going to take it home, instead. Just bring me a glass of chianti while I wait."

He sat on the bench, sipping his wine, trying to distract his attention from the hostess flitting about in her not-too-short skirt pulled taut on her hips. She reminded him of another girl, also forbidden, so many years ago. She was several years older, but the similarity of her features was striking.

The television over the bar had a soccer game on. He could never understand the passion so many had for the game. Ninety minutes to produce maybe three minutes of excitement.

"Would you like another glass of wine?" It was the hostess. Close enough so he could smell her makeup. Cover Girl. He could just imagine...

"No. No, thank you."

"Would you like me to take your glass?"

"Thank you." He stared at her swaying hips as she walked away.

It was too close to home, just a half block from the Queen Anne row-house in which he had the ground-floor apartment. He'd never struck so close to his home or regular routines, not since the first.

With relief, he took the bag containing his dinner of Caesar Salad and Osso Bucco and paid for it, leaving a generous tip for the hostess.

He would need to strike sooner rather than later.

CHAPTER TWENTY-NINE

Wednesday, May 23, 11:19 AM

While Brogan searched for online groups of Taft alumni, Bob and Kim searched for traces of Angelina Farina's family. Granddad's notes showed she had two older brothers and one younger sister. Bob was still searching for the brothers when Kim discovered that the sister, now in her late sixties, was living in Riverdale. "You guys stay and keep at it. I'm going to see her."

***

She parked and walked down the access road to a grand curved apartment building that towered over the Hudson River. The doorman called to announce her, and for a moment she wondered if she should have called, first. But that would have meant stating the reason for her visit, which would have given Ms. Gina Farina Owens reason to decline.

"First elevator on your right," the doorman said.

Gina, whom Kim had already discovered was a former magazine editor and a widow, greeted her wearing tailored slacks, a silk blouse, and a puzzled expression. "Is there something I can help you with?"

"I hope so," Kim said. "You had an older sister named Angelina?"

"Yes. She died many years ago."

Kim dropped her voice. "In fact, someone killed her. And the case was never solved."

"Don't tell me you're trying to solve it now, a half-century later."

"May I come in, Ms. Owens? It would be much better to discuss this in private."

"Yes, please do." Her hesitation was only momentary. "May I offer you something? A cup of coffee or tea?"

"Tea would be fine, thank you."

Gina showed her into the living room, and Kim paused at the bay window with its view of the Hudson. "This is lovely."

"Thank you. I love gazing out that window, especially since my husband passed away. It gives me solace."

"I'm sorry. How long ago was that?"

"Just over a year. Colon cancer." The microwave beeped. "I'll get your tea."

Kim noticed several framed photos crowding the mantel. At the center was a large, formal family portrait with an older couple at the center and several younger adults and many children arrayed around them.

"That was in the summer of 1961," Gina said as she handed Kim her mug of tea. "A family reunion. That summer was such a happy time. Kennedy was president, our family was prospering, and everything was full of promise."

"That's a lot of Farinas."

"They're not all Farinas. My dad's sister," Gina pointed her out, "married a Triscari. A Sicilian name. Dad said it caused a mild uproar in the family because we're *Napolitán*, and *Napolitáns* look down on Sicilians."

Kim spotted Angelina immediately.

A sad smile from Gina. "Yes, and that's me next to her."

"Such a sweet-looking girl."

"Everyone always said so," Gina replied. "But I never saw her that way. She was my big sister, already on her way to womanhood. She was a woman of the world to me. I tried to copy everything she did. I so desperately wanted to catch up. Then, we lost her two years later, and I caught up. And I was miserable."

"I'm sorry, Ms. Owens."

"Thank you. You haven't said what you want."

"I'm investigating a murder. I can't tell you much about it, although perhaps you can guess."

"That poor girl in Brooklyn?"

"Yes. But others, as well. Before I go any further, I must ask you not to mention anything about this conversation, not even the fact that we've had it, to anyone. Not even your brothers."

"My oldest brother is dead, and my other brother moved away. We don't keep in contact." Gina gestured toward the reunion photo. "Angelina's death shattered this family. Mom and Dad remained married but were strangers to each other. My brothers fled as quickly as they could. I struck out on my own. Sometimes, I look at that picture, and I wonder how it all fell apart."

"My mom and dad divorced when I was ten, and I was an only child. I have a sense of what you mean." But Kim didn't want to go there.

They sat on the sofa together.

"So, is my sister's murder one other you're investigating?"

Kim took a sip of tea before continuing. "Yes. We're convinced we're looking for a serial killer. We suspect Angelina was his first victim."

"But how can you possibly restart something that old?"

"I have an advantage. My grandfather was the original detective on her case. I've found the notes he kept. Did she attract a lot of attention from boys?"

Gina nodded. "It started in eighth grade, but really picked up when she started at Taft. Andrew said it was because guys thought she'd be easy to seduce."

Andrew, she recalled from Granddad's notes, was the younger of the two brothers. "Was there anyone, an older boy, who might have been interested? In school or out?"

A momentary flicker of hesitation. "No."

"Gina, if there's someone you have in mind, we can not only secure justice for Angelina, but for several other victims as well. This man remains a threat."

"There isn't. I just needed to think for a moment. If I knew, I'd tell you." Her eyes began to tear. "I miss her so much. Even now."

"Was she seeing anyone on the sly?"

"No. And she'd have told me. She told me everything."

"Was there anyone who liked her, but she didn't like?"

"There might have been a couple, but it was just that 'I think he likes me' kind of thing. Sorry."

***

He was on the prowl, now. Normally, he'd strike in a different borough to keep the police off balance. But what could be better than striking in the same area the police assumed they had covered? Imagine the uproar.

Not Domino Park. Too open. But somewhere not too far, so the narrative that so many felt compelled to believe could continue.

He drove along Meeker Avenue, next to the Brooklyn Queens Expressway. He reached the point where there was parking under the highway. There, on the far side. A retaining wall. And the wide steel support next to it would be perfect. He pulled in and parked his Jeep against the wall and between a supporting girder and a plumber's van. He'd already scouted the neighborhood. A pizza place nearby where teens hung out. What better place to find a target?

He checked the back seat. The cane, fake walking cast, and gallon disinfectant container filled with sand were all there.

Nothing left to do but take the bus to Metro-Tech and a subway home and wait for nightfall.

***

"There's a Facebook group for Taft alums," Brogan said when she returned. "I got in under a false name and claiming I was in the Class of '64, but so far, no other participants from that year. It may take some time." His cell trilled, and he turned away to answer.

"Any luck?" Bob asked Kim.

"Not much. Looks like she's the only Farina left, in New York, anyway. How about you?"

"I found an obit for the oldest brother. Died in Boston two years ago."

"Andrew moved away, but she had no forwarding address for him."

Bob snorted. "That narrows it down."

Brogan tossed his cell on his desk. "Shit."

"What's wrong?" Bob asked.

"That was Holly. She thinks she found a lump. Doctor wants her to go for a mammogram. She's going next Tuesday."

"Is she okay?" Kim asked. "You need some time off?"

Brogan laughed. "She's fine. Meets everything head-on. She doesn't want me to worry. Or take time off."

"Best to do it her way. Keep me posted." Kim punched up Ken Taylor's number. "Quick question. Does the FBI conduct or facilitate genetic genealogy investigations?"

"We have some firms we work with. But only when every other available avenue has been exhausted." Kim told him where they were. "Try to do some more digging, first. Try to track down the other brother."

They spent the balance of the afternoon scouring the internet for Andrew Farina. Brogan got a reply from a Taft alumnus who'd known him but didn't know what had happened after graduation. Kim tried the DMV database, but his New York driver's license had expired in 1970. Bob found no records of him having served in the armed forces. They divided up the databases.

Finally, Kim said, "What the hell? Why not try one of those lookup services?"

"You have to pay to get any useful information out of them," Bob said.

"True. But I just want a city and state. I can contact the local police department from there." She input his name but left the city and state blank. "Five pages of hits. I guess it could have been worse."

A text came in from Joanna Dunbar. *We need to talk. Meet me outside the Sunrise Deli?*

***

Senator Brandt was dreading returning to Albany. The state budget had passed, there was nothing pressing pending, and he would have preferred to remain here in the city, sniping at his opponent in the upcoming special election. What he needed now was a good reason to stay.

An aid, Justin Cates, knocked at his office door, and the senator waved him in. "So, what's the latest?"

"She drove over to Riverdale this morning."

"Any idea who she was seeing?"

"No, sir. She entered a building overlooking the river, and after about thirty minutes, she came out and drove back to Brooklyn."

"Why the hell is she spending so much time in the Bronx? Could she possibly have a suspect there?"

"It's possible. But something else is strange. She's pulled records on some old cases from the archives."

That caught the senator's interest. "What cases?"

"I couldn't find that out without showing myself."

"Do they think the Ramirez murder is related to old cases? Like maybe they have a serial killer on their hands?"

"Could be, sir."

He flung the pencil he'd been toying with across the office. "Fuck. I should be able to get some information out of the department on this." But he'd burned that bridge, thanks to his patron. "All right, Justin. Thank you. Stick close, stay hidden, and report to me if anything develops."

CHAPTER THIRTY

Wednesday, May 23, 12:02 PM

Joanna Dunbar was leaning against the refrigerated case of the Sunrise Deli and Grill on Myrtle Avenue. Her expression was grim and didn't change as Kim approached.

"Is this seat taken?"

Joanna snorted. "Hilarious."

They started walking toward the door leading to Central Avenue. "What's wrong? You look upset."

"You've already had a busy day, up to Riverdale and back. That's your second trip to the Bronx in two days."

Kim turned serious. "I don't suppose you'd like to explain how you learned that."

"Glad to. You're being tailed."

"That's obvious."

"I don't mean by me. Technically, I've been tailing the guy who's tailing you. Justin Cates. I'm not surprised you haven't picked up on him; he's one of those mousy little men you rarely notice. He's one of Brandt's staffers. I've seen him at some odd places—crime scenes and such."

Kim's first thought was to wonder why Brandt would have someone tailing her. But it was obvious. "Brandt's desperate to get a handle on this case in order to spin it his way."

"Or to obstruct it. If Prinz is right."

"He isn't. This murder has nothing to do with gentrification or real estate projects."

Joanna's eyes met Kim's. "You sound rather sure of that. Care to... shit. There he is."

"Who?"

"Cates. He must have followed you here. He's standing at the corner."

"If he followed me here, he wouldn't have seen you. Has he spotted me?"

"No, he's looking around."

Beyond the window was a thin wisp of a man in his late twenties or early thirties, dark hair, dark shifty eyes, thick lips. He was casually dressed in a nondescript navy-blue windbreaker and a snap-billed cap pulled down over his forehead.

Without another word, Kim slipped out the other exit, on to Central Avenue, and circled behind Cates. "And the hunter becomes the hunted."

Cates jumped and turned to face her. "I beg your pardon?"

"I know who you are, who you work for, and that you've been tailing me. As I'm involved in a difficult investigation, that annoys me. And as you may have heard, I dislike having meddling amateurs fuck up my investigations."

"I assure you I don't know what you're..."

She dropped her voice to a growl and took a step closer, forcing him to back away. "Cut the shit, Mr. Cates." He blanched at her use of his name, and she backed him into a doorway. "You go back to the senator and tell him you are out of the private detective business, because the next time I see you tailing me, I will arrest you for obstruction. The charge won't stick, but the headline will stick to your boss like glue. Now, get the fuck out of my sight."

***

Back at the Castle, she briefed Bob, Tim, and Bostwick on this latest development.

"For someone who loves to paint himself as a friend of the department's," Bob said, "this guy sure is one gold-plated pain in the ass."

"Please tell me you didn't really threaten him," Bostwick said with a groan.

"Hey, I didn't threaten to shoot him. Anyway, now that I've seen him, I'll spot him if he turns up where he shouldn't."

She returned to her desk and the five pages of hits she'd gotten in her search for Andrew Farina.

***

"God damn it." Senator Brandt pounded the desk, making his aide shift with discomfort. "How the hell did she spot you? Who told her who you were?"

"Maybe someone from her unit recognized me. She was with her partner in Belmont yesterday. Maybe he tipped her off."

"Did she ever stare at you?"

"No."

It didn't add up. Or maybe it did. "Have you seen her with that reporter at all?"

"Last week, at Millie's…"

That was it. "All right. Drop the shadowing for now. If she made a stink, it wouldn't be good for us.

***

There it was. Andrew Farina. East Stroudsburg, Pennsylvania, age 73. The relatives matched. With a little more digging, she had the address and a phone number.

She checked her watch. Almost four. End of tour. "Bob, how long would it take to get to East Stroudsburg from here?"

"About two hours, but that could vary a lot based on traffic. Planning a quick getaway to the Poconos with Jake?"

Lovely thought, although St. Thomas, not the Poconos, would be her first choice. "No. I may have found Angelina's brother. If we left now…"

"Whereabouts in East Stroudsburg?"

She checked the address. "It's on Mt. Nebo Road."

"Mt. Nebo isn't East Stroudsburg, it's further north, off Route 209, which at certain times resembles a parking lot." He shrugged. "Back in a prior life my wife at the time and I had a cottage in the Marshall's Creek area."

"You were married? Sorry."

"Yep. We divorced shortly after I made second grade detective. Don't look like that. She didn't understand about the job, and I didn't understand about marriage. I salute you and Jake. You're one of the few couples who make it work."

"Most of the time." It slipped out.

Bob softened his voice and his manner. "I won't ask what you mean by that. But whatever it is, if you two can't, no one can." He gestured toward her laptop. "Before we rush out to the boondocks, check that phone number."

Jake texted her. *No meetings tonight and no games to scout. How about dinner at Al Di la Trattoria?*

She tried Andrew Farina's number and got an automated message saying it was not in service.

So much for Andrew. She texted Jake. *Great.*

CHAPTER THIRTY-ONE

Wednesday, May 23, 8:10 PM

Senator Brandt looked up from his corner table at his favorite restaurant, Al Di la Trattoria, and did a double take as the hostess escorted a young couple to a table by the window. The woman bore a striking resemblance to Detective Brady. It took a few moments to realize it was the detective, wearing a dress and high heels. But as he watched, there was no doubt.

What a stunning woman.

And what an incredible piece of luck, a commodity that had been in short supply of late.

***

"Something's been bothering you," Jake said as their dinner plates were cleared away. "You haven't been the same since the dinner Sunday night. I realize this case is a bear, but you've been distant with me, and you've never been that way even on your toughest cases."

"I've never had a case like this one."

"You said you could be objective." His smile took some of the sting out of it.

"Well, I can't." Not that she'd ever admit that to Bostwick. "The leads are incredibly thin. And the killer is still out there."

"Okay. But something happened Sunday night, because I felt it at dinner before you and Jim started talking about your grandfather. It was like a wall going up."

It was so minor. And perhaps he hadn't meant anything by it. "When Jim's wife asked if we had any children, I said, 'No', and then you said, 'Not yet'. It felt like you were pressing me."

"I wasn't. I'm sorry you thought that. But we were going to talk about it once you got settled at Brooklyn North. Having second thoughts?"

And third thoughts and… "What kind of mother do you think I could be when I'm on a case like this?"

"Come on, Kim. This is a once-in-a-career case."

"Which makes it my third once-in-a-career case in eighteen months."

"So, what are you saying?"

***

He'd seen her entering the pizza place with two other girls, having passed the church. "More oregano," she'd yelled, and they'd all dissolved into giggles. The voice, the face and the body were all familiar. She'd been in the park that night. Who knows what she'd seen?

Fate was smiling on him once again.

So, he'd waited.

Now, she was leaving. As she turned toward North Eighth Street, he bent to pick up the shopping bag with the gallon container full of sand, leaning on his cane. As she crossed the street toward him, he called out in his best feeble voice. "Young lady, could you please help me?"

"Sure. How?"

He could smell traces of marijuana on her. "I parked my car under the expressway. Could you carry this for me? I can't manage it with the cane." He gestured to the walking cast. "Foot surgery."

She weaved a little. "Um, okay." She picked up the bag.

"What's your name?"

"Martha."

"In high school?"

"Uh huh. Tenth grade."

Perfect. "Well, Martha, you are as lovely as you are kind."

She giggled again. High. Defenseless. He made sure she was on the outside as they walked.

The light at Meeker Avenue, which ran alongside the Brooklyn Queens Expressway, turned just as they got to the corner, and they crossed. He turned his face away from the few cars stopped at the light. "My car is just a little further, by the wall."

They reached the point where Meeker Avenue was well above their heads. He dropped his cane next to the car. "Damn."

Another giggle. "I'll get it."

As she turned to hand it to him, he grabbed her by the throat. Hard.

***

Kim was struggling to put her answer to Jake into words when a familiar voice broke in from her right. "Excuse me, but aren't you Kim Brady?"

She decided to be polite. "Senator Brandt. This is my husband, Jake Dudek."

"Director of Analytics for my favorite basketball team." The senator shook Jake's hand and then hers. "May I join you for dessert and coffee? I've already instructed the maître d' to put your dinners on my tab."

"Thank you," Jake said, alarmed, "but that's..."

"It's my pleasure. And I owe your lovely wife at least that much for, shall we say, past inconveniences." He turned to her and grinned at her stunned expression. "My frankness surprises you. While obfuscation is a common political tool, sometimes, complete honesty is quite helpful."

Time for her to push back. "Does this have anything to do with my confrontation earlier today with your Mr. Cates?"

The senator glanced around. No one sitting nearby. "It does, indeed. And my apologies for that, as well. Desperate times call for desperate measures."

"Like this one?" she asked.

"Detective, this is not desperation. This is an honest effort to gain information in as non-public a manner as possible. I'm quite sympathetic to the needs of your investigation. And while I may have been, shall we say, indiscreet in the past on such matters, such will not be the case, now. And if I can be of any help, you may call on me at any time."

"As pleasing as that is to hear, Senator, I'm not sure what you need to know or why. I rarely discuss ongoing investigations with public officials outside the department."

The server brought three cups of espresso and three slices of Italian cheesecake and then withdrew.

The senator took a sip of espresso. "You've put in a lot of time in the Bronx, lately. Claremont Park, Belmont, and then Riverdale. Odd for an investigation of a murder in Brooklyn. I had my staff do some digging. Claremont Park, scene of a young girl's murder in 1963. Belmont, scene of another murder in 1963, this time a hero detective named Brady." He held up a hand. "Don't worry, Detective, I won't publicize it."

"Not even to Kyle Emory?"

It worked. The senator paused for several moments.

"I've done some digging, myself," she added.

"As I see. Fair enough, Detective. In that case, let me assure you that Mr. Emory never makes public disclosures and will keep any details I provide him in the strictest confidence."

"I'm not concerned about his public disclosures, just his private ones. And you can guess who I mean."

He shook his head. "I hope I never again make the mistake of underestimating you, Ms. Brady. Here's my problem, though. Mr. Emory thinks the boyfriend did it, as do many other New Yorkers. You and I know he didn't. If I've connected the dots correctly, you're looking for a serial killer, a guy in his seventies, and Mr. Emory pressing certain parties to arrest the boyfriend is counterproductive. If you tell me where you are, I can steer him in the right direction, and I promise I will disclose only what is necessary, and on the condition that he exclude it from any pillow talk."

"And in return?"

"I will protect your flank from political interruptions, which I understand was a problem for you at the end of your time in IAB. I'll even smooth things over for you with the Brooklyn DA's office."

She tried to ignore Jake's expression of alarm. No missteps here. "Senator, I appreciate your offer of support, but it's best if my interactions with the DA's office take their natural course. Mr. Emory…"

Her cell buzzed. A text from Nolan. *Meet me at Meeker and Skillman, ASAP!*

On my way. She jumped up and grabbed her jacket. "Sorry, Senator. We'll have to finish this another time. Thanks for dinner."

CHAPTER THIRTY-TWO

Wednesday, May 23, 8:40 PM

No time to change. Kim drove and had Jake hold her cell in case any additional texts came in, but none did. The BQE was still stop-and-go. So, secondary streets all the way. Peachy.

Once she skirted Grand Army Plaza, she pushed it to fifty going up Vanderbilt Avenue, which was uncrowded. She ran the light at Flushing Avenue and made a racing right turn at the Navy Yard. As she drove east on Flushing, the lights were rolling with her, so few red, and those she encountered, she treated like a stop sign.

Jake had just said something. Was he looking to pick up where they'd left off when Brandt invited himself to their table? "I'm sorry, what was that?"

He snickered. "I asked what happens if you get pulled over."

"Best thing that could happen. I flash my badge and get an escort." She skidded into a turn onto Union Avenue. "What the fuck happened?"

"Want to pull over and text him back?"

"No time."

"Kim, what do you think it is?"

"I don't know." But she did. Her gut never lied.

A patrol car with lights flashing appeared in her rear view. With the road ahead free of traffic, she had no reason to stop. Once she hit a light, she'd pull over and let him lead her the rest of the way.

Meeker Avenue was just ahead. She saw the flashing lights of a dozen emergency vehicles even before she made the turn. The patrol car pulled up right behind her.

This was why she'd driven.

"Stay in the car, ma'am," the uniformed officer called out.

She got out holding her badge aloft. "Detective, NYPD. I'm responding to a call."

"Just hold on, ma'am." He checked her badge. "Jesus, Detective, you ever hear of sirens and grill lights?" His eyes drifted down to her high heels and legs.

"Private vehicle, Officer." She turned away, signaling Jake to stay put. The Crime Scene guys already had a yellow taped perimeter.

Bob called out to her. As she approached, he looked her up and down. "That's a different look for you."

"Don't ask. What do we have?"

"Number eleven. Complete with bite mark. Tim Brogan's here. I figured this should be all-hands-on-deck."

Sergeant Vitello approached. "Dress and heels at a crime scene? That's a first, Kim. Think you'll set a new fashion?"

"Hope not. My feet already hurt. Gotta remember to leave a pair of trainers in the car. Talk to me, Phil."

A teen girl's body was lying with her head against the wall. "Looks like she was thrown against it after she was dead. Defensive wounds suggest she put up a fight, and there's some skin under her fingernails. The ME will need to do a complete exam, but she was raped, bitten, and possibly strangled."

Kim bent over. "I don't see any ligature marks."

Vitello shone a flashlight on the girl's neck. "There's some bruising all around."

But Kim was studying the girl's face. "Shit."

Bob heard it. "What?"

"That's Martha Perez. Lulu's friend." She took a quick photo of the girl on her cell.

A guy from the Medical Examiner's Office interrupted. "She probably didn't die from strangulation. Looks like a blow to the head."

"Yeah, thanks. What else we got, Phil?"

114

Vitello pointed to the steel girder. "We took some paint from that. Freshly scraped by the look of it. We'll get it to the lab, pronto. Looks like he was in a hurry. We took the same paint off this van's front quarter panel."

She pulled up her Notes app and entered the name and phone number of the plumber. "I'll call to find out when he parked it here. With luck it will have been sometime today."

Tim Brogan approached. "Kim, there's something under the van."

"Yeah," Vitello replied. "A walking cast and a cane. I'm waiting for my guys to bring back evidence bags large enough for them. There's also a small pile of sand next to the wall. Not sure if that means anything."

Kim mulled it over. "The cane and cast might mean he was playing the injured old man."

"A copycat?" Bob asked. "This one's a lot sloppier than Lulu was, or any of the others."

"It's also the shortest interval, by a huge margin, between known attacks." She walked over to the van, knelt, and peered underneath. It was as much to give her aching feet a break as to look at the evidence. When she stood, Bob, Brogan, and Vitello were all staring at her.

"Sorry, Kim," Bob said. "It's just that this is a side of you we've never seen."

She waved Jake over. "You've all met my husband."

But her three colleagues just laughed and shook Jake's hand.

"Okay, enough. We need to canvas the neighborhood. Let's start by locating every building within, say, three blocks in every direction, with video surveillance. We'll follow up with them tomorrow to collect what we can. Let's also check any apartment with a sight line to this spot."

"The raised roadway above the wall doesn't allow for much of a sight line," Brogan said.

"No. But the overpasses at the intersections of the cross streets do." She turned to the guy from the Medical Examiner. "I need everything from the autopsy when they get it."

He nodded.

"What do you want me to do?" Jake asked.

"Phil, how long are you going to be here?"

"Till we're done. At least until tomorrow afternoon."

"Great. Jake, my feet are killing me. Please go home and get my new trainers."

He suppressed a smile. "The pink ones?"

"Yes. And a pair of sweat socks. If I'm not here when you come back, just leave them with Phil." She kissed him. "Sorry our dinner got screwed up."

***

He parked his Jeep down the block from his apartment. He'd misjudged this time, and that wasn't like him. Everything had gone so well, according to plan, until just after he'd left his signature. Then, he'd heard the approaching voices. He'd barely had time to ditch the props before bugging out. At least they hadn't seen him.

But now, he examined the passenger side toward the rear. A scrape that hadn't been there before. He'd hit something. A closer look, and he saw traces of pale green paint.

The girder where he'd parked. He'd hit it on the way out.

And on the passenger side next to the hood, an indentation that hadn't been there before. Where the girl's head had struck. Were those speckles of blood surrounding the dent?

He recalled now hitting something else pulling out. Something on the driver's side. And there it was. White paint. The plumber's van.

He'd traded paint on both sides.

The only thing to do was to ditch the Jeep. He'd never worried about leaving evidence behind, like fingerprints or DNA, because he wasn't in the system. And so long as he lived his exemplary life—save for his one peculiar hobby—he would stay out of it. But this was evidence of a different kind. It could help them discover who he was, of getting pulled into the maw of a system that, once it took hold, would never let him go.

It was time to head back out on the road.

CHAPTER THIRTY-THREE

Wednesday, May 23, 9:52 PM

Senator Brandt, having arrived home, showered, and changed into pajamas. He lit a cigar and tried to put a philosophical light on the evening.

"You seem troubled," his wife said.

He'd married her just after graduating from law school near the bottom of his class. She'd been a hottie back then, but now, as they were both progressing through their forties, she was turning frumpy. And she couldn't even claim childbearing as the excuse. "No, just politics."

"I wish you'd tell me. You used to share everything with me."

That he had, back when they shared enthusiasm for causes, before he'd hit the brick wall after passing the bar, discovering that grades in law school did matter.

"Who did you have dinner with?"

There, we've moved past friendly and on to digging for dirt. "Someone from the police department." He tried not to think of the lovely Kim Brady, whom he'd only seen as a tough cop until tonight.

"Anyone important?"

"Could be. It's about a departmental matter." Tonight had changed his view of the detective who, until now, had been a thorn in his side. Tonight, he'd seen the woman. And she was...

"I wish you wouldn't treat me like a member of the press, someone to fob off with non-answers. Who was it? A man or a woman?"

"There were two, a man and a woman." His cell trilled. Cates. Saved by the bell. "Yes?"

"Heard some activity earlier tonight on the police scanner, so I followed it."

"And?"

"Murder in Williamsburg. Under the BQE, near Union Avenue." Cates paused. "She's here."

So, that's where she'd gone in a rush. "Must be related. Anyone see you?"

"That was my thought, too. Don't worry, I've kept out of sight. In fact, I'm leaving now."

"Do me a favor. Swing past the local precinct and the Castle. Find out if there's any monkey business going on."

As he ended the call, his wife was giving him a questioning look.

"Sorry, dear, something has come up." He retreated to his home office before punching up a familiar number on speed-dial.

CHAPTER THIRTY-FOUR

Wednesday, May 23, 10:03 PM
Kim decided, as she entered the pizzeria with her calves and lower back aching, she might never wear heels again.

Behind the counter stood a Latino man who appeared to be about fifty. She showed her badge. "Had many kids in here tonight?"

"I get lots of kids in here all the time."

She placed the photo on the counter. "What about her?"

He stared at the image, wide-eyed. "She's dead?"

"Was she here?"

"Yeah. Came in with two other girls around 8:30. They were giggling a lot. Thought I caught a whiff of weed on them."

She slipped out of her shoes. "What time did they leave?" The cold linoleum felt exquisite against her aching feet.

He nodded toward the photo. "She left a little after nine, maybe 9:15."

"They didn't all leave together?"

"No. The other two stayed another twenty minutes."

"When she left, did you see which way she went?"

"She turned to the right."

Toward North Eighth Street. "What about the other girls?"

"No, I didn't notice. Sorry."

"Thanks." She stepped back into her shoes and handed him her card. "If you think of any other details, anything she said, please contact me."

***

"Wait a minute." Emory wasn't following the senator. Not surprising. It had taken three calls before Loretta answered, and then several minutes before Emory finally took the call. "You spoke to her yourself?"

"Earlier this evening, yes," Brandt spoke with exaggerated patience, grinning at the realization that he had dragged his patron from the throes of the deepest carnal pleasures. For the third time, he described the conversation in the restaurant, her sudden departure, and the report from Cates at the crime scene.

"So," Emory said, "now you don't think it was the boyfriend?"

"Why would she be sniffing around the Bronx? If Cates is right, we've been barking up the wrong tree."

"But you don't know who she's looking for. No idea at all."

"No. And we will not find out with pressure or threats. You need to let me work this one my way."

A long silence. "What did Cates uncover about her visits to the Bronx?"

"Just one item for certain, and I can't imagine what it might have to do with the Ramirez case. She visited the spot where her grandfather was killed."

"Fuck. I'm looking for facts, and you're giving me sentimental drivel."

"You asked. I'm telling you they've locked the department down tight on this one, and it all starts with her. Let me work this my way. Sorry I interrupted your evening entertainment."

CHAPTER THIRTY-FIVE

Wednesday, May 23, 10:48 PM

Jake was waiting when Kim returned to the crime scene, holding her pink trainers aloft. Bob and Tim gathered while she sat in the passenger seat of the car with the door open pulling on her socks and comfortable shoes. "She was at the pizza place a block over. The owner said she turned right when she left, which means she was heading toward North Eighth. There's a church on the opposite corner, so I'm betting he was waiting by the wall in front of it."

"Why there?" Brogan asked.

She kissed Jake, handed over her heels, and thanked him. "Sorry about tonight. Please don't wait up." She watched as he drove away.

Back to Brogan. "Too little space on the near corner, and too easy for someone to notice him before he was ready. Besides, he needed her on the far side of the street. Follow me and I'll show you why."

"Mind if I join you?" Vitello asked with a smirk.

"Not at all." She led them across Meeker, staying to the left side of North Eighth Street. "This is the first of two surveillance cameras along this side, and there are none across the street." She walked to the beginning of scaffolding that ran for nearly two hundred feet. A second camera was pointing into the pathway underneath. "No way he'd want to be hemmed in here, with that camera in his face as he emerged."

"You think he noticed that?" Brogan asked.

She was in that zone, now, the one that felt like she was in the criminal's head. "He notices everything. Just like when he killed Lulu. He'd scouted the surveillance cameras he'd be passing, and he turned his head so we couldn't see his face. Tim, please check both places with the cameras. If we get more than a blurred glimpse of him, I'll be stunned."

"The one closest to Meeker might have caught him," Bob said.

"Nope. She'll be walking closest to the street, and he'll turn his face away from the camera." She led them to the far end of the block. "See what I mean? Much less space." She crossed to the other corner, by the church. "With his broken foot act, this wall made a handy prop. Perfect setup for him: an elderly man, struggling with something heavy and a cane. 'Oh, honey, won't you be an angel and help me carry this to my car? It's just a block away'. And Martha, being a sweet kid and probably not at her most alert, agreed."

"But if she was in the pizza place, why would he expect her to walk this way?" Tim asked. "How was he even aware she was there?"

Good question. "He might have seen her going in. It's too much of a coincidence that Martha also was in the park last September." Sudden thought. "Tim, one storefront near the pizza place has video. Check with them tomorrow as well, just in case he scouted the pizza place, first."

***

Back at the scene, Kim noticed the van from *City News*, the local cable news station. Joanna Dunbar had to be nearby. A casual stroll around the perimeter was all it took to find her.

The reporter looked Kim up and down. "Nice. But the trainers sort of kill the look."

"I was at dinner with my husband when the call came in." She raised her right foot. "Had to send him home for these."

"Too bad. Hope you at least got to finish dinner."

"Barely. Had an interesting guest for dessert. A certain politician of local renown."

Joanna's eyes grew wide. "What did he want?"

"To make nice. He's called off his hound. He's frantic to find out anything on this case."

"A rare, shared concern." Joanna nodded in the general direction of the still-busy members of the Crime Scene Unit. "No one's talking."

"And they won't until we notify the family."

Joanna turned serious. "This is going to get worse, Kim. I accept that you have a job to do, but Felipe Prinz and his gang will blow the place up when this comes out in the morning. At the very least, let me say the two killings are linked, and it's a serial killer."

"I can't go on record. The department would fry my ass." Kim's thoughts turned to the traces of paint on the girder and the plumber's van. He'd been sloppy this time. He'd made mistakes. And if there was dark blue paint on the plumber's van, there had to be white paint on the killer's vehicle. He could have it repainted by tomorrow. And in another state.

CHAPTER THIRTY-SIX

Thursday, May 24, 6:43 AM

He'd arrived at dawn after driving all night, straight out the Long Island Expressway and back. The auto body shop—or, more accurately, the chop shop—was one of several such businesses clustered together in a community of corrugated shacks in the shadow of Citi-Field in Flushing. It had surprised the shop owner to find him waiting when he arrived at 6:30.

Easy terms. Nothing written, no names, straight cash deal. The owner regarded him with caution, as if unable to decide whether he was dealing with a crazy old man or someone more dangerous. Good.

The repainted Jeep, a nice fire engine red in acrylic enamel, would take forty-eight hours for two coats to dry. A professional job. The dent would take no time to fix.

***

"Another teen Latina was murdered last night in the Williamsburg section of Brooklyn. The community is still reeling from the as-yet unsolved murder of Lourdes Ramirez. Police would not release the victim's name until the family is notified. Felipe Prinz, speaking for the activist group Come Home Ernesto, pledged that there would be no peace in Brooklyn until justice had triumphed."

***

Kim got off the B38 bus on the corner by the Castle. Traffic on DeKalb Avenue, both pedestrian and vehicular, was heavy. But she spotted Justin Cates with ease.

"I'm not tailing you," he said. "The senator told me…"

"It's all right. Where is he?"

Cates pointed. "The black Suburban over there."

She spotted it just as it pulled away. "You mean, it was right over there."

"Just walk down DeKalb toward Myrtle."

She took a few steps. "How far should I…" She turned, but he'd vanished. The black Suburban pulled up, having circled the block, and the rear door on the passenger side opened.

Senator Brandt waved her in.

"Been catching up on your John LeCarre readings?" she asked as they pulled away from the curb.

He chuckled. "I could get to like you. Especially after seeing you last night." He turned serious. "You left me to respond to that murder. This is no lovelorn teenager you're dealing with."

"Nice to hear you admit it."

"I never thought it was, if that matters to you."

"Lowers my opinion of you a few notches."

He didn't flinch. "We each have our limitations. We each resent them. And we each look for ways to break free. I'm here because I got an anonymous call at two o'clock this morning from what appeared to be a prepaid cell. The voice sounded an awful lot like yours. After a couple of months of observing you from afar, it strikes me you are a cop who often thinks like a lawyer, and I'm a lawyer who sometimes thinks like a cop."

"I don't like being pushed."

"I'm not pushing you, Detective. Two people are pushing you. One is a serial killer; the other is a terrorist."

"If you're fishing…"

"I've already fished. Last night was not just a murder, it was also a rape. With an as-yet undisclosed signature. Later today, Dr. Lloyd Shelton of the Medical Examiner's Office will submit a specimen from the rape kit for DNA evaluation, which, I would bet, will match the DNA from Lourdes Ramirez's rape kit. Disclosure of those facts will satisfy even Felipe Prinz that you are on the trail of the killer."

"It may also spur him on to greater violence, believing as he does the killer is white."

"The killer probably is white. Most known serial killers are."

How much to tell him? She couldn't decide that unless she figured out his game. Nothing to do but continue fencing. "I can't risk letting word slip out on this because serial killers often travel widely to avoid detection."

He peered at her. "You have something more." When she only stared back, stone-faced, he said, "For God's sake, I'm on your side. You may not realize it, but that entire business with Cadman taught me a lot."

Cadman. The rookie cop they'd stuck her with in her last weeks with Internal Affairs. Kyle Emory's assistant's brother, whom Emory had sought to push through the NYPD. Until Cadman nearly sank the case of the five murders.

"If you're concerned about your serial killer taking off, you've likely already reached out to the FBI. Can you just tell me that so there's no doubt we're on the same page?"

"Yes."

"And you were recently in the Bronx. Was that connected to this case?"

"Yes."

"Two more questions, for now. First, will you call on me if you need additional resources and get resistance from within the department, understanding that I would never mention your name? Second, can you at least tell me how many you think this guy has killed and over how many years?"

"Yes to the first."

She expected him to explode, but he only sighed. "Okay, play it your way. Call me if you need me."

***

The long ride on the subway had allowed him a chance to think things through. It wasn't like him to panic, and that's what he'd done. Twice. First, last night, when he'd heard voices just as he was finishing after

126

taking longer than expected, another cause for concern. Only after pulling out of the parking spot had he realized the voices were from the street above and the owners could not have seen him. And the second was after he'd arrived home and saw the scrapes and the dent.

He was old enough to have more discipline. He'd never gotten so much as a parking ticket and appeared nowhere in any criminal database. And in having the Jeep repainted, he'd just eliminated the one path through which he could be traced, using someone who had almost as much to hide as he did. He'd also had the presence of mind to put counterfeit plates on it last night, and to remove the registration and insurance card from the glove compartment.

On his way home, he stopped at the convenience store at the corner and bought a copy of the morning *New York Post*.

Another Brooklyn Girl Slain in Williamsburg. The photo was of the crowd under the BQE around his parking spot.

"Terrible, isn't it?" The woman at the register shook her head. "I got a granddaughter, she's twelve. I don't let her go out. City not safe anymore."

"Terrible indeed. Someone should do something." He paid for his paper and left. Twelve-year-old Chinese girl. Must remember that.

***

Bob was the first one to find his voice. "Holy shit."

Kim had just laid out the details of her interactions with Brandt, complete with his offers of help, as well as a recap of the previous evening's events.

Bostwick had listened without a word, just the muscles in his neck and jaw working as his agitation increased. "Yeah. Holy shit. Realistically, what could he do for us?"

"Nothing. Which is why I told him nothing other than what he already knew. He's desperate to use this, either to his advantage or Emory's, possibly both."

Bostwick considered it. "Maybe he assumes we'll want him on our side if he gets elected mayor."

"Big deal," Bob said. "Like, he'd cut the NYPD budget if we didn't give him what he wanted."

Brogan knocked. "Hi, guys. I got a look at last night's surveillance videos from all three places. First, the tattoo parlor between the pizza place and North Eighth showed lots of people passing by between six and nine o'clock, but no old guys."

"Maybe this one wasn't the old guy," Bostwick said.

Brogan held up one finger. "I'll get to that. Second, the camera aimed under the scaffolding showed nothing. No sign of the girl, no sign of the guy. The final camera, two doors down, caught this." He handed Kim a printout. "You called it."

Just barely within the camera's focus, she could see Martha Perez walking toward Meeker Avenue, and on the side of her away from the camera was a man in a cast with gray hair, his face turned away.

Bostwick took it from her and grimaced. "So, we're still nowhere."

Brogan pulled out another slip of paper. "Not quite. Dr. Shelton has completed his exam. He's sent the rape kit for DNA analysis and tox screen to the lab. But he found something else that he wants to talk to you about, Kim."

Two sharp raps on the door. It was sergeant Ramos. "Sorry to interrupt, Lieutenant, but I think you guys better check this out."

***

Brandt stood tall behind his portable podium. "I've called this press conference because of the horrific murder in Williamsburg last night. While certain elements have already twisted matters to serve their own destructive purposes, it is important to allow the police department to complete their investigative work. Harassing them with ridiculous charges will not bring the killer to justice. My understanding is that the department has its very best people on this case."

"Senator," one reporter called out. "Is it your opinion that the murders of Martha Perez and Lourdes Ramirez are connected?"

"Yes."

"Based on what?"

"I'll let the police decide when and how to answer that question. But we may well be dealing with a serial killer."

"Are you saying," another reporter called out, "that you admit these crimes weren't committed by someone within the community?"

"I don't know who the killer is or where he lives, only that he has robbed two young girls of their lives, and he must be caught, tried, and punished."

"Senator," Joanna Dunbar called out, "only a few days ago, you criticized the police for not moving fast enough on their investigation. Now, after a second murder, you say 'the department has its best people on the case'. What caused this change of opinion?"

"My support for the police has never wavered. They are our sole line of defense against the barbarians of lawlessness."

"Nice speech," Dunbar replied. "Now, please answer my question. Have you gotten any inside information on this case?"

"Criminal investigations conducted in the press will always fail. Tipping off the bad guy and all that."

***

He turned off the television. A self-indulgent politician who thinks he knows more than the police, who think they're smarter than me. How delightful. None of them get it. What few traces I left have been eliminated—a repaired quarter panel, and a repainted vehicle. Even if they were to locate the right chop shop, the owner doesn't have my name, and it was a cash transaction.

The twelve-year-old Chinese girl was on his mind, now, along with all the factors that had made last night's escapade less than fully satisfying. He'd seen her in the convenience store, stocking shelves and helping behind the counter. She was now Lotus Blossom to him. None of his victims had been Asian, but then none of them had been Hispanic before the first Williamsburg girl, either. Nice that he was becoming more international in his tastes. In their own way, they all reminded him of the very first, the girl who should have been his forever. Lovely, sweet Angelina.

But it had been all about rules. And he hated rules. So, he ignored them. And if he couldn't have Angelina, no one else would, either. And the same for any girl who reminded him of Angelina. As, in her own way, Lotus Blossom did now.

CHAPTER THIRTY-SEVEN

Thursday, May 24, 11:13 AM

Once Brandt's press conference ended, Kim drove to the Medical Examiner's office. "I got your message."

Dr. Shelton led her into an examining room. Martha Perez was on the table, but the doctor held up a small plastic envelope. "I found these in her hair and in the small wound in her scalp."

Kim peered at the contents, a few tiny dark blue flakes. The color was familiar. "Paint chips? From a vehicle?"

"Paint chips from someplace. The crime lab will probably determine where."

"The crime took place in a parking area under the BQE. Apparently, the killer left in a hurry. He left paint samples on a girder and a plumber's van."

Dr. Shelton nodded toward the girl. "He probably also left traces of her DNA on whatever part of the vehicle her head hit. Had to be a sharp edge."

"And a painted one. CSU has already gotten the other paint samples to the crime lab."

"These will follow. I'll make sure they're all examined by the same technician."

Kim stared at Martha's inert body. "She was a nice kid. She wanted justice for Lulu."

"Who?"

"Lourdes Ramirez."

"I've asked for expedited analysis on the tox screen and DNA. Not sure if it will help. The volume recovered for the rape kit was significantly less than what we recovered from Ms. Ramirez."

"Thanks." And then she had an idea. Once outside the ME's office, she made a phone call.

***

"What have you found out?" Emory sounded agitated. "You sounded like you know something."

"The police established a wide perimeter at the scene last night, as they did with the other one, and they are being just as closed-mouthed. Cates saw them huddling around the body."

"Tell me straight. Did someone tell you they suspect it's a serial killer?"

"No, but I have good reason to think it is. Pushing the boyfriend as a suspect will do more harm than good. So, we're stopping that, now."

"That's my decision."

Line in the sand time. "Not anymore it isn't. I've got to protect my credibility with the public and being on the wrong side of a criminal investigation is the worst thing I can do. I've already promised you free rein in real estate deals if I'm elected. Sabrina Dunn wants to turn all your projects into public housing. She also wants to play Robin Hood with some cockamamie universal basic income program that will tax you more to pay her supporters to stay home and do nothing. And let's not forget doubling down on so-called criminal justice reform so that anyone who loots your properties gets nothing more than a 'please don't do it again.'"

"Point made."

The senator was just congratulating himself when his assistant walked in with a note. "She's here."

"Sorry," he said to his patron, "something's just come up. I'll call tonight." He ended the call, and his assistant showed his visitor in. "Nice to see you again so soon, Detective Brady. How can I help you?"

***

She took a seat. "First, thank you for your supportive comments at your press conference this morning."

"I wanted you to realize I was keeping up my end of the bargain."

"Yes, that's how I took it. You offered to help if we needed it. The ME's office completed the autopsy on Martha this morning and submitted the tox screen and rape kit to the lab."

He leaned forward to study her. "Martha? You knew this girl?"

"I had interviewed her, and we walked through Domino Park together. She wanted to help."

"I see."

"The lab usually takes four to six weeks to process a tox screen. DNA analysis can take almost as long."

"You'd like me to apply some pressure to move things along."

"So would my lieutenant."

His grin evaporated. "You told him of our conversations last night and this morning? We agreed…"

"You agreed to keep everything confidential. I agreed to call on you if you could help. I informed my lieutenant of the resources we have available. And he has specifically asked me not to go outside normal channels without consulting him first, and this is certainly going outside normal channels."

He took a moment to digest that. "I'd ask you how quickly you want it, but I get it—overnight, like on TV. Well, Detective, I'll do my best. Now, are you ready to answer the other question I asked you this morning?"

She'd discussed it with Bostwick, who'd advised against it, but had left it for her to decide. A major step forward. "Why are you asking? I need complete assurance you will not reveal it to anyone, including Kyle Emory."

"Fair enough. In answer to the second part, I was on the phone with Mr. Emory just before you came in, telling him I, not he, would determine my actions in dealing with the NYPD from now on, and that he had to trust my judgment."

She couldn't hide her surprise. "And he accepted it?"

Brandt turned sheepish. "Well, I also told him that if elected mayor, I would be much more reasonable about his real estate deals than my opponent." His expression turned to one of alarm. "And that, my dear detective, is not to be revealed to anyone under any circumstances." He relaxed a bit. "Just another gesture of trust between us."

"Understood. And your reason for asking?"

"Mark Twain once said, 'It ain't what you don't know that gets you into trouble, it's what you know for sure that just ain't so.' But in criminal investigations, either can sink you. Having already made one mistake in this matter, I'd prefer not to make any more. Also, the more facts I have, the better I can assist you, if you'll let me."

She told him of the link to the nine cases in the FBI's files, including the 1963 case.

He didn't appear shocked. "One other question that may well be none of my business. My Mr. Cates observed you in the Belmont section of the Bronx the other day. Why were you there?"

Perhaps he didn't genuinely need to ask. But she suspected he'd already guessed. So, she told him.

CHAPTER THIRTY-EIGHT

Thursday, May 24, 1:37 PM

"Think it will help?" Bostwick asked when she got back.

"Can't hurt. Any wait less than four weeks on either result will make it worth it."

Bob joined them. "Got the first results back from the crime lab. The flakes of paint from the autopsy match the paint samples recovered from the girder and the white van. They should have a line on what make and year of vehicle tomorrow."

Bostwick snorted. "By then, it will probably have been repainted."

"And at a chop shop that won't have any paperwork," Bob added. "Of course, if we can find out which chop shop, we can squeeze them, but, but by the time we do, the killer will surely have sold it to someone out of state."

"Our favorite state senator has promised to get the labs off the dime on the DNA and tox screen," Bostwick noted. "Not sure that will do much more than confirm that this girl was Number Ten on this guy's hit list. I wish like hell we could find another way to track him."

Now was the time. "I asked Ken Taylor about Investigative Genetic Genealogy. He said they could facilitate an investigation, but only after we've exhausted all other avenues. I think we're there, and last night's attack suggests our killer has shifted to another gear. There may be more attacks in the not-too-distant future."

Brogan joined the conversation. "What makes you say that?"

"Because the last known attack before Lulu was nearly two years ago. The next previous attack was two years before that one. Now, just seven months."

"Explain to me how this genealogy stuff works," Bostwick said.

"We submit a DNA sample to a firm recommended by the FBI. They check their database to see if there are any close matches, which occur when someone who shares DNA with the criminal does an ancestry search of their own."

"Yeah," Brogan said. "But only if a company that makes their database available to law enforcement did the search. Several of them don't."

"So, we may be screwed before we begin," Bostwick said.

"It's possible. But assuming there's a hit, the genealogist would then build out a family tree by establishing a list of close matches through the usual methods of genealogy researchers. They develop a list of likely suspects for us to investigate."

"How long does this all take?" Bostwick sounded doubtful.

"That depends on how close the matches are to begin with and how many clusters there are. Could be two or three weeks, or it could be as long as six."

"Okay, then we'd better get moving. I'll tell the chief when I didn't hear from him, I took that as his approval. Tell Taylor in the morning you've gotten clearance from me."

In the morning, not now. It would give the chief one last chance to kill it. Oh, well. At least Bostwick was talking tougher.

***

"Hey, Kim." Joanna Dunbar was sitting atop the Korean Veterans' Wall of Honor at the Tillary Street entrance to Cadman Plaza as Kim stepped off the B38 bus. Darkness had fallen.

"Kind of disrespectful to our war dead, sitting on the memorial like that, isn't it?"

"Nah. My grandfather was wounded in Korea. I feel like I'm a little closer to him." She hopped off the wall. "Mind if I walk with you?"

"Not at all."

"I must ask. Have you kissed and made up with Brandt? His performance today was…"

"Not completely. Let's just say we've reached an understanding."

Joanna's expression turned sour. "About what?"

"Getting him to stop pushing stupid ideas and making an already difficult investigation impossible."

"So, you told him it's a serial killer?"

"He'd already guessed. He also told me he'd pushed back on Emory and stopped pushing the boyfriend theory."

Joanna perked up. "You think they've split?"

"Didn't sound that way. More like the good senator is simply asserting a little independence. Anyway, is this the reason you waylaid me?"

"One of two. The other is that we got another anonymous tip about…"

Kim held up her hand. "What the hell is that?" She turned toward the source.

A block away, a steady stream of protesters poured off the pedestrian promenade of the Brooklyn Bridge onto Tillary Street. She still couldn't understand what they were yelling. Angry shouts from drivers in traffic already backing up along Tillary and Brooklyn Bridge Boulevard mixed with the chants.

Joanna sidled up to her. "Holy shit." She pulled out her cell. "I gotta get a van here."

A block away, a car blocked by protesters burst into flames.

Kim pulled out her own cell and called 911. She gave her name and shield number. "Violent protesters coming off the Brooklyn Bridge. One car burning." She gave the location. She then notified Ken Taylor.

"Thanks, Kim. Now, please get the hell out of there."

The stream turned toward them. Sounds of shattering glass. Several protesters pulled a driver out of his car. Kim reached for her Glock but decided against it. They'd swarm her, and if she hit anyone, she'd never work again. Another car burst into flames.

She grabbed Joanna's arm. "Come on."

"I'm waiting for the van."

"Not here. Let's go, before it's too late."

The mob was approaching Cadman Plaza East. Kim jerked Joanna's arm, and they both rushed across Cadman Plaza West. More shattered glass, as the mob hurled rocks at the Post Office building. A bright light cut a low arc through another window, and a moment later, flames were licking outward.

"A Molotov cocktail," Kim said as they crossed Clinton Street. But the mob was still pressing toward them. What if they kept coming toward their home on Monroe Place? "Oh, shit. Jake." She pulled Joanna a few steps toward Clark Street.

The mob reached Cadman Plaza West, hurling rocks at the cars still passing by. One windshield shattered, and the car careened into the scaffolding of a high-rise under construction.

The sounds of sirens pierced the air. Molotov cocktails were hurled into the condo, starting several fires. Within minutes, an entire section of the building was ablaze.

A cluster broke off from the primary group and turned toward Kim and Joanna.

CHAPTER THIRTY-NINE

Thursday, May 24, 6:36 PM

"You're in a good mood, for a change," Mrs. Brandt said as they sat down to dinner.

He rarely discussed his politics with his wife anymore, but he was feeling so good, he couldn't resist. "Told Emory a thing or two. Laid down a few ground rules. And it felt wonderful."

"Biting the hand that feeds you? Not like you at all."

"Changing times, my dear. He now needs me at least as much as I need him. It's a changed dynamic." Kim Brady's legs. Now, there's a dynamic. He shook himself. "Things are likely to get…"

His cell rang. He fished it out of his shirt pocket.

"Oh, please," she said. "Not during dinner."

He glanced at the screen. It was Cates. "Sorry, this could be important." Although he couldn't imagine what. "Yes, Justin. What is it?"

"All hell's broken loose."

***

Smoke and flames were now pouring out of the second-floor windows of the post office building.

Vehicles from the Strategic Resource Group rushed along Cadman Plaza West, and Kim could see flashing lights from the other direction as well. Teams of police in riot gear, including gas masks, deployed, forming a phalanx that spanned Cadman Plaza West, cutting off the group that, moments earlier, had been coming toward Kim.

"Come on, Joanna."

"No, I have to stay."

"Not without a gas mask, you're not."

As if on cue, several cannisters landed amidst the crowd, producing plumes of thick mist.

"Tear gas," Kim said. "Let's go."

"You go. I'm staying."

The tear gas had an immediate effect, as the mob panicked. Their chants turned to cries.

Several fire engines arrived from the direction of the river, but the rioting protesters still choked off their path to the stricken buildings. The news van Joanna had been awaiting pulled up right behind them.

Joanna called over her shoulder as she rushed to meet the van. "I'll be fine, now. I'm going to work."

Kim's cell rang. It was Bostwick. "Where are you, now? I hear you called the riot into 911."

"Corner of Clinton and Cadman West. A detail from Strategic Resource Group is here, and they're working to contain and push away the rioters to make way for the fire department."

An SRG captain approached. "Push them back," he called over his shoulder. "Then, full kettle."

"Are you sure you're safe?" Bostwick asked.

"I'm fine. There's an SRG captain here who looks like he wants to talk to me. I'll check in with you later."

The captain held up his hand as Joanna drew near, microphone in hand, cameraman trailing behind. "That reporter said you're NYPD?"

Kim showed her badge.

"And you were here when this all started?"

"I was here when they arrived. I didn't see where or how they started." She described what she'd seen. As she spoke, a large contingent from the SRG pushed back along Tillary Street, splitting the rioters into two groups. "I live over on Monroe Place. What's a 'full kettle'?"

"It means we surround the group and contain them, allowing us to arrest them all." He glanced at the incomplete condo. "That's a serious fire. Post office, too. Are you sure you saw cars firebombed?"

"Yes, and their drivers pulled out and beaten."

"Did you recognize any faces in the crowd? Say, Felipe Prinz?"

"No. To be honest, I was more concerned about where they were heading and the safety of a friend."

Joanna joined them, without the camera man. "May I..."

The captain wheeled on her. "No." He resumed his conversation with Kim. "Thank you, Detective. I may have more questions for you later or tomorrow."

As he walked away, Joanna said, "Kim, please let me interview you."

"I can't."

Screams pierced the air as the SRG units surrounded and constricted the mob, slowly pushing them further south. They pushed the group on Tillary further east. Fire engines moved into position behind both groups and began efforts to contain the two rapidly spreading infernos.

A shot rang out, and a firefighter stumbled and fell. An FDNY ambulance crew rushed in.

More shots.

Kim moved closer to the surging mob, her eyes tearing from the spreading gas. At the center of the crowd, despite being pushed by the SRG, a path was opening leading toward the burning building.

And then she spotted a male, white, medium height, tangled long hair, rubbing his eyes as he ran. She slipped across the street, under the scaffolding, as he broke free.

She drew back against the wall surrounding the construction site.

He was holding a piece.

She had to time this right.

She pulled her Glock from the shoulder holster inside her jacket and switched it to her left hand.

It was a gamble. She wasn't a good left-handed shot. Then again, she wasn't planning on shooting him.

His footfalls grew closer. He was gasping.

Three, two, one...

She stepped out of the shadows and smashed the Glock against his face.

The impact knocked her back against the wall.

His weapon skittered across the concrete sidewalk as he stumbled and fell.

She blocked his path and pointed the Glock at him. "Freeze. You're under fucking arrest. One move, and I blow your worthless head off."

"Okay, okay."

"Now, nice and slow, get to your feet and put your hands on your head. Any other move, and I shoot."

"You'd like that, wouldn't you, Pig?"

"You have the right to remain silent, which I suggest you invoke."

He was on his feet, now. "You pigs can't stand the truth, can you?"

She shrugged. "You also have the right to an attorney, and if you can't afford one, the state will provide one. Talk all you want. I've advised you of your rights."

"Yeah. I committed the heinous crime of protesting a repressive regime. A night in Rikers or the Brooklyn Detention Center, and I'll be out, no bail due."

"I'm arresting you in the attempted murder of a firefighter. And if we find any traces of accelerant on you, we'll throw in arson. Now move your sorry privileged ass."

CHAPTER FORTY

Thursday, May 24, 7:22 PM

Lieutenant Bostwick, Bob, and Tim Brogan were waiting when she emerged from under the scaffolding, all wearing stunned expressions. Bostwick spoke first. "I had a premonition you'd get into mischief here."

"Who's this fine upstanding young citizen?" Bob asked as he prepared to cuff him.

"Fuck you, pig." His nose was still bleeding from the impact with Kim's Glock.

Kim turned serious. "Get his jacket first, Bob. And under the scaffolding, about thirty feet from the corner, there's a handgun on the sidewalk. Looks like a twenty-five caliber."

"There are gun boxes in the car's trunk," Bostwick said to Brogan. "Grab some evidence bags, too, just in case."

"Immediately after the shot that took down the firefighter, I saw the crowd making a path for him to escape. He was working his way toward the sidewalk under the scaffolding, so I headed him off. He dropped the weapon when I tackled him. If ballistics matches it to the slug…"

Bob searched the rioter's pockets and found his wallet. "Wesley Hammond, from Old Brookville."

"Wesley?" Kim asked. "Not Fidel?"

He struggled against the cuffs. "Pig bitch. Tell me, at break time, you fuck these guys or suck 'em?"

Brogan returned, wearing latex gloves, with the handgun already in the box. "Walther Model 9."

Bostwick nodded. "Give Bob an evidence bag for the wallet, then take Mr. Hammond, here, to Central Booking. Now. The charge is attempted murder. If we get further word on the firefighter, Kim will call your cell."

"And arson," Kim said. "He was part of the crowd that set two buildings and two vehicles afire. He shot the firefighter. Once he's incarcerated, get his pants. We'll have the lab check for traces of accelerants."

"Good point, Kim." Bostwick turned back to Brogan. "Get moving, I don't want him processed with the entire mob. If the firefighter doesn't make it, I want to book him for murder up front."

Kim called Rick Conti to give him the latest.

"You mind telling me what the hell you're doing there?" he asked. "Bucking for a transfer to the SRG?"

"I was on my way home from work. Tim Brogan took the suspect for booking. Right now, it's attempted murder, but if we hear bad news on the firefighter…"

"Got it. Okay, thanks for the heads-up. How's the FDNY doing with the fires?"

She peered across Cadman Plaza. "Post office fire looks like it's almost out, but the high-rise is in awful shape."

Sudden thought. She texted Phil Vitello. *Am at the riot, arrested suspected shooter, have his jacket which may have traces of accelerants. At the corner of Clinton and Cadman Plaza West. Any chance you can get it to the lab ASAP?*

Shouting and cries from the mob were growing more intense. They all turned to look.

"The kettle is compressing the pocket," Bob said. "I don't envy those SRG guys at all."

***

"Pull up there behind the ambulances," Senator Brandt ordered his driver.

"Sir, I just heard gunshots. You ain't safe here."

"Sometimes a politician's life is expendable." Not that he believed that for a second. But with so many police in front of him, the danger couldn't be that great. And then he saw her. Cates had been on the money once again.

He stepped out of the car and strode to where his favorite detective, her partner, and her lieutenant were standing, slightly crouched, behind an ambulance. "I heard about this and…"

"Get out of here, Senator," the lieutenant said. "You are definitely not safe here."

"I don't trust what the media will say about this in the morning, so I'm seeing for myself. If it's safe enough for you three, it's safe enough for me."

Another familiar face rushed toward them. That woman reporter. He stiffened himself for a confrontation but, to his dismay, she rushed past him.

"Kim," she yelled. "Can you tell me anything? What's going on? Who was that guy they took out of here?"

"Joanna, I can't tell you anything." Detective Brady glanced his way.

Dunbar turned on him. "What the hell are you doing here?"

But he was still digesting the fact that Dunbar and Kim Brady were on a first name basis. That could have enormous implications. And then he noticed the flames shooting from the construction site, the condominium in which Emory had invested millions.

"Senator, are you with us?"

God, he hated this woman. "The same thing you are, Ms. Dunbar. Seeking information." He turned to Kim Brady. "Did you arrest someone tonight?"

***

The directness of Brandt's question caught Kim off guard, but she had a duty to answer. And if someone from the press overheard, she couldn't help that. "Yes, I did."

"Who? A rioter?"

The cries and shouts were growing more intense, and Joanna turned away. No worries about the press, now.

"Yes. They shot a firefighter earlier, and I caught someone trying to escape the kettle. He had a handgun on him, which we've taken as evidence."

"What's his name?"

Message from Vitello. *On my way.* She then texted Ken Taylor. *Have anything on a Wesley Hammond of Old Brookville, Long Island? Arrested him tonight.*

"Detective?"

"I'm sorry, I had to check that." She repeated the name as Joanna turned her attention back to them. The reporter's eyes went wide for the briefest moment. Kim expected her to break in with a question, but Joanna stepped back a bit.

The game's afoot.

"Where did you arrest him?" Brandt asked.

She pointed to the scaffolding. "Under there."

Another group from the SRG pulled up and deployed. Brandt nodded with satisfaction. "Watching for any who wiggle free of the kettle." He wiped his eyes. "They use tear gas?"

"Yes, before they formed the kettle."

"Interesting term," he said. "Not the first name I'd have given to a containment strategy. Isn't a kettle for boiling?"

Kim gestured toward the mob, now compressed into half the space in which they'd started. "Isn't that what's happening, now?"

"You disapprove?"

"In situations like this, no."

Bob approached. "Kim, I just got word. The firefighter who got shot? Name was Jared Davis. He never made it to the hospital."

She felt like she might explode. "God damn it!" Control. Calm. Work to do. She called Brogan. "Have you booked Hammond, yet?"

"No, still waiting. Why? The firefighter buy it?"

"Yes. Died in the ambulance. Make it murder." She called Conti and repeated it as Joanna was beginning her report, the camera's arc light casting an eerie glow.

"Got it, Kim," Conti said. "Sorry to hear it, but great work."

"Kim?" It was Joanna. "Please. Come on the air with me."

"You know I can't. Talk to Senator Brandt."

CHAPTER FORTY-ONE

Thursday, May 24, 9:06 PM

He'd been following the riot story from the moment it broke.

"This is Joanna Dunbar reporting from Brooklyn Heights, where tonight an angry mob clashed with police to protest what they consider police apathy towards the death of two young Puerto Rican girls. Both murders occurred in Williamsburg, the most recent one Tuesday night.

"The large group poured off the Brooklyn Bridge and onto Cadman Plaza West, where they set two large fires and clashed with anti-riot police, who had to force the crowd away from two buildings, including the post office, to give access to firefighters. One firefighter was shot and pronounced dead on arrival at the hospital."

The reporter paused, turning off-camera. "Kim? Please..."

A side conversation included with the report? How unprofessional. The camera caught a woman just out of focus, and a graphic appeared at the bottom of the screen: "Detective Kim Brady, NYPD." The detective's reply was faint, but he clearly heard, "... I can't..."

Brady? No, it couldn't be. It was a common name.

The camera was back on the reporter. "I'm talking now with State Senator Raymond Brandt, who arrived at the scene about a half hour ago. Senator, do you have any additional information on this incident?"

"This was no spontaneous outburst of emotion, but a planned attack. The mob split into two groups with military precision as they came off the bridge, one setting fire to the post office, the other to the apartment building under construction. They then deployed themselves in such a manner as to block access to firefighters when they arrived in the scene. The FDNY could not begin containing the fires until the police moved the rioters away. That struggle cost a firefighter his life. I'm pleased to say the police already have a suspect in custody."

"Senator, are you aware that the police deployed the SRG, whose tactics, such as the kettle, have been criticized as violating human rights?"

"The police had no choice but to respond to a situation that has already resulted in three deaths—a firefighter and two civilians. Sabrina Dunn, whom I do not see anywhere around, will undoubtedly engage in much hand-wringing, but if the SRG hadn't responded, all of Brooklyn Heights might have been in flames by now with many more dead, including you, your crew, and the finest detective on the force."

He turned off the set.

The only detective they'd shown was that Brady woman. Kim Brady.

It was time to do some research.

CHAPTER FORTY-TWO

Friday, May 25, 2:20 AM

"You okay? I've been worried sick." Jake threw his arms around her. "You smell like a burning building."

She recapped the evening's events.

"I can't believe you got the guy who shot the firefighter. You amaze me."

"We won't be sure he's the guy until ballistics matches the slug to his pistol."

"I recorded something you need to see. Brandt said something nice about you." He pressed a button on the remote, and the frozen image of Senator Brandt and Joanna Dunbar sprang to life.

And her name appeared on the bottom of the screen.

"What the fuck?"

"It gets worse, Kim." He let it play. "... the finest detective..."

She shucked off her jacket and returned her Glock and the Chief's Special to the safe on the top shelf of the foyer closet. "That's great. Just super." She fished her cell from a pocket and dialed Joanna's number.

Joanna answered with, "I'm sorry, Kim. It wasn't my idea."

"I don't give a shit. You had no business asking me to come on camera, especially while you were on the air."

"I'm sorry. I was amped up, we all were. We were on a 7-second delay. I assumed they'd bleep it out."

"And who the flying fuck plastered my name all over the fucking screen? The killer can probably figure out who I am and that I'm on his tail."

"That's ridiculous…"

"Is it? How did they even know to do that?"

"I'd… when I first called in, my director asked me if I was safe, and I said I was with you, that you'd gotten me out of the path of the mob…"

"And you told him you might get me on camera? We're done, Joanna. You hear me? Done." She ended the call.

***

His eyes were burning with fatigue, but this wouldn't wait. There was precious little out there on Detective Kim Brady. But an article in the Brooklyn Eagle only a month old caught his eye. Something in connection with a case against a domestic terrorist whom a police officer had waterboarded, and Brady had testified that they hadn't relied on the information they'd squeezed from him.

And the judge had bought that? He kept reading. "The defendant's attorney made repeated references to her father, who had also been a detective, and his alleged misdeeds. Detective Brady maintained her composure and cited her grandfather, yet another detective in the family, who'd died in the line of duty."

So, she was Dan Brady's granddaughter.

He'd dealt with one. A second would be a challenge.

CHAPTER FORTY-THREE

Friday, May 25, 7:17 AM
Sleep had finally claimed Kim through sheer exhaustion, but it was short and fitful. A shower revived her. She was ready to leave.

Jake stopped her. "We never finished our conversation at dinner the other night."

The conversation. About last Sunday and differing expectations. Her life since had been Exhibit A on why the last thing they should consider was having children. "I understand. But a homicidal sex maniac may at this very moment be planning my demise. I must find him before he finds me. "

"That's a reach, Kim."

"He ambushed my granddad. That took some doing. And Granddad had way more experience than I do. Gotta run. I'll check in during the day."

As soon as she stepped outside, she saw Brandt's black Suburban. She considered ignoring it and turning for Clark Street, but he rolled down the window and waved to her. If she turned away, he'd follow and that would only draw attention.

He moved over to the driver's side to make room for her. "Your reporter friend didn't do you any favors last night."

"Neither did the station. I still can't believe it."

"My apologies, Kim. When I made my statement, I didn't realize they'd done that. I assumed no one would know who I meant except the person for whom I intended it."

She didn't like him calling her by her first name. She'd suspected the night in the restaurant his interest had grown more personal. Great. Another problem to deal with. "In my experience, Senator Brandt, it's usually best to avoid personal references in such situations. It may work in sitcoms, but not on the street."

"Call me Ray."

"No, thank you, Senator. As you've seen, I'm a married woman. Happily married."

"You'll forgive me saying so, but you didn't look happy at dinner the other night."

"Then you shouldn't have joined us." Before he could respond, she added, "Let's not make a bad situation any worse. You've offered to support our investigative work, and I appreciate that. I realize last night's unrest plays right into your politics, but it's also part of the shit show within which I'm forced to conduct this investigation. So, please, do not mention my name in public. Ever."

"Of course."

A red light came on and the driver's voice broke in from a small speaker. "Tillary is still blocked off, Senator. I'll have to go around the north end of the park. Flushing Avenue is probably the best bet."

"Fine." Brandt spoke to her as the red light blinked off. "You'll at least allow me to drop you off at the Castle?"

"Please make it the Sunrise, instead. My fellow officers are likely to be on edge this morning."

Her cell signaled a text. It was from Ken Taylor. *Prinz has dropped off our radar.*

***

Kim didn't stop to listen as several of those present in the Castle yelled epithets at the acting mayor on the screen complaining about police tactics. Bostwick stood in the door of his office, waiting.

She draped her jacket over the back of her desk chair and joined him. Might as well get this over with.

"You okay?" he asked as they both sat. "It's okay if you take some time off. Phil Vitello's crew is giving last night's scene a good going over. How'd your chat with the good senator go?"

He has the hots for me. No, best not to mention that. "He was pleased to be asked and said he would do what he could."

Bostwick shook his head. "And then sang your praises on television, right after the station had told the world who you are."

"Serves me right for trusting a reporter."

He studied her. "You need a break. That was a nightmare last night. The labs are all going to need time before they get back to us, even with Brandt's help. Take a few days. Unwind. Recharge your batteries. Bob or I will call if anything pops."

Great idea. Take a few days to argue with Jake about having children. Or about talking about having children. Maybe they could work in time for a colonoscopy or something.

"Kim?"

She snapped back. "Sorry. Thanks for the suggestion, Lieu, but I'm much better off staying on the job. Maybe we'll catch a slow day on this case. Maybe not. I heard from Taylor this morning. Felipe Prinz has gone underground."

"He's not your problem."

"I beg to differ. He's setting the fucking city on fire in the middle of a difficult investigation. But that's not the point. We need to keep moving. So, as we agreed yesterday, I'll request the FBI's help to do a forensic genealogy investigation on Lulu's killer's DNA."

"Yes, the chief approved last night. Proceed. Oh, and Rick Conti called."

***

His good fortune was still holding. After picking up his newspaper, he perused the magazine rack, glancing around the convenience store.

Lotus Blossom was alone.

He turned his back as another customer entered and bought a small container of orange juice and paid without comment. He picked up a copy of *Sports Illustrated*. And stole another glance at the girl.

Delicate features. Soft curves. In so many ways, she reminded him of his beloved Angelina when she was the same age, the summer he'd first realized she had to be his.

He took his two purchases to the register. "Where's your grandma this morning?"

"She opened but then wasn't feeling well. She went home when I came in. School's closed today." She flashed a grin. "So, I'm in charge."

"Wow. That's some responsibility. But I bet the rest of your family will help."

Her grin grew wider. "Nope. My dad is running the restaurant and my mom is visiting relatives in Taiwan. My brother is away at college. All me."

"I hope they don't keep you here too late, though."

"No, my grandma told me to close at six."

He paid her. "I hope you have a very successful day." No cameras in the store. None outside it, either. And rain was forecast for the afternoon.

Still a little risky, since he lived in the neighborhood, but that's what made it exciting.

CHAPTER FORTY-FOUR

Friday, May 25, 10:16 AM

Kim met Rick Conti at the Brooklyn Detention Center, where Wesley Hammond was being held. He held out his hand. "This time, I need to assure we stay on the same side."

She took it. "Thanks. The problem is, I didn't see him shoot, I only saw the path open for him."

"And you got the weapon."

She shrugged. "I hope Vitello's guys can find the shell casing, but I'm not optimistic. I also got his jacket."

Conti nodded toward an approaching figure in a suit, tie and fedora. "Here comes the help."

"Looks like top-drawer help. I guess daddy decided Legal Aid wasn't good enough."

"Stanley Wyckoff."

"Hair is too long to be Georgetown Law. I'm thinking Harvard."

"Yep, he's Crimson."

A moment later, Wyckoff gave Conti a curt nod, looking down his nose at Kim. "This it?"

"And your client," Conti said.

"We don't need him."

Kim broke into a humorless grin. "Afraid he might torpedo your defense?"

"He is a spirited boy but misguided. Since our discussion will revolve around legal matters…"

"I'm not here to discuss purely legal matters," Kim said. "I need to interview him to get facts."

Conti stepped in. "Counselor, I'll be glad to discuss options with you after we've interrogated your client. In your presence."

Wyckoff gazed skyward and spread his arms apart in his best what-can-one-do-with-such-dolts gesture. "If you insist. I assume the Inquisition still allows me to confer with my client before we proceed?"

Conti rolled his eyes. "Yes."

Kim brightened. "It'll give me time to get my thumbscrews ready."

While they were waiting, Kim received a text from Vitello. *We found what could be the shell casing, but partially crushed and no identifiable prints.*

"Anything important?" Conti asked.

"No. Just my husband checking in."

Five minutes later, they entered a conference room with Wesley Hammond and Wyckoff, who made the introductions. Hammond slouched in his chair, sullen.

Kim took over. "Congratulations, Mr. Hammond. You are the only rioter who escaped the kettle last night."

"Protester." He spat the word.

"No, protesters march and carry signs and chant slogans to gain people to their cause. Rioters set cars and buildings on fire, trample bystanders, and shoot firefighters."

"You have no evidence that my client did any of that."

She loved when they played into her hand. "I was referring to the mob of which he was a part, which parted like the Red Sea after he shot the firefighter, allowing him to escape the kettle before it had fully closed."

Hammond stirred. "The kettle violates human rights, as every…"

Wyckoff clapped his hand on Hammond's arm with more force than was necessary. "We're not here to discuss general issues. Let her finish."

"Thank you, Counselor. We do have evidence. We have the Walther handgun that he dropped when he stumbled during his attempted escape. When ballistics matches the slug that the coroner pulled out of the firefighter to the Walther and we match the prints on the Walther to his, that's evidence."

Hammond yanked his arm away. "They took my jacket."

Kim shrugged. "More evidence."

"Of what?" Wyckoff asked. "Questionable taste?"

"We sent it to the crime lab for testing." He appeared to be confused. She wasn't about to give him a beginner's course in forensic investigative techniques. "Standard procedure."

Wyckoff recovered. "You're talking about what you might find. As of now, you have nothing but guilt by association."

"We have a lot more than that," Conti said.

Hammond was ready to explode. "Somebody has to stop the madness."

Kim picked up on it. "You mean like setting cars and buildings on fire and then shooting the firefighters?"

"That was an accident. I wasn't..."

Wyckoff turned red in the face. "Shut up, asshole."

But Hammond was rolling, now. "They're conducting genocidal warfare for billionaires to profit. Imperialism is..."

"Thank you, Vladimir Lenin." Kim's voice remained calm and soft.

Wyckoff was seething. "One more word, Wesley, and I resign as your lawyer."

"Ooh," Kim said, "Daddy wouldn't like that."

Hammond sprang to his feet. "Shut up. Just shut the fuck up."

"His arraignment will be this afternoon," Conti said.

Wyckoff calmed down with the refocus on the business at hand. "Good. Which means I'll have him bailed out shortly after."

Conti got up to leave. Kim followed. "Oh, one other thing. I almost forgot. CSU recovered the shell casing from the gun. I'm sure it will have his prints on it. That's evidence, too."

***

Conti said nothing until they were outside. "I thought you always played it straight. That was quite a whopper you told in there."

"I told a lie, but not in there. The text I got before was from Sergeant Vitello of CSU, and they did recover the shell casing."

"Why didn't you tell me before?"

"Because Phil also said it was crushed, and they doubted they'd recover any prints from it."

"So, you did lie in there."

"No, I misspoke. I meant to say I was sure it would have his DNA on it." She turned serious. "Think you can keep him off the streets?"

Deep sigh. "I'll ask for remand, but it all depends on the judge we draw. At least Vickers doesn't work Arraignment Court."

Judge Ronald C. Vickers, "Let 'em run Ron", held the current record for sending criminals back on the street. Kim's last encounter with him, involving the domestic terrorist case, still rankled. "Thank heaven for small favors."

***

Senator Brandt grew alarmed when he saw Loretta Cadman at her desk as he arrived for his appointment with Emory. As always, she wore a designer skirt suit, satin blouse, and designer heels, but her hair was less than perfect, and her face creased with worry.

"He in?" Although Emory had sent for him, so it was unlikely he'd be elsewhere.

"Yes. I'll announce you in a moment." His heart jumped, but she brought him right back to Earth. "I'm worried about him. He's not himself."

He suppressed the urge to quip, "Who is he?" Instead, he took a seat in her visitor's chair and tried not to stare at her cleavage. "What's the trouble?"

"All this. That fire last night. The violence."

"Won't his insurance cover last night?"

"Yes, but it's not that. He's afraid that all his investments will go bad, that he'll lose everything. You'll see when you talk to him. I'm aware you two have argued lately. Please don't this morning. I'm really afraid for him."

158

Afraid the gravy train was heading for derailment. No, that wasn't fair. She genuinely cared for him.

"You don't believe it," she continued. "But I love him. And he loves me."

"Then he should marry you."

"Neither of us wants that. We're both afraid it could ruin things. Our relationship would become public, and with me as the gold-digger. He has two ex-wives who took him to the cleaners. I'm happy as things are now, and I don't want them to change." She stood. "I'll show you in."

Emory was behind his desk, but his jacket was off, and his tie was loose, in a very un-Emory-like fashion. He sipped coffee from a mug, but the senator caught the odor of alcohol. "Who's doing this, Ray? My building? Another girl killed? Where does it stop?"

"Hitting the sauce before eleven in the morning won't solve anything. You need a clear head. You want my thoughts?"

"I do."

A delightful change. "First, stop conflating the street violence and the murders. Two separate issues. Prinz wants everyone to think they're not, but they are. The killer is a sick fuck, but he doesn't give a shit about gentrification or real estate deals."

"What makes you so certain?"

"Doesn't matter. I'm returning to Albany on Monday where I'll announce my committee is launching an investigation of violence and civil disturbances. We'll question law enforcement officials from the NYPD to the FBI. The looney left is kicking up a fuss about police tactics. I want to give them a chance to defend themselves."

Emory gulped from his mug. "The looney left forms a significant part of your electorate."

"As do homeowners and small business owners. I want them to realize I'm on their side. Now, what are you not telling me?"

"Nothing that concerns you."

Now, there was an answer he didn't like at all.

CHAPTER FORTY-FIVE

Friday, May 25, 12:33 PM

Brandt was on the television screen when she arrived at the Castle, but she paid no attention. Seated at her place in the bullpen, chatting with Bob and Tim Brogan, was a very tall and muscular young African-American detective with a big grin.

"Well, if it isn't the legendary Kim Brady."

"Cordell Washington. What brings you to these parts? Or does Colangelo have you investigating me, now?"

Bostwick emerged from his office. "You mean he didn't tell you? Detective Washington is now a member of our unit."

"That's right," Cord said. "My tour at Internal Affairs ended, and I requested a transfer to Brooklyn North Homicide. I've just been catching up with Bob, here. Sounds like you're in your comfort zone."

"You mean her discomfort zone," Brogan said with a laugh.

Cord turned serious. "You ain't seen her under fire, then. The hotter it gets, the more she loves it."

Enough of the pedestal routine. "Can we focus on the case?"

Bostwick turned serious. "How did the interrogation go?"

"Nothing worthwhile. Hammond's daddy popped for a pricey lawyer; some guy named Wyckoff..."

Bostwick rolled his eyes. "Oh, Jesus. He's a real piece of work."

"No question," Kim said, "but he landed on Hammond hard the first time he started spouting. He knows our case at this point is entirely circumstantial, and he wants that front-and-center, not his client's political opinions."

"Maybe not entirely." Bob handed her a printout from the fax machine. "Crime lab found Hammond's prints on the Walther. No others." He handed her a printout of an e-mail. "Ballistics matched the slug from the firefighter to the same weapon, which is registered to his daddy, Fredrick Hammond."

No bail for Hammond. Excellent. "Have you told Conti?"

"Not yet. These only came in fifteen minutes ago."

She punched up Conti's office number.

His assistant answered. "I'm sorry, he's not here. He's at an arraignment."

"Since when does he handle arraignments?"

"He's not handling it. He's observing a new ADA. Can I take a message?"

She considered asking whose arraignment, but that would take more time. "No, I'll try his cell."

It rang four times and went to voicemail. She tried again.

Four rings and voicemail. "Rick, call me back, now. It's about Hammond."

Maybe he was already at the arraignment and couldn't answer. She texted the news about the prints and the ballistics report.

No response.

She sent another. *Do you copy?*

***

He glanced out his front window. The cloud cover had been thickening since noon, and it was now obvious that it would soon be raining. Excellent.

If he had the Jeep back, he might have used it. But the new red paint job would attract attention, and he didn't want that. He didn't want any of his neighbors to see it for fear they'd remember it had been blue. No, the plan was to sell it as soon as he got it back, and he was sticking to that.

He'd go in just as she was closing. Maybe he'd even help her.

Yes, that would be a nice touch.

CHAPTER FORTY-SIX

Friday, May 25, 4:08 PM

"State Senator Raymond Brandt today announced that his senate committee would launch a probe of public violence and potential links to terrorists. While the police commissioner pledged cooperation in complying with the committee's requests for information, Acting Mayor Dunn charged Brandt is simply grandstanding for the voters. She also announced a probe of the department's Strategic Resource Group, which she said was established to guard against foreign terror attacks but has most recently suppressed demonstrations."

***

Bob stared at the screen. "That's odd. Isn't Joanna Dunbar the station's top political reporter?"

Kim glanced up from her laptop. "Yeah, why?"

"She didn't do that story. Isn't Brandt her personal project? She should be all over this."

Brogan chimed in. "Could be DCPI reamed the station over her outing Kim last night."

She had no time for this. "Anything on Martha Perez's tox screen or the DNA analysis?"

"Still waiting," Bob said.

Her cell rang. Her blood pressure rose when she saw it was Conti. "Where the fuck have you been?"

"Getting roasted by my boss. When I got your text, Hammond was already before the judge. I tried to intervene, but the judge wouldn't allow it."

So much for remand. "How much?"

"Two-fifty."

"God damn it." Heads turned throughout the Castle. "For killing a firefighter? Who the hell was the judge? You said Vickers doesn't work arraignments."

"It wasn't Vickers. It was a guy who once interned for him. And it gets worse. Wyckoff had a check with him and bailed him out immediately."

"How long has he been back on the street?" She was yelling, but she didn't care.

"Since shortly before noon."

She glanced at the clock. "Four hours. You might have alerted me a little sooner."

"I didn't have the chance. I..."

She cut him off and called Ken Taylor at the FBI, relaying the news.

"Fuck. Okay, thanks, Kim. We're on it. We'll advise you when we find him."

When. Nice that someone could still be optimistic. "Thanks."

"Oh, and we've referred the DNA issue to a good firm. It'll take time, but I'll call you at the first thing I hear."

CHAPTER FORTY-SEVEN

Friday, May 25, 5:58 PM

The rain had been falling steadily for an hour and intensified as he walked toward the corner. Third Avenue was nearly deserted, and the few people around walked with their heads down and shoulders hunched, struggling to keep their umbrellas from being blown inside out.

A neon sign turned off as he opened the door. The lights were already off.

No customers.

He locked the door behind him.

Lotus Blossom was turning the light off in the refrigeration unit that housed the dairy products. She jumped at hearing the door.

"Sorry to startle you, my dear. I need a pound of butter."

"I already closed the register."

"But I need it for my dinner. Tell you what. I'll give you five dollars for it, now, and you can ring it up in the morning and keep the change for yourself."

She broke into a smile. "Okay, I'll get it for you." She reached in for the butter.

Two long strides.

When she turned with the butter, he was all but touching her.

"Is Breakstone all…"

He grabbed her neck with his left hand and clamped his right over her mouth. Another Angelina. Easy.

***

With Cadman Plaza still blocked off, Kim opted for the subway. She had just exited the elevator in the lobby of the St. George when she spotted a familiar face. "I thought I told you, we're done."

Joanna Dunbar looked awful, dressed in faded jeans ripped at the knee and a rain-soaked hoodie. "Please give me a minute."

"Forget it. I had a lot of explaining to do this morning. I…"

"They fired me, Kim. The commissioner complained about us putting your name up there, and, like you, the station blamed me. But it's impossible to arrange something like that from the field. I didn't even hear about it until I saw the report on the air. And without the graphic, it's impossible to tell it was you."

"What's your point?"

"Somebody set me up," Joanna replied. "When I called in, I said I was with you, but that's because my boss asked if I was safe. I said nothing about interviewing you. That was just a sudden thought of mine in the heat of the moment."

"So, how could anyone have a graphic with my name ready to go?"

"Exactly."

It hadn't been Joanna's fault. Which meant she'd just been wrongly accused and fired. "What will you do next?"

"I'm out. And because of my on-air goof, the station can say they fired me for cause. In this industry, that's a death sentence. But this is what I do, Kim. I need a way back." She hesitated. "This is a huge ask, but…"

"What?"

"Brandt is kicking it into high gear. He actually sounded mayoral today. And he obviously has a high opinion of you."

Kim grimaced. "Don't remind me."

"Do you suppose you could get him to agree to do an interview with me? He did one last night, but that was at the scene. I mean an in-depth interview. Having his agreement would give me something I could use to sell myself."

She'd already asked for a favor on behalf of the department. This would be personal. Not a direction she wanted to take.

"Please, Kim. This is my work. It's all I have. Please."

***

Jake had the news on when she walked in. A nightly program called Race for the Mayoralty was on, and there, next to the host, was Sabrina Dunn.

"My opponent knows full well that we have a police force whose first choice is always to employ military and paramilitary tactics. Their use of a tactic called the Kettle last night was a case in point."

"But how else was the FDNY going to get through to battle the fires?"

"The crowd would have moved off in the course of their march, as well as to get away from the fire. Keeping them contained actually kept them closer to the danger."

"True. How do you propose to address this concern, and will your opponent's so-called probe in the state senate impair your efforts?"

"I have already met with the commissioner on this, and I have asked him to develop alternative ways to deal with the kinds of threats that the SRG was created to meet. My goal is to disband the SRG."

"Might your opponent claim that will only further encourage this kind of violence?"

"Of course, he will. But it's the expectation of repression that leads to violence. When we stop sending police to interfere with demonstrations, we'll finally have peace."

Jake muted the set. "Glad you're home. How was your day?"

"Shitty. That asshole doesn't help."

"She has a point, Kim."

"You mean like the Crown Heights riots in '91?"

"That was different."

"Ever think she has it backwards? That the more violent the protest, the more necessary it is for police intervention? I was there last night. When that mob came off the bridge, there wasn't a cop in sight. They came with Molotov cocktails and set their fires before the SRG showed up and then shot and killed one of the firefighters sent to put them out."

"You're voting for Brandt?" His accusatory tone was impossible to miss.

"Absent a better choice, yes. Suppose they'd turned west from Tillary instead of east? They could have torched the houses on our block and all around us. After all, we're part of the Gentrification Problem, are we not? And, for the record, I would appreciate it if the next time someone asks if we have any children, you refrain from replying, 'Not yet', because that really pisses me off."

His jaw dropped.

Shit, that was not supposed to come out that way. She glanced at her phone. "Excuse me while I make a call."

CHAPTER FORTY-EIGHT

Friday, May 25, 6:46 PM

The senator ended the call and sat back. Joanna Dunbar had been a major hemorrhoid for years. Now, she needed him. The biggest surprise had been that Kim Brady had acted as her agent. He'd figured that alliance had collapsed less than twenty-four hours earlier.

Women.

He shook himself. Focus on the problem at hand. This wasn't just about a reporter he'd longed to see sidelined. Dunn had gone on TV tonight—Dunbar's former station, no less—and spouted so much nonsense that it beggared belief. He was getting support, though, from other media outlets in the city.

He called the number Kim had provided. When Dunbar answered, he said, "A mutual friend has asked me to contact you. I understand you would like my help. Tell me what you have in mind."

"Would you be willing to allow me to approach other stations with the promise of an in-depth interview with you as a selling point?"

"What would be the primary subject?"

"The election, and any issues related to it. I'd also be open to anything else you wanted to address."

He allowed himself a satisfied grin. "You've changed your tune from a month ago."

"So have you. And the brief interview you gave me last night suggests that you wouldn't be entirely averse to working with me."

"I have to admit, you were fair. Are you willing to approach any interview I agree to do with you in the same manner?"

"Yes. I… I'm not looking to be hostile if that's what you mean. But I'd want to be more objective than, say, Dunn got tonight on my old station."

"Cringeworthy, to say the least. That's fine. Would you want to record an interview to take with you as you try for a new position?"

"I don't have the means for doing that, except in an obvious do-it-yourself. Too unprofessional."

"Do you have any contacts you can approach?"

Her hesitation was impossible to miss. "I'm working on that."

He checked his contacts list. Still there. Ed Lyons, of the Independent Television Network. "Ms. Dunbar, you have yourself an interviewee. But don't approach anyone until you hear from me."

"Why?"

"Trust me." He ended the call and made another.

Lyons' greeting was friendly. "Evening, Ray." A good sign. "Sabrina Dunn doesn't like you very much, does she?" Another good sign.

"Why should she? I'm trying to throw her off the gravy train."

"Are you serious about this probe?"

"Absolutely. Got anyone who'd like to interview me about it?"

"That's a tough one. We've lost a few reporters lately who dislike our editorial policies. I'm not sure our current staff would do you justice."

"I understand one of your competitors just tossed a reporter of some note onto the street."

Lyons hesitated. "You don't mean Dunbar."

"I do. I was there last night, and…"

"She was unprofessional in the extreme. She should have known better. Besides, I'm stunned to see you going to bat for her."

"You weren't there. She showed a lot of backbone. The cameraman should've had the common sense to focus on the fire and kill the mic. Had she been working for you, would you have fired her or waited to get the complete story?"

"Okay," Lyons replied. "Fair enough. So, what's the deal?"

"Your policy is to give reporters freedom on stories so long as they don't editorialize, correct?"

"Correct. We have the same policy as the *Wall Street Journal*. Strict separation between news and views."

"Then I suggest you call Ms. Dunbar this evening and invite her to apply for a position at your station. You will not be disappointed. I will give you her number at the end of this call. However, you are not to mention my name to her or anyone else in connection with this. Ever. If she says she can get an interview with me, you may take her at her word."

"Agreed."

"Good." He gave Lyons the number. "Please wait fifteen minutes before calling her."

"Nice talking to you, Ray. Give 'em hell."

CHAPTER FORTY-NINE

Friday, May 25, 7:18 PM

"Yes, I know," she said to Jake. "I should have said something sooner, but I was trying not to let it bother me so much. This case has hit me in a way like no other."

He looked more forlorn than she'd seen him in a long time. "So, what are you saying? About children, I mean?"

"I'm saying I would like to wait a little longer. At least until we solve this case."

"That could be a long time. You're trying to solve over fifty years of murders. Don't you have to stop taking the pill a few months before you can conceive?"

"Yes. You promised not to push me. But whenever you say 'not yet' it feels like a shove."

"And whenever you say, 'no', it feels like a door slamming shut."

Her cell trilled. She reached for it to cancel the call, but the caller ID said, "Bostwick".

Jake threw up his hands. "Go ahead."

"No." She refused the call. "I'm not slamming it shut. But you are pressuring me." Her cell trilled again. Bostwick again. Something was up. "I'm sorry, Jake."

She turned away and took the call.

"Bay Ridge." He gave her the address.

"Isn't that Brooklyn South's neck of the..." But her gut told her even before Bostwick said it.

"It's fucking connected, Kim. I'll meet you there."

***

Brogan and Cord were already there when she pulled up to the convenience store. The lights inside were on. CSU and the Medical Examiner's office were there.

Brogan tried to say something but couldn't. Inside the store some woman was wailing with grief. Brogan looked like he might break down at any moment.

"Kim," Cord said, "you'd better brace yourself. This is totally bad shit."

"How old?"

"Twelve."

"Same deal as Martha," Brogan said, his voice cracking.

Cord led her into the store. "One difference from Martha. We can't find the girl's cell phone."

A CSU sergeant met her at the door. "You Kim Brady? Phil Vitello told me you'd be here."

"Walk me through the scene." She braced herself as they entered the store.

"The girl was working alone because the grandmother was sick, and she was supposed to close at six. When it got to be six-thirty and the girl still wasn't home, the grandmother got worried and called. No answer, so she got dressed and came down."

He walked with her to the front door. "No sign of forced entry, so the door wasn't locked when he came in. It wasn't locked when the old woman got here, so we assume he left the way he came in. If the lights were already off inside, people would assume the store was closed."

A technician from the ME's office joined them. "I make the time of death between 5:30 and 6:30."

She didn't want them both talking at once. "Let's walk through this, first. What else did you find, Sergeant?"

He led her to the dairy case. "The door was slightly ajar. Only her prints were on the handle, so she must have wiped it down before she closed. We found a half pound package of butter on the floor. The attacker probably came in like he needed to buy something, and that was it. He would have grabbed her when she turned around to get it."

"Where's the girl?"

"In the office in the back."

They pushed through the curtain to the back room. A small desk sat amid stacks of boxes of goods. A young Chinese girl lay on the floor, her jeans and panties down at her ankles, her top torn, her white training bra undisturbed.

Her grandmother sat on the floor next to her, still wailing.

The ME's technician spoke up. "The cause..."

Kim held up her hand. "Not now." She knelt next to the grandmother, who only stared. "I'm so sorry."

"She can't be dead," the woman cried. "She's such a good girl."

"I'm sure she was. What was her name?"

"Lily Ng."

Kim turned to study the dead girl's face. Lily. It suited her. And a monster had snuffed that life out, along with eleven other girls. And granddad.

When I catch him, I will kill him.

No. Deep breath. Block out the emotion. Too much to do.

"And she had a cell phone," the woman said.

"Excuse me?"

"I live upstairs. All she had to do was ring. I ran down because she never rang."

"Will you do me a favor?" she asked the woman. "Will you come outside with me, into the fresh air?"

The woman stared uncomprehendingly, but her sobs abated.

"It will be better for you, and they can make Lily all decent again. You don't want her to be like this, right?"

"No."

Cord knelt next to the woman. "Okay?" Kim took one arm and Cord took the other. Together, they coaxed her to her feet. "This way." Kim led her out to the front of the store, and then outside where a social worker was already waiting.

The woman turned to Kim. "You good person."

Kim thanked her. "One thing, please don't cancel the service on Lily's cell, yet." She paused outside, taking several deep breaths.

"You okay?" Cord asked.

"No. Not at all. But we have work to do."

The ME tech was still in the back. She forced all the anger into the back of her emotional closet and focused on the facts. The girl had been raped. Bruising suggested her attacker strangled her but only to subdue her. Cause of death had been the impact of her head on the pointed edge of the desk. There was the tell-tale bite on her shoulder.

As for forensic evidence, CSU had found no fibers on the girl. They had found traces of wet footprints in the store and the office and had photographed them.

Bostwick was outside, waiting. She tried to keep her voice steady as she gave him the update.

He studied her for several moments. "Kim, listen to me. You are now in overload. Take a few days off. You can pick it up when you get back. But you need a break."

"Are you taking a break, Lieutenant?"

"No. But I'm not hunting my grandfather's killer."

"And I can't stop hunting him, not even for a second." She turned to Cord and Brogan. "The closest subway stop is the 77th Street R station. Check the security video for tonight between 5:30 and 7:00. Then check any security cameras in the area between Bay Ridge Boulevard and Fourth Avenue and between 77th Street and 80th Street, especially near bus stops. You're looking for a white guy in his seventies in good shape and soaked."

They both nodded. "On it."

She waited until they were out of earshot. "Not that they'll find anything."

"What makes you so sure?" Bostwick asked. Bob had finally arrived from Staten Island and nodded a silent greeting.

"He lives around here," she said. "The girl knew him. Otherwise, she would have alerted her grandmother, who lives upstairs. She walked to the dairy case for his butter. That's where he caught her."

"Wait a minute," Bostwick said. "How can we be sure of that?"

"CSU found no sign of a struggle out here. He scouts the surroundings in advance, and normally the grandmother is here, so he must have known in advance Lily would be alone. His vehicle is likely being repainted, as it's the only thing besides his DNA that can link him to the Perez murder. That leaves escape either by public transportation or by foot. On a night when it's been teeming rain."

She rejoined the grandmother, who had calmed down. "May I ask you a few questions? It won't take long."

The woman nodded.

"Do you have many older people as regular customers?"

"Yes, many older people live around here. You think an old person did this?"

"I'm just trying to get a feel for your business. Anyone very friendly, who might monitor things to help you out?"

She sighed. "Most people who come in are friendly. I like to talk to them. But no one like that."

"Any of them friendly with Lily?"

The grandmother looked for a moment like she might start crying again, but she didn't. "Everyone loved Lily. Such a good girl."

This would lead nowhere. "Okay, thank you. If it's all right, I might stop back in a few days."

"Okay."

CHAPTER FIFTY

Saturday, May 26, 7:01 AM

"Brooklyn residents were shaken last night to learn of another killing of a young girl, this time in Bay Ridge. The girl, whose name has not been released, was twelve years old. She was found murdered in her family's convenience store. Police are now classifying this as a serial murder, along with Lourdes Ramirez and Martha Perez, both of Williamsburg. Police would not comment further, saying only that they have leads."

***

He turned the set off. Talk of leads reminded him he had one left to deal with. The black Reeboks he'd worn the night before sat just inside the door to his apartment. As a garbage truck approached, he dropped them into the kitchen garbage can, pulled out the bag and tied it, and walked to the curb to drop it in just as the truck pulled up.

He turned away without making eye contact with any of the crew and slipped out of his New Balance shoes once back inside.

With a Brady on the case, perhaps there was another precaution he should take. He pulled out the prepaid cell he'd known he would need one day and called a number he'd recently checked. A voice he hadn't heard in years answered. "You know what I'm capable of. You are never to reveal my identity to a soul. Ever. There's a good girl."

***

Traffic was finally reopened on Cadman Plaza West, and so she took the bus to the Castle. She stopped at the Fire House Deli and Grill just across the street for coffee before heading inside.

"Morning, Kim," Sergeant Ramos called out. Several others, some of whom she hadn't even worked with, greeted her. Word was out. She was up to her neck in this one.

Cord was already in. "That was some wild goose chase you sent us on last night. We didn't find a fucking thing."

"Sorry, Cord. Didn't think you would, but I had to be sure. I'm surprised you beat me in this morning. How's the commute from Manhattan?"

"Easy. Just hop on the M train at Essex and I'm here in no time."

"Essex? That's the Lower East Side. Don't you live in Chelsea?"

"I was." He glanced around and lowered his voice. "I just moved in with Vera."

"Wow, that was fast. You two have only been seeing each other for..."

"A month. But who's counting? She's funny, brilliant, intense, and sexy as hell. Ain't like no other woman I ever met. Anyway, we got some results back on the Perez girl. Tox screen showed indications of marijuana intoxication. DNA from the rape kit matched the DNA from the other cases."

Message received: he didn't want to talk about Vera, at least not here. "As will the kit from Lily, I'm sure. Anything else?"

He handed her a lab report. "Yeah. The paint chips from her scalp, as well as the scrapings from the scene, are from a Jeep Cherokee, patriot blue, either 2000 or 2001."

"Only those two years?"

"Yeah, the shade of paint changed after that."

"Great. Let's get started on DMV records. We're looking for a blue 2000 or 2001 Cherokee registered to someone in Bay Ridge, possibly with the first name of Paul."

"Except it probably ain't blue anymore, and he's likely already sold it."

"But it may give us a name and address."

He sat back. "This case is fucking with you, big time. Dress it up all you want, but this Bay Ridge thing is a hunch. And that ain't like you."

He was right. But she had no choice. "We're dealing with someone who's stayed off law enforcement radar for over fifty years. He's slippery and cunning."

"Okay, then explain this: if he's so cunning, why would he choose a victim in his own neighborhood? It's not like he's ever done that before."

"Because it's exactly what we wouldn't expect." She booted up her laptop and composed an e-mail to Ken Taylor, explaining the latest. She also repeated her Bay Ridge theory and analysis.

"Is that why you asked the grandmother not to cancel the girl's cell service?"

"Yep. Tweens may get careless about many things, but not their cells." She turned to searching the DMV database for 2000 Jeep Cherokees registered in Bay Ridge while Cord took the 2001s. A few minutes later, she heard from Taylor. *I think the Bay Ridge theory is plausible. Tell me how your vehicle search turns out.*

She read it aloud to Cord, who laughed and gestured surrender. "Okay, you win."

Another text from Taylor followed. *Bad news. Hammond has gone underground. He hasn't been home or to his parents' home, nor any of his usual haunts. Will keep you posted.*

She flagged Bostwick down when he came in and told him. "When Bob and Tim come in, please have them go canvass Lily's neighborhood to see if anyone has seen this blue Cherokee. I'm running over to see Conti."

CHAPTER FIFTY-ONE

Saturday, May 26, 8:22 AM

"The paint is not completely dry," the owner of the chop shop said. "The humidity from last night's rain slowed the process. If you come back tomorrow, should be good."

He studied the paint job. Only the lines gave away the fact that the vehicle was nearly twenty years old. "Fine job. What can you give me in exchange?"

The chop shop owner only stared.

"I don't want it. You've rehabbed other cars. I see them behind the fence. You should be able to get plenty for this. What can I get in exchange?"

"I use those cars for parts."

"Or to sell. Don't tell me you don't. I'm not even asking for equal value. Just fully functional."

"I'll have to look around. Can you come back..."

"No, I'd prefer to wait." A folding chair stood in the corner. He opened it and sat. "I'll just sit here and read my newspaper."

***

For a moment, it appeared to Kim that Conti might explode. "So, Hammond's gone. Gosh, who would ever have suspected that would happen? Of course, you realize that if a judge like Vickers hears the FBI has been tailing Hammond, he might just dismiss the charges for not playing fair."

"Was his attorney complicit?"

"Wyckoff wrote the check." He sat back. "So, rich daddy springs his kid, who just murdered a firefighter. Is that what they teach in parenting classes these days?"

Kim tamped down another source of frustration. "I couldn't say."

Conti stared but said nothing.

When her cell buzzed, he waited while she read the text. "It's from Dr. Shelton. The bite mark on Lily's shoulder matches the others. Another fucking surprise. On Hammond, can you do anything?"

"Nothing that wouldn't reveal he's been tailed."

"What about a proceeding that he must attend? If he showed up, the FBI would pick up the trail again. But if he didn't, because he's tucked away someplace cozy, then he'd violate his bail. So, whenever he resurfaced, he goes directly to jail."

"Interesting idea," Conti said. "But he's not required to attend the Grand Jury unless he wants to testify, and Wyckoff won't allow that. Which reminds me, we're giving them the case Monday. I'll need you to testify. The only other thing I can think of is an evidentiary hearing. That's when…"

"I testified at one for the Cove shooting. It's for a judge to rule on whether there's sufficient evidence to go to trial. Didn't Wyckoff claim that everything we had was circumstantial? Say you want to get a judge's ruling. Wait a few days to see if I can get the DNA report on the shell casing and if it shows anything. That way, if Hammond shows, we can add it to the ballistics report and fingerprint evidence. And if he doesn't…"

"I move for his bail to be revoked and there's no hearing. Like I've said before, you should have been a lawyer."

She was almost to the door when he stopped her. "Have you've heard? Your friend, Joanna Dunbar, got fired."

"I wondered about that. I haven't seen her on TV since Wednesday night. Think anyone will pick her up?"

"Someone already has. ITN." He blushed. "My partner swings conservative in his politics. I saw a blurb this morning that she's going to have an in-studio interview tonight, and you won't believe who."

Conti was gay? Digesting that allowed her not to give anything away. "Who?"

"Brandt. That should be a hoot."

CHAPTER FIFTY-TWO

Saturday, May 26, 9:55 AM

Kim met up with Bob and Tim at the convenience store where Lily Ng had been killed. But her grandmother couldn't think of any older man with whom Lily would have been familiar.

Bob had worked his way east along 79th Street, getting as far as Fourth Avenue before working his way back on 80th, ringing doorbells and interviewing people on the street. Tim had worked his way up Third Avenue to 77th Street doing the same. Both carried stock photos of a 2000 and 2001 Jeep Cherokee in blue paint. The closest either had gotten to a positive response was, "Yeah, I might have seen one, but…"

Kim started west from the convenience store. A store front with a Space Available sign in the window had a surveillance camera. She made a note of the number on the sign. Further down the block she found a small group of attached Queen Anne row-houses and started ringing bells. She got one answer, an older woman who came to the door wearing a faded housecoat. "Have you seen a vehicle around here lately that looks like either of these?"

The woman scowled. "They look the same to me."

Kim tried a smile. "I suppose they do. Have you?"

"No. What's this about?"

"You've heard about the girl from the convenience store last night?" The woman nodded. "I'm investigating. We think the killer drove a similar vehicle. The owner would be an older man, say, in his seventies."

The woman's eyes narrowed. "An old man killed her?"

Best not to make her defensive. "Right now, we're just trying to locate the vehicle and its owner."

"Sorry, I never met nobody would do a thing like that." She closed the door.

Kim decided not to pursue it.

At the end of the block, she got one response. "Yeah. I've seen it around. Not sure when, though, and I never saw who was driving."

Phil Vitello texted her. *Crime lab found traces of DNA on the shell casing. Already submitted it for analysis. Also, they found traces of gasoline on Hammond's jacket, most likely they got on in a vaporous state. Should have info by Monday if the DNA's a match.*

She forwarded the text to Rick Conti.

***

A dingy metallic green 2007 Ford Taurus. He popped the hood and listened to the engine. Smooth. Underneath, the exhaust system looked solid.

"New shocks and struts," the owner said. "Springs are in good shape."

He examined the body with great care. "No rot. And it looks like the original paint job."

"You want, I can repaint it, but that would be another couple of days."

The last thing he wanted was a freshly repainted older car. "No, this is fine." He glanced around. No sign of the Cherokee.

"Sold," the owner said. "To an out-of-state buyer. I hope you don't mind, but I moved the suitcase you had in the cargo area to the trunk of this car."

"Excellent." He thanked the owner and drove away, making his way to the Van Wyck Expressway and from there to the Long Island

Expressway. He'd spend the next few days out east, possibly Montauk, while the police combed his neighborhood in vain.

***

"Sorry, Kim," Cord said as they gathered later that afternoon. "No 2000 or 2001 Cherokees currently registered in Bay Ridge, or anywhere nearby, and none anywhere in New York City to anyone named Paul."

"Could it be registered out of state?" Bob asked.

"Yes." Just what Ken Taylor had been thinking. "I'll ask Ken to check for out-of-state registrations. Although," she added before anyone else could, "those would likely have out-of-state addresses, too."

"And our canvass turned up zero leads," Tim said.

"Folks," Bostwick said, "we're done until the lab results come in. You all have time coming, so take what's left of the holiday weekend to unwind. Kim and Bob, please stay in touch in case anything pops, but take some time away from this thing."

***

"Good evening," Joanna said, looking quite corporate in a dark blue skirt, white blazer, and heels. "My guest this evening is State Senator Raymond Brandt, chair of the Senate Committee on Crime and Correction. He is also a challenger in the upcoming mayoral special election. Welcome, Senator."

"Thank you for having me on, Joanna." Looking into the camera made it easier not to stare at her legs.

"Your committee will begin a probe on Tuesday into the recent outbreaks of violence and the responses to it. What are you looking for, and what action could the state senate take to address it?"

"My committee is investigating the extent to which this administration has impaired the police from performing their basic duties of protecting the populace from violence. I have heard complaints of lack of resources and personnel. If money is an issue, the state legislature can provide additional funding."

Joanna nodded. "Ms. Dunn has called for redirecting spending for police to social services. How do you respond?"

"There needs to be better training, and on an ongoing basis, in the NYPD. There should also be more social workers and mental health experts working within the department. But these should be besides, not instead of, support for the basic police function."

"What do you say to those who've been critical of the department's response to demonstrations, specifically the Strategic Resource Group?"

"You were there Wednesday night. That mob wasn't about to be stopped by a social worker asking them nicely. The animal that killed three Brooklyn girls wasn't, either. There are certain situations that call for force, and there is no way around it. Ms. Dunn's contention that withholding police will guarantee all protests will remain peaceful is utter nonsense, as any reasonable person knows."

"So, you think there is no need for additional funding for social programs?"

"On the contrary. Our schools are a mess. We need a chancellor with significant classroom experience who will uphold academic standards in every neighborhood, not just the well-off ones. And we should encourage vocational training because college isn't for everyone."

***

Jake turned off the set when the interview ended. "I know. You think he was great."

"Not on everything. But even you have to admit he makes a better choice than the current occupant of the office."

"I can't get over the puff balls she tossed him. That's not the Joanna Dunbar I remember."

"She kept her questions balanced. Her job was to elicit responses, and she did. She also challenged him on social services issues. His answers on those probably surprised some people."

He tried a grin. "You mean me?"

She grinned back. "I'm not making this personal between you and me. You vote how you want to vote, and I'll do the same. I can't vote for

Dunn. She's gone from making my job harder to making it downright dangerous."

His grin vanished. "How the hell could I vote for her after that?"

But hers remained. "Up to you." She stood and approached him, her hand extended. "Enough. I need a shower."

CHAPTER FIFTY-THREE

Tuesday, May 29, 10:47 AM

Kim finished her testimony to the grand jury, describing the events leading to her arrest of Wesley Hammond. When the ADA asked if anyone had questions, one gray-haired woman raised a hand. The ADA walked over to her and listened while she whispered her question.

"I'm sorry," the ADA said, "but that's asking for speculation, which is not pertinent to the case. You as grand jurors must base your decision on the facts."

No one else had any further questions.

The ADA followed her outside. "Thank you, Detective. You covered everything. After CSU and Ballistics testify, I'll give them the case. Should be no later than tomorrow."

"What did the woman want to ask?"

"If you would have been able to arrest Hammond had the police not attacked the protesters." He laughed without humor. "Takes all kinds, I guess."

***

He was just letting himself into his apartment when his landlady came down the front steps.

"Been away?" she asked.

187

"Yes. I was visiting my brother out in Cutchogue. Lovely out there this time of year, before the summer crowd rushes in."

"You missed the excitement. That young girl works at the convenience store on the next block sometimes? Someone killed her last Thursday."

"Don't recall ever seeing a young girl working in there. Mostly an elderly Chinese woman."

"The girl was her granddaughter. Raped and murdered."

"Good Lord, that's terrible. But why would anyone leave a young girl alone in a store?"

The landlady nodded. "Yeah, good point. But those people? Work, work, work. Anyway, detectives were all over the neighborhood for a couple of days. Said they were looking for a blue Jeep. Don't you have a blue somethin' or other?"

"That was a Honda, but I sold it a while back. Those Jap cars aren't nearly as well made as they say. Got myself a good American car."

"Good for you. I didn't say nothin' to the cop, seein' as how it had nothing to do with you, anyway. Nice girl, though."

"The kid?"

"No, the cop. A woman detective. Can you beat that?"

"Whatever next?" He grinned at her. "Nice Italian girl?"

"Naw. Looked Irish. Well, you gotta unpack and I got chores. Take care."

He gave a friendly wave and closed the apartment door behind him.

He'd disposed of the only items that could link him to either of his last two attacks. And he was now toying with Brady's granddaughter.

Toying with her.

***

The text from Ken Taylor had only said, *Have something for you. Stop by when you can.* Kim took the train into Manhattan directly from the grand jury. When she got there, she updated Ken on Conti's strategy to haul Hammond back under surveillance.

"I appreciate that, Kim, but I doubt it will do much. I'm sure he's sunning himself right now on a lovely beach somewhere well beyond our jurisdiction. We're trying to work around that another way. But we got something back on the DNA sample."

Kim brightened. "Already? You said that could take weeks."

"That's the genealogical research. This is different. They came up with a CGI sketch based on the killer's DNA. This is groundbreaking stuff." He handed her a print of a young adult Italian-American.

"This is a kid. We're looking for a man in his seventies."

"That's what he would have looked like in his early twenties. DNA doesn't change with age."

"Great. I'll jump into my time machine, go back half a century and use this to track him down." But she calmed herself when she saw his bemused expression. "Granddad was right. He's Italian."

"And a rather dark-skinned one, at that."

She studied the print. "How reliable is this?"

"It gives us the face shape, hair color, eye color, ethnicity, skin tone, and gender. It's a ballpark-accurate image, like that of a police sketch artist except based on known DNA markers rather than the impression of a witness. If you went to his high school reunion and showed this around, someone would likely recognize him."

"Except he probably dropped out of high school." She had the odd feeling she'd seen this face somewhere before. "Can you give me a few more copies?"

CHAPTER FIFTY-FOUR

Tuesday, May 29, 1:31 PM

"New York City's three major police unions today jointly endorsed Ray Brandt for mayor in the upcoming special election, charging the current administration has made their jobs more dangerous while alienating the communities in which they work. Senator Brandt immediately thanked them for their support and pledged to restore law and order to the city."

***

Bostwick stared at the image Kim had laid on the conference room table. "This is a kid."

"And so was our killer, once." She repeated Taylor's explanation and then turned to Brogan. "Tim, have you been able to locate anyone from the Taft Class of '64?"

"A few. They're not much for reunions, I can tell you that." He pulled out a folder. "Here's a list of three I found still in the New York area. Two on Long Island, one in White Plains."

"Okay. Let's get this done as quickly as we can. Cord and Tim, you each take one of the Long Island alums. Bob, you take the one in White Plains." She stopped. "Tim, isn't your wife's mammogram today?"

"Yeah. Ten this morning. She called a while ago. They wouldn't tell her anything. She has an appointment with her doctor Friday evening."

"And how will you be entertaining yourself this afternoon, Detective Brady?" Cord asked.

"I'm going to visit Gina Owens in Riverdale again to see if this rings any bells." As the others dispersed, Kim called to make sure Ms. Owens would be home.

"What's this about?" Ms. Owens asked.

"I've come across something I'd like to show you, to see if you recognize someone."

"A picture?"

"It will be easier to explain in person. May I come by this afternoon?"

The other woman's hesitation was palpable. "All right."

***

The senator banged his gavel to recess the hearing for lunch. It had been a busy morning, with the New York City Police Commissioner testifying. He'd been defensive and refused to criticize the acting mayor. He'd bolted afterward.

Cates was waiting for the senator back in his office. "I spoke to one of the commissioner's aides. The commissioner conveys his apologies for his less-than-helpful answers but feels that it's necessary in the current situation."

"Darling Sabrina is muzzling him. A braver man would have defied her and taken the consequences."

"Yes, sir. That's what I said, too. But his aide replied he felt that would do even further damage to public confidence in the department. He says you have the commissioner's permission to make a public accusation against Dunn, and he will simply reply, 'no comment.'"

"Very well, Cates. Let's do that."

"One other thing, Senator. Four precincts in Brooklyn were vandalized overnight, with swastikas and slogans like 'Nazis work here' spray painted on the buildings."

"I didn't see that reported anywhere."

"Our media people tell me only ITN carried the item in the city."

"Let's go enlighten everyone else."

***

Ms. Owens invited her in as she had the last time. But there was something different about the room, though Kim couldn't put her finger on it. "Two more girls have been killed since we last talked."

"Yes, I saw. And you think they're connected to my sister's murder?"

"They're connected. DNA doesn't lie. Using a new process called DNA Phenotyping, we've constructed an image of the killer that is accurate as to general grouping, such as ethnicity, and for specific features, but isn't a photograph. Since the aging process doesn't alter DNA, it's an image of a young adult—someone of high school age or a little older. Angelina's killer was in his teens at the time, and I wondered if this image reminds you of anyone."

Ms. Owens glanced at it. "No." Her voice was shaky.

"Please, you hardly looked at it. Your sister likely knew her attacker. Which means you may have known him, too."

"No." More emphatic this time. "You don't understand what all this is doing to me. Angelina was my role model. We had a special bond. I never got over her death. So, I buried it and prayed it would go away. Now, you've dragged it all back. I haven't had a decent night's sleep since your last visit. I'm back on anti-anxiety medication." She was sobbing. "Please, get out and don't come back."

CHAPTER FIFTY-FIVE

Tuesday, May 29, 7:03 PM

"Good evening. Mayoral challenger Senator Ray Brandt charged Acting Mayor Dunn with obstruction today when the police commissioner provided few answers to questions about the limitations placed on the department in responding to public violence in recent days. Brandt charged she had muzzled the commissioner to save her own neck as recent polls show public anger rising over street violence and increases in violent crimes around the city. When asked about these fresh charges, the commissioner replied, 'no comment'. Senator Brandt's witness list tomorrow includes the heads of two of the three major unions in the NYPD. This is Joanna Dunbar reporting."

***

The Castle was all but empty when she returned. But Bostwick was still there. "Any luck?"

"No, and it was downright weird. She was like a different woman, worn to a frazzle. Last time she gave me tea."

"You dredged up a lot of painful memories. That can't have been easy for her."

Bob sauntered in. "Struck out in White Plains. No bells ringing."

Next was Brogan. "Nothing. The guy couldn't talk about anything except his time in Nam. Sad."

He looked distracted. Easy to guess why. "Don't worry, Tim. Whatever it is, Holly caught it early."

He gave a weak smile.

"I got something," Cord said. "She couldn't remember the dude's name, but he dropped out at the beginning of their junior year. Before that, he'd given her the eye a few times, and it freaked her out. I asked if his name might have been Paul, but she wasn't sure."

Text from Rick Conti. *Grand jury indicted Hammond. Murder and arson. Evidentiary hearing tomorrow.*

She turned to Bostwick. "Lieu, can we put some heat on the lab for the DNA result on the shell casing from the other night? We might need it sooner than we expected."

CHAPTER FIFTY-SIX

Wednesday, May 30, 9:11 AM

"Anti-police protests increased in intensity last night with attacks on more police stations. Several local politicians have voiced concern that the undermining of police is leading to an increase in crime across the board. The head of the PBA will testify before Senator Raymond Brandt's committee today, where he's expected to quote recent CompStat data showing increases in crime in every borough of the city over this time last year."

***

Kim sat in the back of the courtroom, waiting for the judge to arrive. Rick Conti was already at the prosecution table, but she couldn't catch his eye.

Wyckoff was at the defense table with a junior associate, a woman about Kim's age dressed in her corporate best. No sign of Wesley Hammond.

"All rise."

In walked Judge Ronald C. Vickers. Let 'em run Ron. No wonder Conti wouldn't look at her.

"I call this hearing to order." Vickers turned to Conti. "Proceed, Counselor."

Conti stood. "Your honor, the defendant is not present at this time."

"Counselor," Vickers said to Wyckoff, "may we expect your client soon?"

Wyckoff stood, his expression impassive. "My staff is trying to locate him, your honor."

"Counsel was notified the same time we were," Conti replied. "Are we to understand that counsel could not reach his client?"

"As yet, no," Wyckoff replied.

"Then, your honor," Conti said, "I ask you to revoke defendant's bail and issue a warrant for his immediate arrest."

"Not so fast," Vickers replied. "You requested this hearing less than twenty-four hours ago. I see no sign of 'willful and persistent' failure to appear. I grant defense a delay of 48 hours, during which I expect counsel to urge his client to appear at ten o'clock Thursday morning."

Kim waited outside. Conti didn't look any happier when he joined her. "There's a reason they call him Let 'em run Ron. Nothing to do but…"

"But let a murderer skate on skipping bail?"

"No," Conti said. "He gave him the forty-eight hours required by the so-called Criminal Justice reform the state legislature passed. After that, it's at his discretion how far we keep kicking the can down the road before he decides this is willful and persistent."

She understood, but she was pissed. "What's the back-up plan?"

"There isn't any. Vickers holds all the cards."

Which pissed her off even more.

***

In the past, it had always been a simple matter to put his little adventures behind him and bide his time until the next opportunity presented itself. But the less-than-satisfactory attack on the Perez girl had thrown him, while the thrill of the last attack had whet his appetite for further adventures. He'd always hid in plain sight before, always blended in, amazing himself at how cunning he could be. But the encounter with the Chinese girl had been fraught with risk because it had been so close to home. What he needed now was something further away, something to confound the police.

But it had to be in Brooklyn because she was in Brooklyn. His huntress. He had fantasized that her name would be Diana, and it had been a serious disappointment to find her name was Kim.

It was so aggravating when reality refused to bend to his fantasies.

He glanced around his sparsely furnished living room. She'd come to his home. That discomfited him in the extreme. Even if it were luck, even if it had resulted from his own choice of target, had he not had the good sense to clear out, it could have gone badly. Because he wasn't sure how much of his features those video cameras revealed that night in Williamsburg.

And what if she came back? Because something told him she might— that ever-present sense of survival that sniffed out danger before it was dangerous. The blowhard politician had called her the finest detective in the department. Others had said the same about her grandfather, who had been good, very smart, yet not smart enough to avoid an ambush.

What a joy if he could do the same to the granddaughter.

CHAPTER FIFTY-SEVEN

Wednesday, May 30, 5:06 PM

Kim saw it as soon as she got off the bus on Tillary Street, a poster slapped onto the Korean Veteran's Monument: "Wesley Hammond, hero to the masses!" As she crossed Cadman Plaza West, she saw another plastered to the side of a bus shelter: "Free Wesley Hammond!"

Gotta find him first.

She had just turned onto Clark Street when she saw a familiar face. "Hi, Joanna. How's the new job?"

"Hi. If you've seen my reports, what's your opinion of them?"

"The interview with Brandt was good, although a bit on the soft side. How are you finding it at ITN?"

"Better than I expected. They don't push me into their ideological box. I think they're hoping I bring them viewers who previously saw them as right-wing nut cases. How's the case going?"

"Looks like Vickers is going to stand by while Hammond jumps his bail. No surprise there."

"I heard. I did a piece today on the firefighter's family, a human-interest thing. Should run as part of the seven o'clock report tonight. Real sad. Three kids, one with a disability. And their dad's killer gets to walk. Sucks."

"Is that the basis for a story I hear forming?"

"I would appreciate any help you can provide. You have contacts at the FBI, and I figure they must be involved. So…"

Kim stopped her. "I do and they are, but they're not even telling me much."

"Weren't you at the hearing today?"

"Yes, as a witness to present evidence in our case against Hammond. Nothing else."

"But why even go for the hearing? You can't have all your ducks lined up at this point."

There was a reason Joanna was one of the best. "It was Conti's decision."

Joanna cracked a smile. "And you two don't dance, so you must agree on this. All I want is a name of who to contact with the feds."

"Rick and I have reached something of an understanding. Mutual needs and all that."

"Kim, I realize you put in a good word with Brandt, a great word, because he was nothing but cordial to me. Like I'd never said a harsh word about him in my life."

"He's a politician, and he saw a way to put a critical member of the press in his corner. Nothing to do with me."

Joanna laughed. "Still cynical. Isn't there anything you can do? Because if I can drive this story to a favorable conclusion, it would be quite satisfying."

"You looking to report the news or make it?"

"Yes."

"Okay. I'll talk to my contact at the FBI and tell him your involvement and I'll tell him you tipped us off to the coming disturbance in Domino Park that night. I'll provide him with your number and leave it up to him if he wants to contact you. Fair enough?"

"Thanks."

***

"I must congratulate you," Emory said as the senator sank into a chair. "My latest polling numbers show you've taken the lead."

"Yes. Isn't it amazing what a serial killer and an insurrectionist can do for a campaign?" But his host wasn't laughing, so he changed the subject. "My sources tell me they suspect Hammond has fled the jurisdiction."

Emory dwelled on that for several moments. Good. Maybe something useful would result, something other than financial support for the campaign. But the senator wasn't prepared for what came next.

"They must be anxious to learn where he is." Emory's voice was little more than a whisper.

"Undoubtedly. Most people in this city still frown on killers. Why?"

"Fredrick was almost certainly responsible for whisking the boy away."

The senator snorted. "Stop the presses."

"Do you think they'd be grateful if he turned himself in?"

"Overjoyed. Any other fantasies you'd like to discuss?"

"Would they be grateful enough to shift their focus to the real culprit?"

"If you mean Prinz, I doubt they could make the case. Yes, he fomented the riot, but unless he put the gun in Hammond's hand and ordered him to fire…"

Emory nodded. "A distinct possibility."

"It wouldn't be credible coming from him. He'd need corroborating evidence."

"You'll humor me at least this much. Mention it to the detective. She was in the courtroom today, was she not?"

"And she's the one who caught him red-handed."

Emory shurgged. "Then she's the perfect one to tell."

***

"Did you see the news tonight?" Jake asked. "Brandt's pulled ahead in the latest polls with sixteen percent still undecided. Has to be a kick in the teeth for someone like Dunn, who started out with such high hopes."

"Like a lot of them, she got too wrapped up in her own self-righteousness." She wasn't in the mood to discuss politics tonight. Too much was still swirling in her own mind. She'd called Ken Taylor about

Joanna's offer. His reply—thirty seconds of silence—hadn't surprised her. That he'd taken her number and said he'd consider it had.

Her cell rang. She almost dropped it when she saw the name on the screen.

Senator Brandt.

She took it into the bedroom so Jake wouldn't overhear. "Good evening, Senator. And congratulations. I saw the new poll numbers."

"Thank you, my dear. But I'll wait for the special election before I celebrate. A little bird told me our least favorite jurist sideswiped you today. I also saw Ms. Dunbar's piece on Jared Davis' family tonight. I wonder if I could run an alternate theory of the crime past you, just between us."

CHAPTER FIFTY-EIGHT

Thursday, May 31, 6:56 AM

Ken Taylor met Kim at the entrance to 26 Federal Plaza. "Are you serious about this?"

She waited until he'd closed his office door. "I'm the messenger, that's all. Brandt claims that Fredrick Hammond can convince his son to return to the States from wherever he's hiding out if we promise to take seriously his claim that Felipe Prinz forced him into shooting Jared Davis and charge Prinz with the murder, the arson, the whole truckload."

Taylor sat back. "And, as the messenger, what is your opinion of that tale?"

"I wouldn't care even if it were true. I don't think Brandt believes it, himself. It sounds to me like Emory hoping to squeeze some additional financing out of Hammond's father. But it raises the possibility of bringing Prinz to heel, and I suspect he's counting on that. I wonder if you might want to utilize Ms. Dunbar to figure out where young Hammond is hiding out."

"I'll take it under advisement. In the meantime, the DNA detectives have been working overtime, although what they've come up with is totally out of left field. I'm almost sorry I got you started on this because…"

It hit her before he could say it. "The killer is related to Angelina."

"How the fuck did you figure that out?"

"I've been stewing about it ever since I showed the image to Gina Owens." Kim could still envision the exchange. "Her reaction was off the charts. After I left I realized she was upset before I even showed it to her."

"But that doesn't prove…"

She shook her head. "There's more. She couldn't wait to get me out of her apartment. She threw me out. It was only later that I realized what was different. My first visit, she'd had a group of old family photos on the mantel, including a photo of her entire family. But the day of my second visit, they had disappeared."

"That still doesn't…"

"She had told me her father's sister had married a Triscari, and that some of the family had looked down on them because the Triscaris were Sicilian while the Farinas were *Napolitán*." Kim brandished the image. "He looks Sicilian." She noticed he was holding a closed file folder. "You're now going to open that to show me the cluster the investigator found, and one person is a cousin named Paul Triscari, born in 1946."

And he did.

***

"By her own cousin?" Bostwick said. "That's revolting."

But Kim was pacing while the others on her team watched with nervous eyes. "I pulled Gina Owens' phone records. No calls from Brooklyn as far back as I could check, except one. From a prepaid cell. The cell tower the call originated from was in Bay Ridge."

"Don't tell me," Bob said. "Right by the convenience store."

"Yes," she said. "And made last Saturday."

"The day after Lily Ng was killed?" Cord said. "That's fucked up."

"Perhaps not. Triscari was ditching the car and was likely worried he might have left other loose ends. So, he calls the younger sister of his first victim since she's got a sense of family history. In fact, it was her genealogy search that provided the link to Triscari." She considered it. "He knows how to press people's weak spots."

"So, what's next?" Cord asked.

"I'd like to get Gina Owens into protective custody," Kim replied, "but I'm certain she wouldn't agree."

Bostwick spoke up. "Offer it. Tell her everything you've learned and how you came by it. And tell her you've protected witnesses from madmen before because it's true. Notify Taylor you're off the Hammond case. He's the FBI's problem, now, and Conti's."

CHAPTER FIFTY-NINE

Thursday, May 31, 9:05 AM

There was no doubt now in Kim's mind that Triscari realized who she was and that she was on the case. Her name was on television the night of the riot. He'd known her grandfather's name. Anyone who was smart enough to stay clear of law enforcement for half a century was smart enough to put the two names together.

He'd gone after her grandfather at seventeen. Nothing in Granddad's notes hinted at anything Triscari might have done to lure him to the Belmont section of the Bronx that night. There was just that one cryptic note. "Tracking Paul."

As she drove up the Brooklyn-Queens Expressway, she realized she might not even get to talk to Gina Owens. And she had no backup plan for that.

***

Bob was glad to see no one else in the unit was around except for Bostwick, whose office he entered with one knock.

"Morning, Bob. Early for you."

"I wanted to talk to you about Kim."

Bostwick sat back. "I realize you two have something of a history, but…"

"Nothing to worry about. I once worked with her dad."

"Offed himself if I recall."

"Yeah. Partly out of guilt because of some shit he did on the job, and partly out of guilt he didn't buy it on the job, like her granddad did. She knows about the first part, but I doubt she knows about the second."

"Where are we going with this?"

"She scares me sometimes. Her dad was a bulldog. She's a wolf. Smart, cunning, and, on a case like this, unstoppable." He hesitated. "On this case, it's liable to get her killed."

Bostwick stared at him. "You're asking me to take her off?"

"Good Christ, no. That would be the worst thing you could do. She'd simply keep going on her own, not telling anyone what she's doing. I realize she's unorthodox, and you two didn't hit it off at first, but you need to support her. She needs you to be one hundred percent behind her. That way, you and we can provide the support she'll need."

CHAPTER SIXTY

Thursday, May 31, 9:42 AM

Kim parked the car. In a sudden thought, she wished she'd brought the guys with her. Because Gina Owens might just run.

She walked around the perimeter of the building, checking for potential avenues of escape and for anyone lurking outside. Because she was now in the zone where anything was possible.

All clear.

She punched up the number on her phone. Ms. Owens answered on the third ring. "Good morning, Ms. Owens. Detective Kim Brady. I'm sorry to disturb you so…"

"I'm not talking to you."

"Would you rather talk to your cousin, Paul, again? Because if you don't talk to me, I won't be able to stop him when he comes after you."

She waited for the telltale beep of the call dropping, but it didn't.

Ten seconds…

Twenty seconds…

Thirty seconds…

"Will you talk to me, Gina?"

A sniffle. A sob. "Yes, all right."

The doorman called up to Gina's apartment when Kim presented herself. His frown suggested he heard the strain in the woman's voice, but Kim's shield convinced him it was okay.

Gina answered the door still in her robe and slippers. "How did you know?"

Kim waited until she was safely inside the apartment before pulling out the Genetic Genealogy report. "This was the ultimate proof, but I was certain the last time we talked, and you had taken down all the family pictures."

"What's this mark next to my name mean?"

"It was your family history they based their analysis on. When did you have it done?"

"Two and a half years ago."

Around the same time as the last killing before Lulu Ramirez. "Why did you have it done then?"

A shrug. "I just wanted to feel like I was in touch with my family again."

Kim sat on the sofa. "I want to believe you, Gina. But I've got to be sure. So, let's start with something else. When did you first realize Paul had raped and killed Angelina?"

No answer.

"How were they with each other when you were kids?"

Gina thought about it. "They were close as children. He was always nice to her as far back as I can remember. But the Christmas before she died, something changed. His mother, my Aunt Amalia, saw him kiss her under the mistletoe and said something about kissing cousins. Mama whispered something to Papa—I couldn't hear what. But I also saw Angelina pull away, like she was uncomfortable."

Kim stared at her. "So, you suspected. And he knows it. That's why he called you last week, the morning after he raped and killed that twelve-year-old Chinese girl. Twelve. The same age you were when Angelina died."

Gina started crying again.

Time for Kim to press for what she needed. "Angelina was afraid of him, wasn't she? Something had changed, hadn't it?"

"The following summer, we'd had a big family picnic. All the cousins were there. Angelina wore these cute short shorts. Twice, I caught Paul staring at her. He was practically drooling over her. And then he caught me looking at him, and he fixed me with a glare that was terrifying. I turned away. And for the rest of the day, whenever he was near, he was pleasant and nice, as always. With my sister, too. I convinced myself I had misunderstood."

"What about the night she died?"

"I've tried so hard for years not to think about that night. It was the worst night of my life. The whole family came together for us."

"Even Paul?"

"Yes. At her funeral, I broke down and cried, and he held me and comforted me. I was just feeling a little better when…" She froze.

"When what, Gina?"

"It was that night, after the funeral. Everyone was going home, hugging mama and papa, everyone sniffling, trying not to cry. Paul came over to me and whispered, 'Gina, you are one lucky girl. So much like your sister.' I watched as they left, Paul and his family. When he got to the car, he turned back and grinned at me. Like it was all a big joke."

She broke down and cried again. Kim didn't stop her, only rubbing her back for comfort. At last, Gina calmed herself. "Paul will figure out I've talked to you and kill me. He warned me, so either he suspected you'd been to see me, or that you would soon find me."

"I won't let anything happen to you. I've dealt with people like this before. We can protect you. If you can pack a bag, I'll take you into protective custody."

Gina could only shake her head.

Kim grasped both her shoulders. "Listen to me. It's the only way I can protect you. If you stay here, you're a loose end, and you can guess what he does with those. Pack a couple of bags. I'll wait."

CHAPTER SIXTY-ONE

Thursday, May 31, 9:54 AM

Gina. He hadn't thought about her until recently. He'd glimpsed Gina on his way to the park that night.

And later he'd seen Angelina. His Angelina.

With some skinny-ass mick, holding hands.

She'd stopped him at the corner. Turned and let him kiss her.

For a moment, he'd been paralyzed with rage, undecided whether to kill her or the boy. But then the boy had turned and started back toward the school.

Out of reach.

She'd watched him go for a minute or two. And in those moments, he'd decided.

Angelina was all that mattered.

He'd started across the street but realized someone might see him. So, he'd stepped back into the shadows of the trees.

Watching her as she drew closer, flush with excitement at her first kiss.

"Angelina, over here."

She'd turned, startled. "Paul?"

"Yeah, come 'ere."

She'd started across the street. "I should get home."

"Aw, come on. You always have time for your favorite cousin, right?"

"Sure."

He'd guided her toward the path into the park.

And she hesitated. "Paul, is something wrong?"

"No, baby. Nothing is ever going to be wrong again."

He'd released his rage. Angelina had become his. She'd never belong to anyone else.

A police patrol car passed by, breaking his reverie.

His thoughts returned to Gina, the only one who'd known of the beast inside him. She'd seen it the summer before that night and tried to hide it. But no one could hide anything from him.

She still feared him after all these years. When he'd called her on a whim the morning after Lotus Blossom, it had still been there, almost palpable over the phone.

Fear did strange things to people. And with his exploits now being splashed across the newspapers, he was rethinking having called her. Terrorizing her may not have been enough, and perhaps she now required different handling.

She lived in Riverdale. Retired. His call had made her nervous, so she would stay close to home.

Time to pay her a visit.

Sweet little Gina.

***

Kim reached for her piece as they left the building but decided the sight of a weapon would freak Gina out. They stopped by the doorman, whose furrowed brow signaled deep concerned.

"If anyone asks for me," Gina said, "please tell them I've gone down to the Jersey Shore to visit some friends."

Good, she'd gotten it right.

But the doorman looked at Kim with alarm, so she added a warning. "You will not, under any circumstances, reveal to anyone that a police detective was here." She gave him her card. "And if an older man comes looking for her, call me as quickly as you can."

"Yes, ma'am."

Once they were in the car, Kim could relax. "You okay?"

"I guess. Why did you say not to tell anyone about you being a detective?"

"That's for your protection. In case Paul comes after you. Right now, we're headed back to my unit's headquarters in Brooklyn." Once she was on the road, she pressed a button on the steering wheel activating Bluetooth. "Call the lieu."

A moment later, Bostwick came on the line. "What's the deal, Kim?"

"I'm on speaker and I have Gina Owens with me. She has agreed to be placed in protective custody. I'm southbound on 9A, heading for the Cross Bronx. ETA at the Castle in forty-five minutes. Can you call Rick Conti to arrange it, or do you need me to do it?"

"I've got it covered," Bostwick replied. "I'll have him call you if he needs anything additional. Tell Ms. Owens she's in excellent hands."

Kim ended the call.

"What did he mean by that?" Gina asked.

"Just that I have experience."

CHAPTER SIXTY-TWO

Thursday, May 31, 10:36 AM

Even before he parked the car, something felt wrong. He pulled out the cell he'd taken from Lotus Blossom as a trophy and called Gina's home number. No answer. His sense of something having gone wrong grew stronger.

He approached the doorman. "Can I ask you a question about one of your residents, Gina Owens?"

The doorman blanched. "She's gone to visit some friends at the Jersey Shore." It came out as one continuous word.

He gave the doorman a menacing look. "That wasn't the question." He stood his ground, impassive, lowering his voice to a growl. "Are you all right? You seem quite…"

"I'm fine."

"… nervous." He narrowed his eyes and took a menacing step closer. "When did she leave?"

"You just missed her."

"Did I? Was she alone?"

"Yes. Definitely."

The doorman was ready to shit his pants. "No, she wasn't." He glanced up. He'd noticed the video camera on the way in and had turned his face away, as he always did. It would catch anyone walking through the lobby. "Show me the video."

"I'm not supposed to..."

He backed the doorman against his desk. "Show me the video. Now."

The doorman turned the monitor screen on the desk to face him. In a moment, he saw Gina walking out.

With another woman.

He checked to make sure they were off camera before turning on the doorman. "Who's the woman she's with?"

"I don't..."

He grabbed the quaking man by the throat, the muscles in his arms bulging. "Who is she?"

"Some... detective..."

He squeezed harder. "Give me her card." Because they always left one.

He placed it in his shirt pocket and then squeezed with both hands.

CHAPTER SIXTY-THREE

Thursday, May 31, 11:16 AM

When Kim pulled up to the front of the Castle, Brogan and Cord were standing out in front, just as she'd asked. The nearest parking spot was six blocks away.

"The lieu is working on the protective custody thing." Cord turned to Gina. "In the meantime, we've got some decent coffee for you." He nodded toward the Fire House Deli. "Splendid stuff, not the swill we brew."

Brogan pulled Gina's bags out of the back seat.

Gina looked doubtful.

Kim rubbed her arm. "It's okay. I'll find a place to park. I may be awhile."

"Might be quicker to just drive it home and take the bus back," Brogan said.

Kim laughed. "Don't listen to these guys. They think they're funny, but I trust them with my life every day." She watched as they led Gina inside.

***

He got out of Riverdale, driving down the Henry Hudson Parkway and getting off at 95th Street before finding a parking spot on Riverside Drive. He pulled the detective's card from his pocket.

Detective Kim Brady, Brooklyn North Homicide.

He did a Google search on Lotus Blossom's cell. Police Borough Brooklyn North. Wilson Avenue in Bushwick. Without question, that had to be where they were going.

He turned the card over and saw another phone number written there. Had to be her cell.

No, he wouldn't call her. Not yet. It would alert her to his getting her card, which would mean checking back with the doorman for a description. No, much more fun to keep her guessing.

For now, it was sufficient that they were together, the detective and little Cousin Gina. That could be useful.

***

"Never mind witness protection, where the hell are you?" Conti sounded frantic. "Hammond's hearing is due to begin in half an hour."

Shit. She'd forgotten all about it. Bostwick had told her to focus only on the Triscari case. She explained about Gina Owens. "If I leave now, I can be there in about forty-five minutes. Just don't call me as the first witness."

He mumbled something unintelligible and ended the call.

"You're leaving?" The color drained from Gina's face.

"I have to testify at a hearing and totally forgot about it. I should be back by lunch time. It sounds like it will be a while before you're placed, but you're perfectly safe here." She grinned. "We call it the Castle."

Two choices. She could take the B38 bus or take the M train and switch to the F at Essex/Delancey. The bus was more direct, but prone to traffic jamming into downtown Brooklyn. The subway meant detouring out of borough, plus the potential for delay changing trains.

She decided on the bus.

It was a five-minute wait when she got to the bus stop. She was recalculating her arrival time at the court building on Adams Street as the bus crossed Evergreen Avenue when Conti texted. *Don't bother. Vickers just granted Wyckoff's request for another 48-hour delay. We're postponed until Monday. Please don't make any plans.*

When the bus stopped at the light at Bushwick Avenue, she flashed her badge and had the driver let her off. For once, Judge Vickers had done her a solid.

She walked back to the Castle.

"That was fast." Bob was sitting with Gina, who was relaxing. "Let me guess. Hammond didn't show."

"We're postponed until Monday. So, forty-eight hours has now morphed into a hundred and twenty."

"With an endless supply yet to come," Bob said. "Ain't justice grand?"

Kim turned to Gina. "Don't ask." She finally had the time to return Conti's text. *Good. Now, you can get cracking on getting Gina Owens into protective custody. Not in the Bronx. Or Brooklyn.*

After a moment, Conti replied. *Are we insisting on five-star hotels, or will a 4-star be satisfactory?*

Nice to see he still had his sense of humor. Then again, if Hammond had showed, Vickers might have forced him to call her first. *4-star is acceptable.*

His response was immediate. *Wiseass.*

The alarm blared, and the room burst into activity. Sergeant Ramos rushed over. "Everybody out. It's another bomb scare."

Bostwick took over. "Okay, pack nothing up. Let's go."

"Wait a minute." Kim's mind was racing. "I'm not taking Gina out into the street."

"ESU is on their way, Kim," Bostwick said. "She'll be as well protected out there as she is in here. Besides, this is almost certainly a fake, just like last time."

"Fake, yes, but not like last time. You guys go ahead. I'm taking Gina out back. When ESU arrives, I'll get her into their van."

Bostwick hesitated, then waved everyone else in the unit out. "I hope you know what you're doing."

So do I. She flagged down Sergeant Ramos as he rushed by. "Sarge, who alerted us about the bomb scare?"

"Anonymous caller. Said he's planted a device in the building, and any attempt to remove it would set it off immediately."

"What did he sound like?"

Ramos' eyes went wide. "How the fuck...? Some guy. I called it into ESU. Now get your ass out of here." He rushed off.

Kim pulled her laptop from its docking station. "Come on, Gina." She led her out the rear exit. "We call this the Castle because of the tower on the corner and the façade along the roof, but they're two separate buildings. You can tell from back here. See, the rear of the corner building extends further back than ours, which is a big help right now."

"Why?"

"Because as long as we stay back here in this little cove, no one can see us from the street."

Gina looked doubtful. "That's a good thing?"

"Right now, yes. I've learned from experience it takes a major effort to make protective custody fully protective." She opened the laptop and set it up on the hood of a parked car.

Gina stared at her. "You're working at a time like this?"

"My husband complains I'm always working. Sometimes, even in my sleep." As her fingers flew across the keyboard, she prayed that the Wi-Fi signal from inside would extend to the lot.

"What are you doing? Or aren't I allowed to ask?"

Normally, Kim wouldn't have answered, but keeping Gina talking might allow her to relax a little. "I'm checking the phone records of our main number." She checked her watch. 11:57. So, the call had to come in no earlier than 11:40. A few more clicks, and she had the number. "Called at 11:42."

"What does that mean?"

"By itself, nothing. But I copy the number into a text, and I ask a technician to check with the carrier to get the name of the owner." Vera Koshkin at One-PP had done this work in the recent case of the five murders.

A short while later, she got the response. *Hello, Brilliant American lady detective. Cell phone's owner is Shaofen Ng.*

Lily Ng's grandmother. It was Lily's missing phone. *I need the tower ping from that call at 11:42.*

Another ten minutes, and Vera answered with the location two blocks away.

She called Bob. "The bomb scare call came from a burner right here in the neighborhood. Inform the lieu. And keep a sharp eye out for our guy."

"You think he did this? Why?"

"If he knows about Gina, he might have been looking to flush us out into the open. If he doesn't, it's just to fuck with us. I'll get back to you. In the meantime, you guys check around, but do not come back here."

She texted Vera. *Please get me the list of every tower that cell pinged from last Friday on. Send via e-mail. And ask the carrier to continue monitoring in real time.*

CHAPTER SIXTY-FOUR

Thursday, May 31, 12:09 PM

The second booth from the front window of the little Chinese place on Wilson Avenue provided a fine view of the proceedings across the street while making it impossible for anyone outside to see him. It had taken some doing to convince the manager to open early, but his story that he craved freshly made Chinese sponge cake had done the trick.

As he savored the cake and tolerated the tea—he hated tea, but appearances today were everything—he watched and waited. The police nest had been vomiting occupants for several minutes, now, but had finally slowed to a trickle. Several female officers had been among the early evacuees, but no sign of Detective Brady or Gina.

He could accept the fact that Brady had iron nerves—so had her grandfather. But he worried that she might have seen through his bomb scare ruse.

Two vans from ESU pulled up. One parked on Wilson without obstructing his view, which was considerate of them. The other turned up DeKalb.

Why would they go there? These buildings were all connected.

Unless there was a rear entrance to the parking area. Which might explain why he still hadn't seen the two women.

***

Three calls to the doorman's cell, the number which Gina had provided, went unanswered. A call to the Fiftieth Precinct confirmed her worst fears. They had found the doorman strangled.

"It's connected to an ongoing investigation," she said. "Please give the lead detective on the case my contact information and have him call me as speedily as possible."

Triscari. Anyone else would make it a coincidence, and she hated those. But he wouldn't have gone there cold, so she checked Gina's phone records. Sure enough, there was a call. Ten minutes after she'd whisked Gina away.

Her cell buzzed. It was a text from Vera. *Check your e-mail.*

There were no tower pings before the call to Gina. Triscari had only turned the phone on that morning. He'd made the call from the immediate vicinity of the building. He'd left the phone on after the call, and it had pinged successive towers trailing south on the west side of Manhattan, the last ping coming around 95th Street.

Where he'd remembered to turn it off.

An ESU van pulled into the lot and several members deployed. An FDNY bomb squad unit pulled in behind them. Kim recognized Lieutenant Zimmerman from ESU, but she didn't call to him until he was almost on top of her, causing him to pull back, startled.

Until he recognized her. "Kim Brady, correct? Last time we met, I was afraid you were going to be blown to bits. What are you doing back here? Having another try at it?"

"Hello, Lieutenant. No time to explain. This woman is a witness in an important case, and I'm staying with her until we can get her into protective custody. This scare is most likely related, but I know you guys have jobs to do. In the meantime, I need your help to do mine."

***

He paid the restaurant manager and slipped out the door. Most of the evacuees were milling about, but a few in plain clothes looked a bit too casual. Pretending to be interested, he pulled up his hood and made his way over to DeKalb Avenue.

"Move it, buddy. This ain't safe."

"Thank you, Officer." He walked beyond the barricade the cops had set up to block pedestrian traffic. He crossed DeKalb, figuring it would be easier to get past the checkpoint on Wilson. If need be, he'd walk down another block and then come around from behind.

He had just started across Wilson when he saw a tall black detective in his mid-thirties watching him while trying to appear he wasn't. As the detective moved toward him, he turned and began walking away along Wilson. A cab pulled up, and a passenger got out.

He jumped into the cab and closed the door.

"Hey, buddy, I'm going off duty."

He turned to see if the black detective was still closing. He was not. "Then your light shouldn't have been on. I'm a senior citizen and I have health issues. And I'm not going far, for God's sake. A few blocks. I'll even pay cash." He shoved a ten through the slot.

"Okay, where to?"

"Corner of Suydam and St. Nicholas Avenue."

"No problem." One block to Suydam Street and he made a right. One block to Knickerbocker Avenue before stopping for the light.

Perfect. He yanked on the door handle. "Thanks."

"But we only..." The rest was lost behind the closed door. One block and then he turned down DeKalb. The police were setting up a checkpoint, and an officer called to him. "Hey, you can't go..."

"I live right down here," he called, and picked up the pace. But a police van approached from the other end of DeKalb, and out of caution, he paused behind a large tree.

***

Inside the van away from any windows, Kim did her best to appear relaxed for Gina's sake. But inside, she was tight as a drum.

"Are we safe?" Gina asked.

"You're surrounded by police," Kim replied. "No safer place in the world."

"Amen to that," called the driver. "Where to, Detective?"

An excellent question. She punched up Conti's number.

"Where the hell are you, Kim? Word is you guys had another bomb scare. I thought Prinz would keep low for a while after his last adventure."

"This isn't CHE. It's related to my case. No time to explain, now. I just need to get this woman into a safe place, pronto."

His pause gave her a sense of dread. "I'm working on it. I realize you don't like it, but we may have no choice but a Brooklyn site. It's complicated."

"Complicated, my ass. Call Yvette Driscoll at the Manhattan DA's office and tell her it's for my case. Tell her we've kissed and made up, and it's critical we get someone placed today and in a place no one would look. Tell her I suggest the Manhattan location we used during the last case she and I worked together."

"I'm screwed if I do that. The politics…"

"Fuck the politics, Rick. It's important."

"Why?"

"Long story." Like everything else. "I'll owe you big time."

Long pause. "I'll see what I can do."

A moment later, Cord called. "I think I spotted him. Old dude in a blue hoodie, hood up. But I got a look at him. Dark even for an Italian. He was watching the Castle. He crossed over to our side of the intersection, but when he saw me, he grabbed a cab and bugged out."

"Why do you think it was Triscari?"

"Because his gray hair stuck out from under the hood, same as the dude on the video."

CHAPTER SIXTY-FIVE

Thursday, May 31, 7:34 PM

It was dark by the time he got home. He'd stopped at Luliano's on the way and bought himself a meatball parm hero. He sat at his kitchen table, picking at it with disinterest.

The entire building had emptied in minutes, but neither the detective nor Gina had been among them. Why?

When he'd left the little Chinese place, the black detective had immediately spotted him. Recognized him. How?

And when he'd worked his way around to come at the building from behind, the police had been waiting for him. There was only one way to explain all of that.

She'd known.

The entire police department had thought it was a bomb scare.

But she'd known.

She wasn't as smart as her grandfather.

She was smarter.

This would take a great deal of planning.

CHAPTER SIXTY-SIX

Thursday, May 31, 11:07 PM

"Jake, I won't be home tonight. I've gotten someone into protective custody, and I'm staying with her to make sure she settles in."

"You okay?"

"Sure."

"No, I mean, seriously? Because you don't sound okay. In fact, you don't sound like any way I've ever heard you sound before."

Because she was now in a place she'd never been before, facing an enemy like none she'd ever imagined. "I'm fine, Jake. Just a tough case."

***

"What are you doing in your study at this hour?" The senator's wife's voice dripped with genuine concern. And she was right. Even at his busiest, he was never in his study this late.

But Cates' report an hour earlier of some new storm brewing over competition between the Brooklyn and Manhattan DA's offices was making it impossible for him to sleep. Kim Brady was at the heart of it. And this time, Rick Conti was on her side. Well, at least Conti couldn't have a romantic motive if what Cates said was true.

Not like the senator.

His wife was waiting for an answer. He shook himself. "Sorry, dear. Some things came up tonight and I have to think them through."

"You should put a limit on when Mr. Cates can call. Lately, he's been disturbing you at the oddest hours."

"I'll be up, shortly. I'm fine."

But it was Cates' other piece of information that had shaken him. ESU had been called to the Castle today, and no one was saying why. The official explanation, which hadn't made it into the media, was a false alarm.

It had to involve Kim. The Castle was Brooklyn North Homicide's headquarters. He resisted the temptation to shoot her a text and ask because then she'd realize Cates still had his nose to the ground.

He punched up the number of Rick Conti's section chief. "I hear there's trouble in paradise."

"Yeah, and if you get elected, it will become your headache. I thought we'd taken care of this nonsense of NYPD personnel picking which boroughs to deal with. Didn't transferring that bitch to Brooklyn teach her anything?"

"I hear Conti's on her side."

"Yeah. Well, he ain't on top of her."

The senator laughed to cover his irritation. "Careful with that. What's this all about, anyway? Not judge shopping again, I hope."

"No. She wanted to get some woman into protective custody, and we weren't moving fast enough for her."

"Then you should have moved faster. And you should commend young Conti for thinking outside the box. Good night."

A witness who needed protection. Now, that might trigger a false alarm.

CHAPTER SIXTY-SEVEN

Friday, June 1, 7:14 AM

"Didn't you sleep at all last night?" Gina had slept all the way through.

"I was working." Although Kim had left the Castle without a power cord for her laptop, and she'd run the battery down to thirty percent before midnight. She'd spent the balance of the night staring out the window at the Hudson River, turning the facts of the case over in her mind. That counted as working.

"I'm sorry I've dragged you into this. Your husband must be terribly upset."

"He worries about me, yes. But last night was no cause to worry. We were both safe."

Gina turned thoughtful. "My husband and I didn't have the best marriage. I could never relax and enjoy life, and he lost patience with me. Eventually, he started having affairs, but he was discreet and so I didn't complain. We never had children. Do you have any?"

"Not yet." She smiled at having given Jake's response. "We've been talking about it. If you don't mind me asking, did you see your cousin Paul much after losing Angelina?"

"No. My parents stopped going to family gatherings. My brothers went their own ways, although my oldest brother kept in touch with Paul's older brother. Paul had been in trouble and had run away from home that winter. Papa was sure he'd held up a store or something."

"Did Paul stay in touch with you?"

"No. I only heard from him for the first time last week, when he called me out of the blue and warned me to keep quiet. That's when I put the family photos away."

One other thing had been nagging at Kim. "Since Paul dropped out of school, how has he made a living?"

"When Paul's mother, Aunt Amalia, died, she left her house and possessions to her older son, but she left her money to Paul. Her husband had left her quite a lot in investments. I suppose he's been living off that."

Her cell buzzed. Text from Ken Taylor. *We need to talk.*

"You have to go. I understand. Thanks so much for staying with me."

Kim took her hand. "My pleasure. The officers outside will take care of anything you need. Don't go out unless it's absolutely necessary, and then make sure they take you. I'll check in from time to time to see how you're doing. Use the prepaid cell I gave you. Make sure you keep your own cell off. Okay?"

"Got it. Thanks."

Kim texted Taylor back. *On my way.*

***

Taylor had a hot cup of coffee waiting for her when she arrived, although the brisk walk in the cool morning breeze across town had revived her a bit.

"Didn't think you could make it that fast from Brooklyn," he said.

"Thanks for the coffee. I didn't come from Brooklyn. I stayed in Manhattan last night with Angelina Farina's younger sister. Our suspect killed the doorman in her building yesterday about a half hour after I got her out of there."

"How?"

"Looks like strangulation. The Bronx ME will make a determination later today."

"So, both the victim and the method are out of profile."

"So was my granddad."

Taylor took a sip from his own mug. "Any chance this was related to the bomb scare your building didn't get yesterday?"

228

"Word of that got out?" That was the last thing they needed.

"The department has kept a tight lid on it, so no worries there. But your senator friend has heard from his trusted soldier…"

"Justin Cates. Which means he's still hanging around even though I told Brandt to cease and desist."

"Relax. He's also keeping us informed. Brandt is pushing Emory's idea of offering Hammond a chance to cut a deal. My boss has decided it's worth looking into. Your Ms. Dunbar is reaching out to Felipe Prinz to see if he wants to do an interview, which will get him back on our radar screen."

"Has the DA heard about this?"

"Not yet. It's too early. Right now, we need to find out where both Prinz and Hammond are. Any deals we offer either of them will be under federal jurisdiction and will only take place after the US Attorney for the Southern District of New York and the Brooklyn DA have agreed on terms."

"Can we at least try to remember in all these machinations that Hammond shot and killed a firefighter who was responding to a fire Hammond's group had set?"

"Hey, I'm on your side, Kim. And I trust you to keep this under your hat."

"In other words, don't tell Rick Conti."

"I'm glad you two have reconciled. You're an expert judge of people, and you understand his situation better than I do. I'll leave it to you whether to tell him. But he's got issues of his own in that office right now."

"You mean because he worked with me to find Gina Owens a safe location when his boss wouldn't?"

"No, I mean because his boss is homophobic. Or didn't you know Conti was gay?"

"I didn't until recently. Isn't the DA socially progressive?"

"Bryce Mitchell, yes, but not everyone under him is. If Brandt approaches you about this, please tell me. I've asked Cates to tell him not to, so you can help me gauge if it took."

"Okay. Anything else?"

"Yeah. We're working with you on Triscari. I'll contact you if we find out where he lives and if we can bag him, we will."

"Okay. When I return to the Castle, I'll forward all the information we have on him, the results about his vehicle, everything."

"One more thing. Take care of yourself. That bastard already killed one detective. He won't hesitate to kill another."

CHAPTER SIXTY-EIGHT

Friday, June 1, 8:21 AM

A young mechanic had been checking Joanna out on and off for several minutes, now, as she wandered around the hangar area. It was the attention she'd hoped to draw when she'd chosen the black stretch capris and low-cut form-fitting pink top, but on this unseasonably cool and windy morning, she was now wishing she'd brought a jacket.

"Aren't you cold?" he asked. Not the most aggressive come-on she'd heard.

"A little."

He gestured for her to come inside the hangar. "Want some coffee?"

She gave her sweetest smile. "Thanks." It was an immediate relief to get out of the wind. "Light, no sugar."

"Already sweet enough, I guess." Even he had to blush at that one. When she giggled, he said, "I'm Matt."

"Joanna."

Recognition dawned. "I've seen you on TV. You're that reporter."

She raised a finger to her lips. "Shh. Don't blow my cover."

He dropped his voice. "You looking for a story?"

She decided not to play it coy. "Always. Do you have information about the planes that are kept here? About their owners?"

"The planes, yes. The owners? Depends. Who you looking for?"

"Does Fredrick Hammond keep one here?"

He glanced around. "Um, I could get in serious trouble for that."

She sidled up to him. "I'm not asking you to go on the record. I'm just checking if my instincts are correct."

He considered it, his eyes lingering on her bustline. "See that Lear jet out there?"

"Is he the only one who uses it?"

"No. He flies business associates in and out with it."

"Any family?"

"Once in a while, his son."

She kept it nonchalant. "Recently?"

"Last Thursday. When it came back Friday, his son wasn't on it."

"Where did it go?"

This time he hesitated. "Not sure."

She brushed against him. "Any ideas?"

"When the pilot came in, he asked me to take care of a few things. For a tip, he gave me two bottles of Cane Island Rum. From Jamaica."

***

Loretta Cadman let Senator Brandt into Emory's apartment and showed him into the bedroom, where his patron was still in bed, sipping coffee. A pot sat on the dresser.

"Thank you, Loretta. I'll see you at the office later." Emory waited until she closed the door. "I take it you have some news for me."

"The feds find your offer interesting, but they will not consider it unless they can establish where the junior Mr. Hammond is at present."

"The senior Mr. Hammond won't say. Otherwise, he loses all bargaining power."

"If they find out on their own, he loses more than that. He becomes an accessory after the fact. I suggest we step with great care."

Emory's eyes narrowed. "What have they discovered?"

"Not for me to say." This was great. Emory was aware the senator knew, but he couldn't do anything about it. "But be careful of how much you learn but don't report. They could snag you as well."

"Is that a threat?"

So, Emory was getting nervous, too. "Don't be ridiculous. I'm looking out for my patron's welfare. You look out for mine. That's how it works. I've done as you asked. There is interest at the FBI. I've told you what they need, and I've warned you of the potential danger to your business partner if he doesn't comply. Call me if anything else arises."

***

From Taylor's office, it was a quick walk to One Police Plaza, where Kim figured the best sketch artist in the NYPD would be at work bright and early.

Sheila Gregg burst into a big smile when Kim walked in. "Whoa, what brings you in so early without even a phone call?"

Kim showed her the image of Paul Triscari. "Can you do a sketch of how this guy would look in his seventies?"

Sheila turned serious. "This is the serial killer, isn't it? Anything additional you can give me?"

"He has an Aquiline nose, his hair is thick and whitish-gray, and he likes to wear hoodies. Bits of his hair stick out when he does."

"Like how?"

Kim brought up a screenshot of the glimpse the surveillance camera had gotten by the bus stop the night of Lulu's murder.

Sheila nodded. "I've got someone coming in at ten. I'll shoot you an e-mail just before that. Fast enough?"

"There's a reason you're the best. Thanks."

***

Bostwick was out, so Kim called the guys into the conference room. Cord had already updated the case board she'd started ten days earlier. She handed out printouts of the sketch Sheila had just e-mailed her and posted one on the board. "This our guy, Cord?"

"That's the fucker, all right. Saw him across the street, cool as could be."

"I need you guys to take these to Bay Ridge and do another canvass. Take care to hit any places where no one was home last time. Concentrate on two blocks in every direction from the crime scene."

Bob spoke up. "You're not joining us?"

"No. I want the ME's report on the Bronx murder when they have it, and I'm speaking with Rick Conti about this Hammond thing."

"Not to press things," Bob said, "but didn't the lieu say to let that go, except for testifying, while we're working this case?"

"He did, and I'm not investigating. I just need to find out if my schedule is going to continue to be interrupted every two days."

"Ain't that up to ol' Let 'em run Ron?" Cord asked. "And what do we do if we find Triscari?"

"Arrest him, of course. But you won't find him, and that's not my aim. Your job is to flush him out. Cord, you saw him yesterday, and he saw you. Stay paired with Tim. I want him to see you guys. So, go slow and hang out, find a place to have lunch and talk to people."

"If our purpose is to flush him out, what's your purpose?" Bob asked.

"To be ready when he comes after me." Because there was only one way for this to be resolved.

***

The murder of the Riverdale doorman was all over the morning news shows. He'd lost track of Gina, who by now would have told the whole sordid tale. That meant they'd be back looking for him, which made it a good day to be out.

It was after ten. He'd already cut it close.

Ah, well, that's what he always did.

Jones Beach. That would be a fine place to spend the day.

CHAPTER SIXTY-NINE

Friday, June 1, 10:14 AM

Rick Conti looked like he might explode. "You can't possibly be in favor of this."

Kim wondered if it had been a mistake to tell him. "I'm in favor of whatever brings Jared Davis' killer to justice. Based on what I know, I'd say both Prinz and Hammond should pay the price. Who pays how much? Maybe we bring him in and then tell him there's no deal. Maybe this is to humor Hammond, Senior, and to keep him off balance while the feds make a case against him for assisting a fugitive from justice. To be honest, this Triscari thing is keeping me plenty busy. You're a friend, a good friend, and I assumed you'd be interested."

Conti lost some of his edge. "You think they've gotten anything on the father?"

"I can only say what I'd do in Ken Taylor's position. I'd check to see if Mr. Hammond owned a private jet, and if so, where he kept it. My first guess would be MacArthur Airport in Ronkonkoma. Then, I'd check the flight logs for the time between Wesley's release on bail and the first court appearance he missed. One thing leads to another."

"You'd do that? Or Taylor's done that?"

She laughed. "Definitely the former, and probably the latter although he didn't say. But if you go to your boss about it, we never had this conversation."

"I'm not going to my boss. I'll let him come to me. Thanks for the heads-up. What's the latest on the serial rapist/murderer?"

She brought him up to speed and showed him the sketch. "Bob and the guys are canvassing Bay Ridge with this, leaving copies wherever they can. He's probably not hanging around, so this afternoon I'm calling my lieu and asking him to give it to DCPI for dissemination to the media. By tonight, the public information blitz will be on, and the Twittersphere will be humming."

He stared at her. "You'll just drive him underground." Then it hit him. "Or worse."

She patted his hand. "Don't worry. But watch yourself. I've heard your section chief is a homophobe."

***

A lovely sunny afternoon at the beach, one that allowed him to think things through. He needed a definite plan. That would require patience and consideration. In the meantime, he eyed the few early season sun-worshippers. The seniors gravitated to the tables by the concession stands. So, he wandered down the boardwalk.

Looking for targets.

He saw her close to the water's edge, where the surf was breaking with some power. She was staring out at the ocean, where one ship crawled across the horizon. He slung the camera bag with a brick inside over his shoulder and made his way across the sand, his hood down.

As he got closer, he judged her to be in her mid-teens. She should have been in school.

He glanced around. The beach was deserted.

Perfect.

He fell sideways on the sand, crying out.

She turned and, after a moment's hesitation, ran to him. She had a sweet face with rich dark hair and dark eyes. No more than sixteen. "Are you all right?"

He grabbed his right ankle. "I think I twisted it. The sand just gave way."

She tried to check it for swelling—smart kid—but he prevented that by clutching it, and she only touched his hand.

"If you'll help me, I can make it to the boardwalk." She helped him up, and he pretended to test his weight on his right foot. He took a step and winced. "Can you please just carry my camera bag? If you can do that much for me, I'd be awfully grateful."

"Okay." She took the bag. "Wow, that's a heavy one. Is it an older camera?"

"Indeed, it is. A Leica M6. Heavy, but sturdy, and it gives wonderful results."

About thirty yards from the boardwalk, he stopped. "Sorry, just need to catch my breath. I'm not as young as I used to be." He glanced around. Clouds had moved in, and the wind had picked up. Still no one on the beach. "Okay, I'm game."

He resumed his tortured limp. "You must be in college."

"No, high school. I skipped school today. I just needed to be alone."

"Oh, why is that?"

"Just… things. Family stuff."

"Parent problems?"

She grew guarded. "Something like that. How's the ankle?"

"Hurts like the dickens. You're so kind to lend a hand. What's your name?"

"Erica."

They reached the wooden steps, and he leaned heavily on the railing as they climbed to the boardwalk. The concession stands were far off to the right. He turned left. "I parked in the next lot over. If you wouldn't mind, Erica, I'll be glad to drive you back." He winced as if in pain.

"Sure, okay."

CHAPTER SEVENTY

Friday, June 1, 6:21 PM

Kim reviewed the information the detectives from Bronx North Homicide had e-mailed to her. The doorman at Gina Owens' building had died from a crushed larynx. Bruises around the throat showed he was strangled. The lack of ligature marks suggested the killer had used his bare hands.

A call to Dr. Shelton at the Brooklyn Medical Examiner's office, and she'd learned that, yes, it was possible for seventy-year-old man to have hands that powerful if he worked out regularly with weights.

Bostwick had called and given her permission to send the sketch to the Deputy Commissioner for Public Information. A lieutenant at DCPI assured her it would go out to all media outlets immediately.

"Good evening, Detective Brady." Cord flashed his usual grin.

"Where are Bob and Tim?"

"They signed out. Bob was exhausted and deputized me to report. Tim was freaking out, had to get home to his wife. Tonight's her gig with the doctor about the mammogram."

Another worry. She shook it off. "Anything new on Triscari?"

"Oh, yeah. It's his nabe, okay. A few store owners said the sketch looked like someone they've seen, the little Italian place on Third said he's a regular and a local, and the girl's grandmother freaked out when she saw it. Kept saying, 'It can't be him, he's so nice.' And the landlady you spoke to in the row house just up the street said she didn't recognize the dude in the sketch, but her eyes super-sized when she first saw it."

"What about her tenants?"

"Neither apartment answered when we knocked. She declined to grant us entrance without a search warrant. Can your new best bud get us one?"

She almost laughed picturing Conti's likely reaction to that. "Based on her statement that she didn't recognize the sketch? Sorry, Cord, a facial expression doesn't add up to probable cause, even with the most sympathetic judge. But I'll call the lieu and have him request a detail to stakeout the house."

Cord placed his hand on her shoulder. "And then, go home and chill. Brandt's debating Dunn tonight. That should be good for some comic relief."

***

This time had been different.

She'd fought like a banshee, scratching his arms enough to make them bleed and nearly getting a finger into his left eye. It had taken all his strength to subdue her. And then…

No, he couldn't even think it.

He'd left her body in the dense growth just off Ocean Parkway.

He was still seething as he pulled up a few doors down from the row house. The lights were off in the front window of his landlady's apartment, but he detected a slight movement of the curtain as he approached.

Once in his apartment, he checked his appearance in the bathroom mirror. The girl's fingernail had nicked him just above his left eyelid and there was a trace of blood. He cleaned it.

His forearms were another matter, where deep gouges left a maze of crossing lines that remained red even after he'd washed the dried blood away. The girl had torn one sleeve of his hooded sweatshirt. He'd throw it out, but not here.

The police sketch only caught his eye when he emerged from the bathroom. He was still staring at it when he heard the knock at his door. A single knock.

His landlady nodded toward the sketch in his hand. "I left that for you. They were here today, looking for you. Two detectives, and they mentioned a third."

He said nothing.

"That's a close likeness," she continued. "Not exact, but close. Enough to make folks think it's you."

His mind was racing, trying to decide on a tactic.

When he remained silent, she said, "I ain't stupid. Neither are you. Truth is, you been a good tenant since you got here. Quiet as a church mouse and you pay your rent regular. I have a hard time believing you done the things this guy done. But you never know with people."

"What do you want?" Best to cut to the chase.

"To live my life in peace. I told them I never seen anyone like that sketch. But one of them, this big black guy, he looked like he didn't believe me. This was the second time they been here, and I'm sure it ain't the last. So, you'd best clear out, the sooner the better. Don't worry, I ain't gonna say nothin' after you go, and if they come back, I'll just say you moved out, no notice."

Could he trust her? And did it matter? "Thank you."

"It ain't for you. This is for me. You go your way; I go mine and live my life. That guy in the sketch, they're gonna get him, with or without my help. And if they don't, the Good Lord will have His way in the end." She pointed to his arm. "That don't look so good. Better get some antiseptic on it right away." She left without another word.

It took him ten minutes to pack.

CHAPTER SEVENTY-ONE

Friday, June 1, 8:00 PM

"Good evening, and welcome to our televised mayoral debate. I'm your host and moderator, Joanna Dunbar. I thank both candidates for participating. We'll begin with opening statements. Senator Brandt, as the challenger, you make yours first."

He gazed into the camera and repeated his charges against the administration. "If elected, I will re-invigorate our police force with new recruitment, better training, and responsive management to make our streets and subways safe. I will encourage new development while making certain that we make provisions for affordable housing. This city will welcome new investment that brings well-paying jobs so that more people can afford to live in better neighborhoods. I'll bring in a school chancellor with a history of classroom, not bureaucratic, success."

Jake turned to Kim. "I smell a rout."

She was lost in thought. She'd already called Gina to check in on her, and she was safe. The canvass had convinced her she'd been right about Triscari's whereabouts, but now he'd move on.

She texted Bostwick. *Any luck on Triscari's surveillance detail?*

His response came a minute later. *First shift should be in place by now. I've left them with instructions to contact you if anything pops.*

She tried to relax. That should be enough.

If he hadn't already fled, perhaps she could make him stay.

***

He found a cheap motel on Queens Boulevard with a small parking lot tucked in the back, out of sight of the casual viewer.

The landlady had said they'd get him, with or without her help. For the first time since he was seventeen, he had to admit to the possibility. Today had shaken him, not only because of the landlady's comments, but because of how the afternoon had gone. He felt empty, as he had when his pretty cousin had rejected him. His punishment of her had made him complete, as it had whenever he'd punished another in her name.

Until today.

He'd been in a tough spot after Angelina, with a smart detective hot on his trail. Like now. He needed to deal with this one as he had back then, when he'd made his pursuer come after him and then pounced at the right time.

He studied his image in the mirror. Before leaving Brooklyn, he'd taken clippers and buzz-cut his entire head. He'd thinned those bushy eyebrows. Now, he'd shaved what little hair remained. He'd dumped his hooded sweatshirts in a Goodwill bin and stopped in a nearby sporting goods store to purchase several baseball caps, all different teams.

The whole time, he'd been turning over an idea in his head. The old plan needed a Twenty-First Century twist. He pulled out the detective's card, the one he'd taken from the doorman.

Now was the time.

CHAPTER SEVENTY-TWO

Friday, June 1, 9:12 PM

As the debate ended, the senator and his wife approached the acting mayor for the traditional let's-make-it-look-good-for-the-cameras handshake.

Sabrina Dunn shrank back, as if revolted. "You've got some nerve, Brandt. Acting like you're concerned about the people of this city while doing the bidding of billionaire real estate tycoons."

The senator, knowing the cameras were still rolling, and the microphones were on, gave his friendliest smile. "You know what your problem is? You keep telling the people what you're doing for them without bothering to find out what they want." It was the perfect sound bite.

***

Jake was in the shower when Kim's cell rang. She answered without checking Caller ID, assuming it was Bostwick or someone from the unit.

"Good evening, Detective Brady."

"Who is this?" Although she didn't need to ask.

"Please. You're much too smart to resort to asking questions to which you already have the answers. You can't quite believe that I've had the balls to call you, but that's because you still don't realize what you're up against. But you will, soon. No need to trace the call, since you'll recognize the number."

The call dropped. It had come from Lily Ng's cell.

Jake returned, lending a scent of shampoo. "Who was that?"

She didn't answer. Her mind was racing. A dangerous game of chess had reached the middle game.

"Kim? You okay?"

She was better off going to the Castle than staying here. It was protected, safe. And if she stayed here, Jake wouldn't sleep. "I'm fine. I have to go in."

"Now? It's almost ten."

She gave him a wan smile. "Can't help it. It's this case."

"Fine, as long as you're not running off for a rendezvous with Senator Brandt."

She burst out laughing, grateful for the release. "God forbid."

"Oh, he has an eye for you. I caught it that night at the restaurant. He was checking out those legs I don't get to see enough. But, seriously, do you have to go in?"

A quick kiss. "If I don't, I'll only keep you up all night." She needed to plot out some things on the board.

CHAPTER SEVENTY-THREE

Saturday, June 2, 12:56 AM

The senator's soaring spirits lasted until he and his wife pulled up to his gracious turn-of-the-century home on Surf Avenue in Sea Gate and saw a familiar black limo in his driveway. That Sea Gate was a gated community posed little bother for Kyle Emory.

"You go ahead. I'll be in shortly." He turned toward the limo, praying Loretta Cadman wasn't sitting in the back seat. She wasn't.

"I watched your performance tonight," Emory said. "Impressive."

Not a ringing endorsement. "I felt it went well. My internal polling shows I picked up eight points tonight, some from undecideds and some from Dunn."

"Congratulations." Emory's voice remained flat.

"Something wrong?"

"Not exactly wrong. But you talked about attracting well-paying jobs so that the great unwashed could afford to live in gentrified neighborhoods. At least, that's what I heard you say."

"Isn't that the American Dream?"

"Don't let success go to your head. We have an agreement."

The senator considered it. "We have an understanding. You support me because you realize that no one from your own party could win the mayoralty, and the progressives have created a schism in my party. If elected, I'll encourage redevelopment in all parts of the city. To win the office, I need the people in this city to have reasons to vote for me. Many of whom have different values from you."

Emory didn't miss a beat. "Which brings me to the hypothetical question I raised with you. Any news?"

"The DA's office will listen if Hammond returns voluntarily but will make no guarantees until they hear what he has to say. They're due back in court on Monday morning, at which time Judge Vickers may well run out of patience and issue a bench warrant for his immediate arrest."

"The boy's father tells me someone has been sniffing around MacArthur Airport, asking about flight logs. Sounds like you're being done down behind your back."

It was amazing how naïve Emory could be. "What did you expect? Once I raised the subject, they knew the old man had engineered the boy's departure. Once they have proof, they'll arrest the father as an accessory after the fact, seize the flight logs, and send a team to wherever the kid is hiding to grab him."

"Shit."

"My advice is to tell him to send his plane back to get the kid and bring him back, or else suffer the consequences. If they find the kid on their own, there'll be no dialogue."

"What about Prinz?"

"Gone to ground. Now, if you don't mind, my wife is waiting for me inside."

"Wait. One more thing. Have you seen the sketch the cops are circulating of their so-called serial killer?"

"Briefly, yeah."

"Get a good look at it?"

"Not really. What's your point?"

"He looks Italian. And his latest victim was in Bay Ridge. Lots of Italian-Americans in Bay Ridge. And they vote. I bet most of them have been expecting this killer to be a Latino kid."

"The police said a while ago they were dealing with a serial killer."

"But they didn't say an Italian serial killer. I suggest you make sure things work out for the Hammond boy, or support for you might, shall we say, falter?"

***

Ever since Kim had asked Vera Koshkin to have Lily Ng's cell tracked in real time, she'd been getting updates every few hours. There had been nothing since Thursday.

Until tonight.

Triscari's call to her had originated near the 79th Street Boat Basin in Manhattan, from where he could have gone anywhere. Except Bay Ridge.

It hadn't pinged off any other towers, so he'd only turned it on for the call. No way to track his movements. She made a notation on the board about the call and its location, knowing there would be others, hoping a pattern would emerge but realizing it might not.

This guy was clever.

But they always made mistakes.

She turned to the timeline. One common characteristic among serial killers was that they always had a cooling-off period after they killed until the inner forces that drove them to kill built up over time and they needed to kill again. It was possible there were other victims on whom the FBI had received no reports, but she doubted it because of the notoriety serial killers had begun receiving in the nineties.

"Hey, Kim." It was Sergeant Arman Dhillon, who had the desk on the twelve-to-eight shift. A well-liked Punjabi Sikh who wore the NYPD turban, everyone at the Castle called him Marshal. "Strange to see you here at this hour."

She gestured to the board. "Bitch of a case."

He turned serious. "It is. Why do they do it, these serial killers? I've never understood it."

"I've read some books on it. Lots of reasons, but they all boil down to the same thing: they're sickos."

"But it is worse than that. It is a special brand of evil. I wish I could help you. I have a teenage daughter myself, and I worry for her every day."

She regarded him with warmth. "I'll bet you're a fine father, Marshal."

He placed his hands together and gave a slight bow. "You are most kind. Please tell me if I can help." The grin vanished. "Why do they do it?" He walked away.

She resumed studying the timeline. The attacks up to Lulu Ramirez had been at intervals of two years or more. Then, only seven months until Martha Perez. And Lily Ng two days after Martha.

It had now been over a week since his last known attack, not counting the doorman to Gina's building whom Triscari had killed trying to get to Gina.

Two years, then seven months, then two days. Something was changing with Triscari. He'd also engaged her after attacking a girl in his own neighborhood, forcing him to flee.

The release of the sketch now increased the pressure on him.

She remembered his call from a phone he knew she could trace.

He wants me to come after him, like Granddad did.

CHAPTER SEVENTY-FOUR

Saturday, June 2, 8:04 AM

Kim jolted awake at the sound of the television in the Castle coming on. Sergeant Rojas had relieved Marshal Dhillon. "You okay, Kim? Dhillon told me you've been here all night. Something new on the case?"

"Not sure. I'll let you know if anything develops."

"Okay. Oh, and I just put a fresh pot of coffee on."

"Thanks, but I'm going out for some breakfast." The Fire House deli was open. She was about to head over when she heard from Jake. *You okay? Get any sleep?*

She replied. *Yes, and yes. Will call later.*

As she entered the deli, she received another text. She wished Jake would give her time and placed her order. She checked the text while she waited. But it wasn't from Jake.

It was from Rick Conti. *F. Hammond coming in this afternoon with info on sonny boy. Need you here at 1:00.*

Kim replaced her phone in her hip pocket and paid the counterman. She turned and started.

"Hi." Joanna Dunbar. "Can I ask you about something?"

They walked to the door but didn't leave. Joanna lowered her voice. "Have you heard anything about Fredrick Hammond looking to cut a deal for his son?"

"Did you get that from Ken Taylor?"

"I can't tell you that. I'm just checking if it's true. Because if it is, it's got to piss you off in the extreme that a firefighter's killer is going to walk because of his daddy's money."

Kim turned to go. "I don't have time for games, Joanna." She saw the sketch of Triscari taped to the wall next to the door. "I've got a serial killer to run down."

"Okay, okay. I'll tell you, but you can't tell anyone else. I got it from Justin Cates."

"Brandt's 'fixer'. That's a hoot. How does he know?"

"He's the one making the arrangements. He didn't tell me anything else. So, had you heard?"

"Yes. Just a few minutes ago. Heard from Rick Conti. Don't even think of asking me any when or where questions."

Joanna snickered. "Not in a million years. I want the why. What does Hammond have to trade?"

"Maybe nothing. This could all be smoke."

"Okay. Call me if you have anything I can use."

***

He hadn't slept. The room was too confining, but he dared not go out in daylight. Even with his shorn hair and baseball cap, when he looked in the mirror, the reflection was the man whose image was now plastered all over the city and regularly shown on every news show.

And the pressure that led to Erica hadn't abated at all.

He had to get out. Somewhere. Anywhere. He needed air.

And he needed vengeance.

***

Bostwick was in his office at the Castle. She told him about the text from Conti when he stopped her. "I told you, Kim, you can't go chasing after another case while you're working this serial killer. It's too much."

"It's just this meeting, Lieu. I saw Jared Davis get shot, and I apprehended his killer. I have an obligation to…"

250

"There was another killing. Another young girl, this one in Nassau County. They discovered a body this morning near a softball field at Jones Beach."

"Same pattern?"

"Looks like it. Sexual assault and murder. We're waiting for the report to come in from the Nassau County Medical Examiner. Think our guy has gone suburban?"

"They get a time of death?"

"Best they can figure right now is sometime yesterday."

"That's where he was when Cord didn't find him at home." Then, it hit her. "Wait. You said sexual assault and murder. Not rape?"

"Huh. I hadn't considered that." Bostwick checked his notes. "Yeah, that's what he said. Sexual Assault. You think it means something?"

Kim fired up her laptop and checked the ME reports on Lulu, Martha, and Lily, making some notes. "Yes, it means something. Please alert me the minute the report comes in from Nassau County."

CHAPTER SEVENTY-FIVE

Saturday, June 2, 1:05 PM

A secretary escorted Kim and Bostwick into the Brooklyn District Attorney's office. Rick Conti and his boss were already sitting at the conference table with DA Bryce Mitchell at the head. Kim took the seat opposite Rick. Mitchell frowned when Rick mentioned Kim's name.

"While we wait for Mr. Hammond to arrive," Mitchell said, "let's make one thing clear. We are treating him as a cooperative citizen who is assisting an investigation, not a criminal." When Kim couldn't quite hide her distaste, he said, "I'm sorry if that offends you, Ms. Brady, but..."

"Detective," Bostwick said. "She deserves to be addressed as 'detective'."

Mitchell rolled his eyes. "I'm so very sorry."

I love you, too, twerp. "Are we allowed to ask questions?" When annoyance rippled across Mitchell's face, she added, "I promise to ask nicely." Her silenced cell vibrated, and she held it in her lap and read Taylor's latest text, working hard to maintain a poker face.

A secretary knocked and entered. "Mr. Hammond and his attorney are here, sir."

"Show them in."

Hammond entered wearing a custom-made grey pinstripe suit, white shirt, and blue-and-yellow striped tie. And a worried expression. Wyckoff was with him.

"Gentlemen," Mitchell said, gesturing to the two remaining seats at the table. "Please."

Wyckoff spoke immediately after the introductions. "My client appreciates you agreeing to meet with us on this informal basis. He wants to be of help in this difficult situation."

Mitchell took charge. "And we appreciate his willingness to come forward. I understand that, before we proceed, your client wishes to set out his concerns."

"If you don't mind," Hammond said, his voice like gravel. "Like other boys of his class, Wesley doesn't appreciate the advantages he's had. He's fallen in with evil company, and they've unduly influenced him. He never would have engaged in such behavior on his own."

Kim was about to explode, but Bostwick stunned her. "Excuse me, sir. This misguided lad stands indicted for arson and murder. Detective Brady, here, arrested him as he was fleeing the scene, recovering the weapon that killed Jared Davis. His were the only fingerprints on the weapon. His DNA was on the shell casing recovered at the scene, which means your son loaded it into the weapon. The weapon is registered in your name. Detective Brady, have I left anything out?"

Lieu, we are friends forever. "Just that the crime lab found traces of gasoline on his jacket. The Molotov cocktails that set the fires contained gasoline."

Mitchell shifted in his seat. "We're all aware of the facts, Detective."

She pulled out her cell. "Well, here's one you may not know, and I'd like Mr. Hammond's explanation. Flight logs at MacArthur Airport show his private jet took off at 6:10 Thursday evening, destination the island of Jamaica. It returned Friday morning at 8:05. Shortly after disembarking from said private jet, a witness saw Mr. Hammond, here, handing bottles of Jamaican rum to members of the ground crew." She glanced over at Hammond. "Cane Island. Very nice."

Wyckoff stirred. "Where did you get this?"

She held up her cell. "This is a text from Ken Taylor of the FBI. They have sworn statements supporting the facts I just mentioned. Wesley Hammond is a fugitive from justice, and from where I'm sitting, Mr. Hammond, you are an accessory after the fact."

Mitchell turned red. "That is a legal determination, Detective, and my office will decide whether to make it."

Rick Conti spoke up. "That may be, but Detective Brady is correct that the facts support that determination. It's also possible that since the flight was to a foreign country, and the arson was an act of terrorism, the FBI could turn the case over to a federal court."

"And what about the real terrorist, Felipe Prinz?" Wyckoff asked. "Might the FBI be interested in him?"

One more ace to play. "You mean Phil King?"

Silence.

Kim referred to Taylor's lengthy text. "Phillip King, a/k/a Felipe Prinz, flunked out of Kings University Law School four years ago, wanted for a variety of crimes in New York, Philadelphia, Baltimore and Washington, DC. Believed to be currently hiding out somewhere in upstate New York." She put the cell down and addressed Wyckoff. "What about him?"

Conti turned to the DA. "I suggest we begin extradition proceedings with Jamaica. If you like, I'll inform Judge Vickers of this latest development and withdraw our request for an evidentiary hearing."

The senior Hammond pounded the table. "Goddamn it, you sandbagged me. You won't get away with this."

"Mr. Hammond," Mitchell said, "your son is a fugitive, and the evidence shows you assisted him in his flight. I understand a father's love for his son, but I cannot turn a blind eye to the demands of justice. At the very least, you may be guilty of obstruction of justice. I'll give you forty-eight hours to return the boy to my jurisdiction. If he has information that could lead to the arrest of Mr. Prinz... um, King, my office will take that into consideration. But if he's not here by this time Monday morning, I'll have no choice but to begin extradition proceedings with Jamaica and issue a warrant for your arrest."

Whatever Hammond was about to say in response, it died when Wyckoff grasped his shoulder.

Mitchell turned to Rick. "Inform Judge Vickers of this fresh development and that we are withdrawing our request for the hearing. Ask for Hammond's bail to be revoked. Mr. Wyckoff, if you oppose his motion, I'll withdraw my offer."

Hammond and Wyckoff stormed out without another word.

CHAPTER SEVENTY-SIX

Saturday, June 2, 1:58 PM

As Bostwick drove, he chuckled. "Looks like we both stepped in political shit this time."

Kim grinned at him. "Yep. Sure felt good."

He turned serious. "One thing. I hope that text from Taylor was authentic."

She laughed. "Oh, yeah. I'm not that big a gambler." After a moment, she added, "Looks like Mr. Mitchell may suffer a drop in campaign contributions."

"Don't go there, Kim. None of our concern."

"It is for me. I live in Brooklyn." Cord texted. *ME report just came in from Nassau County on Jones Beach victim. ID'd as Erica Caruso, age 16. Cause of death multiple skull fractures. Signs of sexual assault but no rape kit, no DNA except lots of skin under her fingernails.*

She read it to Bostwick. "We gotta check out Bay Ridge."

"Bob and Tim are there now."

"I want to talk to that landlady again."

"Maybe it wasn't our guy. No rape, and it sounds like he really whaled on her."

"It's him." She texted Cord back. *We're heading back to Bay Ridge. Please get DNA profile from Nassau ASAP.*

***

The landlady didn't answer. Kim peaked in the front window of the ground-floor apartment. No sign of life. Back up the steps, she leaned on the middle bell button, listening to it ring inside.

It worked.

"What the hell do you want, now?"

Kim remained pleasant. "Good afternoon. What happened to your downstairs tenant?" She displayed the sketch for the landlady. "Him."

"I told you before, I ain't seen him in days, and I still ain't. If you find him, his rent is due." The landlady tried to close the door.

Kim blocked it. "I don't believe you. If you like, I will stand here, preventing you from closing your door, while my lieutenant here gets a search warrant for the apartment downstairs and an arrest warrant for you for obstruction."

"I ain't allowed to let you into his apartment. I seen that on TV."

Great. Another Law and Order fan. "You can if he doesn't live here anymore."

The landlady lost her bravado. "Okay. He moved out late yesterday."

"Was he around yesterday during the day?"

"No."

One more thing. "When you spoke to him last night, did you notice any scratches on his arms, neck, or face?"

The landlady blanched. "Sweet Jesus."

"Is that a 'yes'?"

"He had scratches on both arms. Deep scratches, like gouges. Deep enough to bleed. And he had a minor wound near his left eye. Under the brow."

"Thank you."

Once back in the car, Bostwick said, "Looks like Erica was another of his victims."

"And she put up one hell of a fight."

"Which is why he didn't rape her?"

"No. And I don't think that's why he beat her so severely, either."

Lily Ng's cell number appeared on her screen. *You won't be able to find me, but I'll find you.*

"What's that?" Bostwick asked.

"Just my husband checking in." No, she would not tell him. "Can we take one more detour on our way back to see Dr. Shelton?"

*****

Emory let Senator Brandt in, himself. Loretta Cadman was nowhere to be seen. Odd. "Do come in."

"I understand the meeting did not go well for your friend. In fact, it sounds like it was an utter disaster."

"Which is not what we paid... what we planned."

Emory's naivete had grown intolerable. "You mean you didn't suspect the FBI was doing their job? Or that the police would push back? Or that Felipe Prinz was just a half-Jewish, half-Puerto Rican law school dropout named Phil King who liked to read Karl Marx in between bong hits? Look at it on the bright side. Let 'em run Ron is probably the only judge in Brooklyn who still wouldn't revoke Hammond's bail."

"I am not amused. You were supposed to make this work."

"And I told you it was a longshot."

"Your man should step on Conti."

The balance of power between them had finally shifted, and it felt so good to press his advantage. "Two problems there. One, Conti was right. Two, Bryce Mitchell backed him up. Conti's section chief must now step lightly, as his animus against young Conti is becoming apparent."

"Is it true that Conti and Brady have kissed and made up?"

"Figuratively, yes."

Emory snorted. "Certainly not literally." He didn't hide his disgust.

"You are now making the same mistake Conti's section chief is making. The guy is gay. Deal with it. My advice is..."

"You are not here to give me advice."

"I'll give it because I'm closer to the situation than you are. Tell Hammond he has no more cards to play. Have him get his brat kid back from Jamaica and turn himself in. If the kid really has hard information on King's whereabouts, he'd best spill it and cut the best deal Wyckoff can get for him. Time to pay the piper. That's my advice. Do with it what you will."

CHAPTER SEVENTY-SEVEN

Saturday, June 2, 3:18 PM

Back at the Castle, her suspicions confirmed, Kim took a moment to respond to the anonymous text. *If you find me, it's because I want you to find me.*

After a few minutes, she checked for tower pings for Triscari. There was only one, from the text she'd received that morning. It had been in East Williamsburg.

He wasn't staying in East Williamsburg. She'd bet on it. His continue use of Lily's cell meant they could track his movements, however fragmented. Since he was engaging her in an exchange of texts, he'd likely stick with the same cell.

In the meantime, she read through the report from the Nassau Medical Examiner. The list of injuries soured her stomach. Paul Triscari was capable of almost anything.

Her cell vibrated. Same number. *Of course you do.*

"What the hell is that?"

She jumped at the sound of Bob's voice.

"Just a text."

"Who from? This is your partner asking." When she didn't answer, he said, "Kim, if you want to keep secrets from Conti, or Brandt, or Bryce Mitchell, or even the lieu, that's fine. But your grandfather kept something from his partner, and it cost him his life. Don't make the same mistake."

Partner's radar.

She waved him into the conference room and closed the door.

"It's Triscari, isn't it?" Bob asked.

She nodded. "We're fencing. I'm trying to get him into a texting war to track his movements."

"So why the secrecy?"

"Because I can't see where this is going."

He examined the board. "Bullshit. We both see where it's going. You said yourself he's going to come after you. You want to take him down. Revenge for a hero grandfather."

No way was she going to put him in a position where he might someday have to lie for her. "This is not about a grandfather I never met. It's about a serial killer with a problem that's getting worse and may get more innocent people killed. I will do whatever's necessary to stop him."

Bostwick's voice was audible through the closed door. Bob stared at the door.

"Don't even think about it, Bob. We need to stick together. You need to trust me, and I need to trust you." She spread out a street map she'd printed on the table. She marked the approximate location of the East Williamsburg tower. Without another word, she opened the door and returned to her desk. She checked the tower ping on his latest text. Jackson Heights. "Uh huh. Next one will be from a tower near the East River."

Bob shook his head. "A wild guess."

"Not wild at all. He can't venture out much because the sketch is plastered all over the city and the media, and he can't run because he needs to kill Gina and me. I'll go further than that: no further south than Greenpoint, no further north than the Queensborough Bridge."

"If you're right, I'll eat my hat."

She decided on a response to Triscari's last text. *I know you far better than you realize.*

CHAPTER SEVENTY-EIGHT

Sunday, June 3, 6:39 AM

Kim had given herself over to a night of lovemaking with Jake, as much to keep him from asking questions as for the release she needed. She'd showered first this morning, and while he was showering, she checked her texts. Nothing new from Triscari. She texted Bob. *No response to yesterday afternoon's text and no tower hits. It's his move.*

Bob's response was immediate. *His next text might be from a different location than you expect.*

Not a chance.

Jake came out from the bedroom, his hair still dripping. He frowned, seeing her dressed for work. "You really should give yourself a day off here and there."

She didn't resist when he pulled her into a tender embrace. "True, but today isn't a good day for it. Two cases going, and something could pop on either of them any minute."

"Didn't Bostwick tell you to forget the Hammond case?"

"He did. But he realized yesterday that isn't possible." She flashed a teasing grin. "Besides, this will keep you hungry for more fun tonight."

But once she was on the street, all jollity died. Her city was a war zone, and the sight of the burned-out condo on Cadman Plaza West only made it worse. She was grateful to find a B38 waiting for her.

No sooner had she climbed aboard than someone took the seat next to her.

"I hope I'm not disturbing you this quiet Sunday morning." It was Justin Cates.

"You still tailing me? I thought we'd settled that."

"Relax. I'm on your side."

"As nice as that is to hear, when you see me on the street, you don't know where I'm going or why, if I'm being shadowed or if I'm liable to come under fire at any moment. Worst of all, you don't know if your proximity to me might put me in danger or blow my cover."

He stared at her. "Why do I think you're serious about that?"

"Because it's not something anyone would joke about. You may relay my thoughts on the matter to your employer. Was there something specific you wanted to discuss with me?"

"Yes. First, the senator heard about your participation yesterday. He applauds you for it."

"Considering that my comments frustrated his goal, you'll forgive me for taking that with a grain of salt."

"He had no goal in that meeting," Cates said, "other than it taking place. Like most politicians, he sometimes finds himself in positions he would rather avoid. This was one. Despite the benefit to his campaign, the last thing he wants to see is Wesley Hammond get off lightly. That's why he's glad the FBI could discover where Freddie Hammond keeps his jet and where it went last Thursday night."

She looked into his eyes. "I wonder who told them." Her cell, lying in her hip pocket and set to silent mode, vibrated. A text. She ignored it.

Cates shrugged. "I wonder. Perhaps it was just good investigative work, or help from an honest, law-abiding citizen. I also wanted to discuss the identity of the serial killer. No, I'm not asking his name. But from the sketch, he looks Italian, and you've visited Bay Ridge several times. That's the heart of the senator's district, and Italian-Americans comprise much of his support. It would be..."

She tried not to wonder about the content of the text. "We don't get to pick the ethnicity of the criminals we hunt. Nor their neighborhoods. He has to live with it, just as we all do."

Cates nodded. "I understand."

"Do you?"

His face spread into a knowing smile. "I understand a great deal. One of my better skills is being a good listener. The senator was especially pleased that you and Rick have not only buried your differences but are working as an effective team." He pushed the STOP signal button. "This is my stop." He stood.

"Wait. How could he possibly know that?" When Cates only grinned, she reflected on what he'd said. Rick. With an element of warmth. "You're close with him, aren't you?"

"The senator? No, I just work for him."

"Not him. Rick Conti."

Cates blushed.

She lowered her voice. "You're his partner."

***

Joanna pulled up behind the ITN van on Pond Road behind Strathmore bagels in Ronkonkoma and checked her watch. 7:45. Come on, Tony, get your ass in this car or we're going to miss it.

The rear passenger door to her Chevy Bolt opened and her cameraman slid in, cradling the TV camera in his lap. "Okay."

She pulled away, casting occasional worried glances at the sky. "We miss this, we're fucked."

"I like girls who talk dirty. Especially petite ones like you."

"That's one." Where the hell was the gate?

"What's that mean?"

"An Amish farmer and his bride are riding in a horse-drawn carriage on their wedding night, and the horse bucks. The farmer says, 'That's one.' They ride further, and the horse bucks again. The farmer says, 'That's two.' They ride a little more, and the horse bucks one more time. The farmer says, 'That's three.' Then he shoots the horse. His bride yells, 'Why did you do that? He's our only horse.' And the farmer looks at her and says, 'That's one.'"

Tony shrank down in his seat.

She found the gate and turned in. Another glance at the sky as a plane approached.

"That ain't him, is it?" Tony asked.

"No. Prop plane. Our fair-haired boy is coming home on a jet." She located the hangar where she'd chatted with the friendly mechanic to whom she hoped to talk dirty, and who had called her at four this morning with the information that had brought them here.

"Hey there, news lady."

"Morning, Matt." Oh, no. She was blushing. "This is Tony, my cameraman. Any news, yet?"

"Just got the word they're on final approach. Should be on the ground in a few minutes. Where's the van? Don't you guys usually have a van with your station name plastered all over?"

"Left it by a bagel place. Didn't want to tip anyone off. The FBI might be even more pissed at the media being here than old man Hammond."

"Smart girl." He winked.

Focus. This was big. "Where will the plane taxi once it's down?"

"Normally, to the terminal building way over yonder. But Hammond's car is parked behind this building, and the old geezer doesn't like to walk any further than required. Besides, the FBI has given the tower instructions to order the pilot directly over here." He pointed to the spot where the jet would stop. "If you look, you can see a few agents."

She glanced around. "Okay, Tony, we'll take up our position here, where we should get a good view as they get off the plane. Shoot it all from when the plane touches down, and I'll do a voice-over."

"You don't want to do an intro?"

"No, we need to keep out of sight as long as possible."

Matt cocked an ear. "Sounds like a Lear."

The whine of jet engines grew stronger, and Joanna watched as the lithe aircraft passed overhead and touched down before slowing, turning, and taxiing back toward them.

She took the microphone. "Joanna Dunbar at MacArthur Airport in Ronkonkoma, Long Island, where the private jet of Fredrick Hammond has just touched down on its return from the island nation of Jamaica. On board is Wesley Hammond, suspect in the shooting death of New York City firefighter Jared Davis. Police expect him to surrender immediately upon deplaning."

The jet had nearly reached the hangar area. Several FBI agents were now visible on all sides of the space the jet was approaching.

"Law enforcement stands ready to take Wesley Hammond into custody," she continued. She paused as the jet came to a halt, waiting for the whine of the engines to abate. As the engines shut down, the door behind the cockpit door swung up into an open position and steps folded out downward. Two men stepped down. Federal agents quickly surrounded them.

"Wesley Hammond and his lawyer have deplaned, and Hammond is now in custody." She watched as agents handcuffed Hammond and led him to a nearby sedan. "From here, they will drive him back to New York City for interrogation. A Brooklyn grand jury has already handed up indictments for murder and arson. The next expected step is for a judge to revoke Hammond's bail. Joanna Dunbar for ITN."

Tony lowered his camera.

Two agents were walking directly toward them.

She turned to Matt. "Is there a back way out of here?"

"Yes, but don't take it because I guarantee there will be agents waiting there. You two slip into that storage room back there, but don't touch anything. I'll tell you when the coast is clear."

***

You know me? How? Been communicating with the dead? Did Grandpa tell you?

Kim had checked the text as soon as Cates left the bus. She had waited to reply, both to see if she could track his movements better and to not appear as if she were waiting for each message. In the meantime, she was updating her map with the location of the latest text when Bob walked in and checked out the map.

"I don't believe it." He glared at the newest mark. "Hunters Point."

"Good morning, Detective Nolan. Our special this morning is fried fedora on rye."

Marshal Dhillon poked his head in. "Kim, Bob, you guys need to see this."

The TV was on. Joanna's voice described the scene at MacArthur.

266

"So, they got the little bastard," Kim said.

She received a text, and Bob watched with expectation as she checked it.

"No, Bob. It's from Ken Taylor. He's pissed that Joanna went public with the story. What did he expect?"

Another text, this time from Rick Conti. *FBI in-bound with Hammond. Need you here in an hour, with or without Bostwick.*

CHAPTER SEVENTY-NINE

Sunday, June 3, 9:33 AM

Emory was already scowling when Senator Brandt entered the bedroom. "I take it you've heard. Who alerted the media?"

"No idea."

"It wasn't your Mr. Cates, was it? He seems to be everywhere these days."

"I don't see…"

"Because he has other loyalties."

"I doubt that the Brooklyn DA was thrilled at today's morning news coverage…"

"It will raise the public's expectations."

The senator allowed himself a grin. "Which would make a sweetheart deal much harder for the public to swallow. I told you this wouldn't work the way Old Man Hammond wanted." He made a show of looking at his watch. "If you'll excuse me, I must be going."

***

Bostwick met Kim and Bob outside the DA's office. He hadn't had time to shave. "Anything new on Triscari?"

"I'm trying to track him. He sends me texts intermittently. He's playing head games."

"What texts? Anything I should worry about?"

She hoped the lieu didn't catch Bob's alarmed expression. "Nothing specific, yet. He's using Lily Ng's cell, and we're tracking tower pings. It gives us clues as to his movements."

"So, you might snag him before he strikes again?" Bostwick kept his voice down, but the tension in his voice was clear.

"That's our goal."

They crowded around the conference table—Bryce Mitchell, Rick, Rick's section chief, Wesley Hammond, Wyckoff, Kim, Bostwick, and, at the last minute, Ken Taylor. Bob and the two agents who'd brought Hammond in sat in chairs along the wall.

Mitchell took charge. "First, I want to thank everyone for handling this in an expeditious and low-key manner."

"My client and I did not appreciate seeing his arrest splashed all over the media this morning," Wyckoff said.

Taylor spoke up. "No one in our detail revealed anything to anyone about this. Our operation was deep and dark."

Wyckoff turned on Mitchell. "Perhaps ginning up the jury pool?"

The DA laughed. "When this goes to trial, we won't need to do anything to the jury pool. Jurors don't like people who lure firefighters out and then shoot them."

Hammond exploded. "That was Prinz. It was all his idea."

Taylor raised a hand. "If I may, the media thing is irrelevant. This is the second time you and your client have raised Prinz being responsible. Okay, I'm listening. How was he responsible and not you?"

"Considering," Kim put in, "that all the forensic evidence points to you, and you were the one fleeing the scene. How's your nose, by the way?"

Hammond clenched his teeth. "Bitch pig."

"That's not helpful, Mr. Hammond," Mitchell said. "Detective Brady is quite right. The murder weapon belongs to your father and has your prints on it. We recovered the shell casing which has your DNA on it..."

"The pigs planted that evidence..."

Kim laughed. "Yeah? And where would we have gotten your fingerprints or your DNA?"

"You have ways. You can't deny it."

Rick turned to Mitchell. "Sir, this isn't getting us anywhere. Either he has something to tell us, or he doesn't."

Before Mitchell could reply, Taylor asked, "Where is Prinz now? Where is he hiding?"

A deer caught in the headlights.

"It's put up or shut up time, Mr. Hammond," Kim said.

"I don't know." Hammond's reply came out as a whisper.

"Upstate New York?" Kim pressed.

"I don't know." Louder this time.

"He doesn't have that information," Wyckoff said with annoyance.

"And," Conti said, "his explanation about how Prinz, not he, is guilty of murdering Jared Davis?"

Hammond could only stammer. "I... he..."

Mitchell threw up his hands. "This is a waste of time. Mr. Wyckoff, I am calling a press conference in thirty minutes to announce that your client is in custody, and that I'm demanding Judge Vickers grant our motion to revoke your client's bail and remand him. And, should he not grant my motion, I will appeal his decision and will also file a complaint against him with the State Board of Judicial Review seeking his removal. If you and your client wish to discuss a plea deal on a more rational basis, please contact Mr. Conti. This meeting is over."

***

It didn't surprise Kim when Ken Taylor pulled her aside outside the building. "Dunbar's a friend of yours, and she'd been sniffing around us for a lead on Hammond. How did she get it?"

"I don't know, Ken. I'd tell you if I did. But she's a determined and resourceful reporter. MacArthur wasn't a hard guess for where Hammond keeps his plane. Even I'd guessed that. She probably did some digging out there. And I think she can help you if you let her."

His eyes narrowed. "With what?"

"Running Prinz to ground. She mentioned something to me about wanting to interview him."

"For ITN? You can't be serious."

"Never more so. I'm sure Prinz would love to shove his Leninist rant in the faces of ITN's right-of-center audience. Stick it to the bourgeoisie. And if he accepted, however they set it up, whether by phone or in person, you'd be able to track him, right?"

"Probably yes. What do you suggest?"

"Leak it through Joanna that Hammond tried to cut a deal by naming Prinz. That should piss him off. Then Joanna can make a public appeal to interview Prinz to get his side of the story."

Ken considered it. "Which only works if Prinz watches ITN."

"Both items will quickly make it into mainstream media."

"Okay, it's worth a shot. If she agrees, have her call me immediately. I'll need the details."

As she rejoined Bob and Bostwick, her cell buzzed. *Have I left you wordless already?*

CHAPTER EIGHTY

Sunday, June 3, 11:53 AM
Back in his home in Sea Gate, Senator Brandt was scouting the Sunday morning news shows.

"You look disgracefully pleased with yourself," his wife said.

"They've got young Hammond back in custody."

She took a sip of coffee. "Your Mr. Emory can't be happy about that."

"No. But then, life is full of little travails. I just saw Bryce Mitchell throw an open threat at ol' Let 'em run Ron. Threatening to go to the State Board of Judicial Review. When did he grow a pair of brass balls?"

"Dear, please. Your language. Must you be so crude?"

"Fits the subject. But, to answer your initial observation, I suspect the heat is getting to him. He needs to straighten up and fly right, because Old Man Hammond has deep pockets and was counting on a deal to spring his little communist. But the little..." He paused a moment to consider his wife's sensibilities. "... punk didn't cooperate, according to Justin."

"And how would he know?"

Ah, the same old complaint. "The usual means, I imagine."

She put down her cup with an expression of disgust. "I wouldn't think they've had time for pillow talk today."

"Now, who's being crude?"

"Well, I'm sorry, but I can't see how a God-fearing man like you can not only countenance a filthy character like that but employ him."

272

"My dear, I don't approve of his... tendencies. But he is free to do as he will, and in all other respects he is reliable and loyal."

"Other than that, Mrs. Lincoln, how was the play?"

"The world is changing, and we must change with it, I suppose. If he doesn't flaunt it and his work remains excellent, I can't complain."

"And suppose someone makes it public and reveals the identity of his lover? What happens then?"

It was something he hadn't considered.

***

"He moved." Kim made additional marks on the map. "The first text was from Hunters Point. He didn't ping another tower for quite a while. Based on the location, I'm guessing it was in an eatery."

"Having breakfast?" Cord asked. He'd welcomed them back from the DA's office.

"A definite possibility. There are a few places in that area."

"Maybe we should get over there and show his sketch around," Bob said.

Cord agreed. "Yeah. Let's see if it rings a bell with anyone."

"You guys go ahead. I'll stay here for the moment."

Cord turned to Bob. "She don't think he's still there."

"No, I don't. The tower pings continued along Hunters Point Avenue to Skillman to Queens Boulevard. He's not on a subway, he's in a car. Then along Queens Boulevard until Forest Hills, from where he sent his most recent text."

Cord shook his head. "He left it on the whole time?"

"Heading east again," Bob said. "That's the pattern, going east and west, back and forth."

"So far. The question is how much north-south variance will he work in." She considered it. "He may not have worked that out, yet."

"Any pings since he sent the last text?" Cord asked.

"No. I suspect he realized leaving his phone on was a bad move. But he'll turn it on again before he ditches it."

"What makes you think that?" Bob asked.

Cord replied before Kim could. "Because he'll be looking for her reply."

Which was why she was so happy Cord had transferred in. She decided now was a good time to reply. *I have more important things to worry about than your texts.*

Bostwick joined them. "All the local stations, plus ITN, carried Mitchell's news conference. I wonder who is busting the biggest gut: Prinz, Vickers, or Hammond Senior."

But Kim had gotten an update from Vera. "He got the text, and his cell pinged a tower along Queens Boulevard. Rego Park. He's heading back west." She pulled up Google Maps on her laptop. "There are several hotels along there between Elmhurst and Long Island City." She jotted down the names and addresses. "Forget the diners. Cord and Tim, you guys start in Elmhurst and work your way west, Bob and I will start in Long Island City and work our way east. Ask the desk clerks if anyone who looks like our sketch is staying there. Whoever gets a yes will notify the other group and we'll camp out for him."

Everyone but Bostwick saluted.

One other thing. "Tim, how did it go with your wife's mammogram?"

He looked relieved. "Came up clean."

***

Ed Lyons, the head of ITN, was waiting for Joanna when she finished recording her follow-up piece for the noon update. "I just heard about this. You're soliciting an avowed communist and insurrectionist to come on the air? Here?"

She led him to an empty room. "Did you hear my piece?"

"Yes, as you were recording it. Ms. Dunbar, your work has been of the highest quality. We are the envy of every 24/7 news station in the business. But I can't approve..."

"I'm working with the FBI. If Prinz agrees to be interviewed, either in person or remotely, they can trace it and arrest him."

Mr. Lyons considered it. "So, we might just tape it and not actually broadcast it."

"I wouldn't count on that. I'm sure he'll insist on doing it live."

"Then I can't..."

"Mr. Lyons, I realize this interview would be an affront to most of our viewers. But I could follow it with a strong editorial piece stating that we do not agree with his views and that our purpose has been to educate the public."

"You're not in full agreement with our editorial views, and our viewers are aware of that. This could paint you as more radical than you are."

"That's why I'd be willing to do the editorial piece. I could've been killed, thanks to this maniac. So could a good friend of mine."

He pondered the matter for several moments. "I suppose I can do my bit to help the FBI nail communist scum."

***

Do you, indeed? And here I thought I was your top priority.

Triscari's response came in just as Bob was crossing Newtown Creek onto 11th Street in Hunters Point. She texted Vera Koshkin. *Please text me the location of each new tower ping. Hope you're getting some sleep.*

Bob had just turned onto Jackson Avenue when she got Vera's response. *Queens Blvd and Woodhaven Blvd. I sleep between pings.*

She probably was. "Queens Center Mall."

"Shopping for new clothes?" Bob allowed himself a laugh. "Or hoping we'll chase."

"I wouldn't put it past him. He's smart enough to expect us to track his movements."

"So why doesn't he turn it off?"

"Sometimes he does. It's all one big head game."

"Do we chase him or do we stick to our plan?"

She liked how Bob's thinking was complimenting hers. "Stick to the plan as long as he stays on the Queens Boulevard axis. If he breaks off, we may want to chase, depending on his direction." She texted Cord and Tim the latest.

"What about responding?"

"I'm doing it now." It would encourage him to keep his phone on. *Oh, you are. Perhaps we can meet face to face and discuss it.*

Bob turned off Thomson Avenue into the tiny parking lot of a Days Inn. "First stop."

A text came in from Vera. *Another ping. Same location.*
But no response from Triscari.

***

The call came into the station's main number, and Joanna had to be paged. Before she took the call, she texted Ken Taylor the number on Caller ID.

"This is Joanna Dunbar. To whom am I speaking?"

The caller was a young woman with a Spanish accent. "My name is Inez. I'm calling for Felipe Prinz. Why would you, a reporter for a fascist network, want to interview him?"

"Wesley Hammond blames him for the shooting of Jared Davis. It stands to reason Prinz would want to defend himself."

"And help you convict Wesley. Why would he do that?"

"They don't need Prinz's help to convict Hammond. He's going down for murder and arson."

"You want Felipe to turn himself in. That will not happen."

"I'm just offering him an interview to give his side of the story. Public opinion has turned heavily against CHE since the shooting. He's losing whatever momentum he once had. He doesn't have to come here to do an interview, I can take a camera crew and van and come to him…"

"No."

Joanna allowed herself a laugh. "Didn't think so, but it's an option. We can also do one by phone."

"You can?"

"Sure. I'll give you my personal cell number. Tell him to call me if he's interested."

"I don't know if he…"

"Inez, it's nice talking to you, but I must talk to him if this is going to happen." She gave Inez the number. The call dropped.

A short while later, she heard from Taylor. *Burner phone, call originated in Brownsville. Doubt Prinz is anywhere in NYC. We'll check out Brownsville, tell me if he calls. Good job.*

CHAPTER EIGHTY-ONE

Sunday, June 3, 12:54 PM
They'd worked their way through Sunnyside, but no desk clerks had seen the man in the sketch.

"Forty minutes since you texted him," Bob said as they drove east. "Woodside is next."

Kim's cell buzzed. *You're making the same mistake Grandpa made— underestimating me.*

She waited for the text from Vera. *Last ping was on tower in Woodside. 61st Street.*

Kim checked her list. "Winfield Country Inn is a block away from the tower, and five blocks from here. Holy shit, that's the place." She texted Cord the address. *Get here as fast as you can.*

Next, she texted Triscari again. *Underestimate you? Never. I know who you are and what you are.* She kept it short. She needed a read on where he was.

Text from Vera. *Tower ping, same location.*

"We're going to bag him," Bob said.

"Hope so." Could it really be this easy? She stared at her cell. No response.

"Shit." Bob pounded the steering wheel. "There it is, other side of Queens Boulevard."

"Make the next left." Still no response.

Bob made two left turns and then pulled up in front of the Winfield Country Inn. No one around. He checked the small parking lot in the back while Kim entered the lobby. It was desolate, and the air was stale.

She showed her badge to the desk clerk, a heavyset man in his fifties with oily skin and unkempt greasy hair. "Have you seen the man in this sketch?"

He didn't look up from his newspaper. "Nah."

She reached over and snatched the paper away from him. "I'll assume that's a 'yes'. Where is he?"

Bob came in from the lot. "No one outside."

Kim leaned over the desk. "Where is he?"

"Sorry," the clerk said. "Lemme see that again." He blanched. "Holy shit. He just checked out."

"When?" Kim asked through clenched teeth.

"Like five minutes ago. Maybe ten. Paid cash."

"How long was he here?"

The clerk took the register. "Checked in Friday. Room 410."

"Show us," Kim said.

"Wait," Bob said. "You've got surveillance cameras. Show me the last half hour."

The clerk looked helpless. "Can't be in two places at once."

"Give me the fucking key," Kim said, "and show Detective Nolan what he needs to see." She took the elevator up to the fourth floor. As she passed 408, cries of intimacy echoed from within. Afternoon delights.

She entered the room.

Nothing. Clean and bare. She checked the drawers, but only because it was procedure. Triscari might make a mistake, but not such a basic one. She returned to the lobby and again brandished the sketch. "Is there anything obvious in his appearance now that differs from this sketch?"

"Yeah. He wasn't wearing a hoodie, and he's bald. Wears a baseball cap most of the time."

She turned to Bob. "Must have shaved his head. Cute. You find anything?"

"Not much," Bob said. "Camera caught a shit green Ford Taurus about fifteen minutes ago. Couldn't see the driver."

Cord rushed in with Tim right behind. "Get him?"

"No," Kim replied. "He'd gone by the time we got here." She needed to get out of the stale lobby and into the fresh air.

Another text. *Perhaps. But then you were certain you knew where I am. Wrong.*

***

Joanna was already in her apartment when the call came in on her cell. "Inez told me to call you."

"Who is this?"

"I just told you…"

She'd consented to the FBI tapping her cell line. "Yeah, yeah. And you could be another go-between. I need verification of whom I'm talking to, for real."

He chuckled. "And just how can I convince you?"

"Tell me who you are, what your real name is, and something that I would have confidence that only you could know."

"Felipe Prinz. That's my real name. My given name, if that's what you want, was Phillip King, a son of a petit bourgeois business owner. I'm not sure what will satisfy your last requirement, other than Wesley Hammond was determined to kill someone, anyone, that night to prove his manliness after I'd called him out for being a coward. But I'll also give you something you can check out, because no one in my group knows it. I changed my name partly to give myself street cred in the movement, and partly because Phil King got thrown out of law school for assaulting his contract law professor."

"Wouldn't that also have given you street cred?"

"No. She was sixty-two. But you can check it out. If they won't tell you, maybe they'll tell your detective friend."

"I'll do that. Assuming it checks out, does this mean you agree to an interview?"

"On three conditions: I pick the time, we do it by phone and we do it live. Not even a seven-second delay."

"Precisely the conditions I expected. I agree to all of them if you agree to one more. We do it on Facetime. My viewers will need to see your face to be sure it's really you."

"My burner phones do not support Facetime."

"Then you'll need one that does. If you like, the station will provide you with one."

He laughed. "Right. You'll be happy to send it to me Fedex, with the feds right behind the delivery truck."

"I was thinking more like giving it to one of your local supporters, who could then bring it to you."

"And the feds could follow her. Or him. Sorry, no."

"Up to you. No Facetime, no interview. You have your needs, I have mine."

"I'll get back to you."

CHAPTER EIGHTY-TWO

Sunday, June 3, 7:13 PM

"What are you still doing here?" Bob had just come back from getting dinner at the Firehouse Deli. It was after seven, and the Castle was a ghost town.

Kim was still staring at her map. "Triscari's last text pinged off a tower on Woodhaven Boulevard, south of Metropolitan Avenue. He must have turned it off at that point, because there wasn't another ping until a few minutes ago, at Broadway and Malcolm X Boulevard."

"Shit. That's only a few blocks from here." He laid his prosciutto and provolone hero on the desk and opened his laptop. "The Hotel RL is over there."

"It's a feint." Her voice was flat. "There are three places I'm sure he isn't staying tonight: Bay Ridge, the RL, and the Winfield Country Inn."

"You okay? You don't sound good."

"He was toying with me, and I fell for it. That back-and-forth along Queens Boulevard was simply baiting me."

"That assumes he knows we can track his movements via cell phones."

"Which anyone who has ever watched a true crime show knows."

He picked up his hero. "Want half?"

"Thanks, Bob, but no, thanks."

He took a huge bite. "So, you figure we're back to square one?"

"No." She'd gone for the first feint, but if they'd been a little quicker at the early stops, they might have caught him. "He doesn't know how close he cut it today. And I have no intention of telling him. He's leading me somewhere, but I just haven't figured out where, yet."

She returned to her study of the map. West side of Manhattan, to East Williamsburg, to Hunters Point while staying at a hotel in Woodside, to Forest Hills, back to Elmhurst, then bugging out of Woodside. "He went east-west on his first baiting trip. I have to believe he's going to go north-south on the next, which explains why he's hanging near the RL right now."

"Or northeast-southwest, or northwest-southeast."

She shook her head. "Only by degrees. This guy wants contrasts. He thinks he's befuddling me. But just because I fell for the feint doesn't mean I'm not learning from watching him."

She walked back to the map to mark Triscari's last position. "Whoa."

"What is it?"

"You were right, Bob. Look." She waited for him to join her. "From the boat basin to East Williamsburg was northwest to southeast. Then northwest to Hunters Point. From there to Forest Hills is southeast, though more east than south. Now, look at this last move, from the Queens Center Mall to the RL. Northeast to southwest."

"So, his next move will be northeast?"

It would be the very change she'd suggested, but with the directions slightly altered. It would be logical and neat.

She had printed the map from Google Maps. It showed restaurants and hotels and subway stops. She traced a line northeast from the RL. No hotels until one got into Maspeth, and then no more until the belt along Queens Boulevard. And he wasn't going back there.

He also wouldn't be logical and neat. "No. And he's not stopping at the RL. He's heading over to my neck of the woods. Look, near the site of the riot, you have seven hotels in a tight cluster."

"Why not further southwest?"

"Three more clustered between the Barclay Center and the Gowanus Canal. And cheaper, so a definite possibility. We'll start checking them tomorrow."

"Aren't you afraid he might move again?"

"You forget. I have my indicator." She held up her cell. "And this will give me some time to test my theory."

***

It was ironic that the lovely view of Lower Manhattan from the window of his hotel room, a major reason he was paying $169 a night, meant nothing to him. But the cost was worth every penny because he'd just convinced his pursuer that he was going bargain-basement on this little sojourn. The best hotel in downtown Brooklyn was the last place she'd look.

And the location had other advantages.

She'd been at Cadman Plaza the night of the fire. After work hours. It stood to reason she lived in the area. And tonight, returning from his little reconnaissance mission, he'd seen her alighting from a bus on Tillary Street. He'd wanted to accost her right there, but that wouldn't have been according to plan.

And this had to be according to plan.

His plans hadn't been working too well of late. This afternoon's adventure had cut it a little too close. But then, that wasn't all bad, either. It had no doubt added to her frustration. He would want to cultivate that.

Seeing her getting off the bus had given him a chance to study his prey. An attractive woman, with her brown hair pulled into what looked almost like pigtails. Gave her a sort of young girl look. And he so liked young girls.

But, no, she was much older than his preferred targets. Still, if his plan worked as well as he hoped it might, it would provide a delicious conclusion to this adventure. The stirring he now felt reinforced the idea.

But first, the plan.

The Borough Hall subway stop on the Four and Five line was only two blocks from the hotel. Easy. It could also be reached through connecting passageways from the Borough Hall stop on the Two and Three line and the Court Street stop on the R. Lots of options.

He'd spend two hours on the platform timing the intervals between trains. Two lines meant more traffic, but at night, it slowed to a workable level. With the platform deserted on a Sunday night, he'd make certain his plan was viable.

CHAPTER EIGHTY-THREE

Monday, June 4, 9:06 AM

"The FBI has confirmed the arrest of CHE leader Felipe Prinz last night in upstate New York near Chenango Lake. Mr. Prinz has been implicated in the riot that led to the shooting death of firefighter Jared Davis by the alleged gunman, Wesley Hammond. Neither Brooklyn DA Bryce Mitchell nor the federal attorney for the Southern District of New York would comment on the arrest of Prinz. Acting Mayor Sabrina Dunn said, 'I hope no demonstrations disrupt access to the polls for tomorrow's special mayoral election.' Joanna Dunbar, ITN News."

***

Kim turned away from the set. "I guess that kills Joanna's Prinz interview."

"Nice attempt to get demonstrators out there so people can't vote," Bob said.

Bostwick chimed in. "She's desperate. I saw on the news yesterday the polls now have Brandt up by ten points."

Cord looked up from the *New York Times.* "You ask me, the only thing demonstrations would do is make Brandt voters more determined than ever to come out. Folks are tired of this shit."

No time for this. "Come on, guys, we've got hotels to check out. Seven in the Downtown Brooklyn cluster, three in the Gowanus cluster."

"Nothing from our friend this morning?" Bob asked. "That's odd."

Yes, it was. The bastard had something up his sleeve. "Let's stay in pairs. Cord and Tim, Bob and me."

"Won't that slow us down?" Tim asked. "Might go faster if we each work on our own. We're only looking to see if he checked in to any of these."

"I can't take the chance that he might try to take one of us out if he sees anyone alone. Safety first."

"I agree," Bostwick said. "What about monitoring his cell activity? Shouldn't someone stay here for that?"

"Vera's on it," Cord said, a little too quickly.

"She tell you that over breakfast?" Tim asked.

"Yeah." Cord grinned at him. "Suffer, fool."

Tim held up both hands. "Hey, man, I'm married."

"Okay, let's go, guys," Kim said. "And don't just ask the desk folks, because they probably weren't on last night when he checked in. Show the sketch to housekeeping people and staff in lobby stores or stores close to the hotel."

***

With sunglasses and a baseball cap, it was easy for him to blend in with the crowds of downtown Brooklyn. He'd spent time in the business center checking the evening schedules of the Four and Five trains. The last Four train every weeknight was 11:52PM, while the first one in the morning was 12:09AM, and the Five didn't run at night. Seventeen minutes was more than enough of a window.

His mind turned to his prey. By now, she must be growing anxious, with no text from him in over twelve hours. But she would have someone tracking his cell activity, which is why he'd left her that one breadcrumb last night. Outside a hotel right near her headquarters. How maddening that had to be. And she'd have nothing to feed on but dead air until he decided otherwise.

He was in control. That had to upset her to no end.

He was still chuckling to himself as he approached Smith Street on Livingston but stopped when he spied his prey coming out of the Park Fast on the opposite corner with a middle-aged man. He slipped into the entrance to the Civil Court building.

A detective paying for parking? Brady was either off duty or keeping a very low profile. He crossed Livingston to a construction site. The scaffolding over the sidewalk gave him ample cover.

She and her friend turned left onto Smith Street, following a parallel course to his, heading south toward the Hilton.

He hadn't left a clue for her. She was very lucky or very smart.

If he texted now, she'd realize she was hot on his tail, and he would likely have to start his plan tonight. He could also withdraw, take a subway several stops in any direction, and throw her off the scent.

Across the street, a breeze blew her jacket back, revealing a blouse of teal blue.

She must have been quite enticing as a high school freshman.

***

The senator settled into the seat behind his desk in his district office and allowed himself a moment of self-congratulation. Normally, he'd be in Albany on a Monday, but not with the special election a day away. He'd just ended a conversation with the commissioner, who had assured him that the department was prepared for any civil disturbances over the next forty-eight hours. He'd also issued a statement to the press condemning Dunn's irresponsible musings on the subject, which could only be interpreted as a call for insurrection. Fortunately, the most likely architect of any such insurrection was now in federal custody.

The intercom buzzed. "Mr. Cates to see you, Senator."

"Send him in."

As usual, Cates looked perfect, with not a hair out of place. He tried not to think about Cates' proclivities, or of Rick Conti. "What's the latest?"

"Rick's not getting any intel, Senator. His section chief is locking him out."

"Does Mitchell know?"

"Not yet. Rick's afraid to say anything. He's afraid Mitchell will think he's bigfooting his boss. The official line is that Mitchell and the Southern New York District Attorney still haven't agreed on who will handle prosecuting Prinz. Ricky suspects they'll pull Hammond back in to get something coherent out of him to make the state case against Prinz stronger than the federal."

The senator tried not to wince at Cates' using the nickname, Ricky. "Does he have any idea what Mitchell thinks?"

"He probably agrees, but who knows?"

"Okay. Keep me posted." Cates got up to leave, but the senator stopped him. "One question, on a personal note. Are you and Rick planning on, um, formalizing your arrangement?"

Cates broke into a winning grin. What was wrong with this guy? Women would go nuts for him.

"If you're asking if we're planning on getting married, the answer is no, at least not anytime soon. We've discussed it, but we agree that since I work for you, it would place us both in an awkward position."

That was a relief.

***

Kim had just finished interviewing a housekeeping worker at the Hilton, Brooklyn when her cell signaled another text. *That blouse is a lovely shade of blue. Looks nice on you.*

Bob approached. "Nothing. You get anything?"

She shared the text.

"He's commenting on your clothing, now? That's creepy."

"It's more than that. He's stalking us."

"I'll check outside while you contact Vera."

Kim texted Vera and asked for activity.

Text originated from the same tower as your cell. No further pings.

Either he'd already turned off his phone or he hadn't moved. If the latter, getting an answer might prompt another text from him, making the picture clearer. *You like it? I wore it just for you.*

Another text came in almost immediately, but it was from Cord. *Nothing in any of the three places near the Gowanus. Two had no check-ins last night, and the last only had two women check in. What now?*

That made it easy. *Meet Bob and me at the corner of Livingston and Smith. Park in the lot on the corner.*

Bob returned. "No sign of him anywhere."

She repeated Cord's news and texted Vera.

Immediate response. *Still in your area.*

CHAPTER EIGHTY-FOUR

Monday, June 4, 1:32 PM

By one-thirty in the afternoon, they had finished interviewing employees in all seven hotels in the downtown Brooklyn area. No one had recognized the man in the sketch.

"Picture him bald," Kim had prompted each one. "Or wearing a baseball cap."

"What team?" they had all asked.

"Unbelievable," she said to Bob as they stood in the lobby of the last hotel, the Marriott, Brooklyn Bridge, just across from the Kings County Supreme Court. With luck, Wesley Hammond would stand trial there one day soon.

She checked her cell. The only text she'd received was the one from Vera an hour earlier reporting she'd tracked no new tower pings anywhere from Lily Ng's cell.

Tim returned from his part of the sweep. "Nothing."

Cord approached from the opposite direction. "This guy must be a fucking chameleon."

"Either that," Tim said, "or he hopped on any of the eight subways that stop near here."

Kim glanced around again. Nothing. "No. He's around here, perhaps closer than we think."

***

He allowed himself a self-satisfied smile. Even closer than that, my dear detective.

Sitting behind the barrier of potted palms that separated the entrance from the lobby, with a herringbone snap-billed cap pulled down close to his eyes, he studied the three men standing with his adversary. The older guy was the same one who'd been with her in front of the Park Fast. The other two, younger, must be colleagues from her group. Or unit, as they liked to say, aping the military.

"So," the colored fellow said, "what do we do, now? Just hang?"

She didn't answer right away. That was good. It suggested confusion.

"No," she said at last. "He pulled us out here for a reason. But now that he's accomplished it, he'll lie low for a while, then poke us again."

That's right, my dear. That's exactly what I'll do. And you'll come running when I do.

Because you don't know it yet, but I own you.

***

The senator listened carefully as his campaign manager laid out the itinerary until the polls closed. "Two big rallies tonight, sandwiched around a Knights of Columbus event, followed by a day of meet-and-greet events tomorrow while campaign workers get out the vote. Our campaign ad blitz started over the weekend and will go full blast right until the polls close. We've booked time on every Mets, Yankees, Islanders, and NYCFC telecast, hitting the crime issue hard."

"What about the Red Bulls?"

His campaign manager snickered. "They're in Joisey. We've booked a ballroom and an executive suite at the Marriott at the Brooklyn Bridge for tomorrow night."

"Rather pricey, isn't it?" he asked.

"Yes, but it will make a big media splash. Besides, our campaign fund is in fine shape. We have a start on your re-election campaign."

He pointed a finger at his guest. "We take nothing for granted."

"That's my line. And with Prinz in the slammer, I doubt we'll have too much to worry about on the demonstration front. Too bad, really. Might have made for some nice, free campaign video."

***

While Cord and Tim returned to the Castle, Kim and Bob stopped in to see Rick Conti.

"I was about to call you," he said. "Bad news. Prinz's attorney has filed a motion in federal court to dismiss the charges for lack of evidence. He and the US attorney meet with the judge tomorrow morning to make their arguments. Mitchell wants us to meet with Hammond and Wyckoff this afternoon for a final attempt to squeeze whatever we can out of him."

This couldn't be happening. "You mean you might let him plead out? The whole point of the ruse was to get Hammond back into custody."

"The feds want to make sure they keep Prinz in jail, since he's much more dangerous on the street than Hammond. They're hoping Hammond will give them enough. Mitchell wants to play nice."

"And if he lets Hammond off with a wrist slap, what does he plan on saying to Jared Davis' family? Or to the men and women of the FDNY?"

Rick waved a hand. "Slow down. I'm on your side, Kim. And Mitchell is keeping my boss out of this."

***

It was a short walk to the Brooklyn Detention Complex. Ken Taylor was waiting when they arrived. Kim kept thinking about Triscari. Where he might be, and what he might be planning.

Wyckoff and Hammond were already in the conference room. Wyckoff nodded a greeting to Rick. "I see you brought a posse with you."

Rick took charge. "The FBI has Felipe Prinz in custody. Your client has implicated him in the murder of Jared Davis but has provided no corroborating evidence. The Brooklyn DA has authorized me to reduce the charges against him in return for such evidence."

Wyckoff sat back. "Reduce them to what?"

"That would depend on how much evidence he provides, and whether it indeed mitigates his own guilt." Rick turned to Hammond. "Let's hear it."

Hammond bristled. "Fuck you. I'm not selling out my…"

Wyckoff placed a hand on his client's arm. "We need to discuss this privately."

They all stepped outside the room while Wyckoff and Hammond conferred.

"What's the plan if Hammond doesn't give you anything?" Kim asked.

Conti laughed. "That's easy. I go back and report it, the charges stand, and the FBI figures out another way to keep Prinz contained. My job only gets sticky if he talks."

Wyckoff waved them back into the room. Hammond sat, staring at the table and pouting.

His lawyer ignored him. "I have advised my client that, at the very least, we should hear what you have in mind in the event the information he provides satisfies you, and the cost to him if he refuses."

"If he refuses," Rick said, "he is facing a charge of murder in the first degree, twenty-five years to life; terrorism, life; arson in the third degree, maximum of 15 years; and riot in the first degree, maximum of four years. So, he's going away and never coming out."

Taylor spoke up. "If you can provide enough information for us to make the case against Prinz on terrorism and inciting to riot, the US attorney will request that the Brooklyn DA drop the terrorism charge and reduce the murder charge."

"Reduce it to what?" Wyckoff asked.

"It depends on what else he has to say for himself," Rick replied. "He also must testify against Prinz. If he does, we can reduce the murder charge to voluntary manslaughter if the feds convict Prinz, second degree murder if they don't."

Buried in her hip pocket, Kim's cell vibrated with a text. Damn, it would have to wait.

Wyckoff turned to Hammond. "With the judge we drew, you could be out in as little as fifteen years."

Kim saw red. She was about to say something when Bob's knee pressed against hers under the table.

"It's a gift," Conti said, taking the words out of her mouth.

Hammond bristled. "Yeah, a gift for selling out a noble leader."

Wyckoff gripped Hammond's arm again. "Wes, don't."

Hammond yanked it away. "Fuck you. These fascists come in with a load of bullshit charges, and you want me to sell out Felipe? No way."

"They're not bullshit." Kim rattled off the long list of forensic evidence against him, then continued, "You were in the middle of the riot, which clearly was an act of terrorism. You're going down, you little shit, and I'll be there to testify against you."

Hammond jumped up. "Fuck you, bitch."

Kim stood. "Want to mix it up, little boy? Wanna dance?"

Bob stood to block her.

Wyckoff shoved Hammond back into his seat. "Shut up, asshole."

Conti remained calm. "I'll put that down as a 'not interested', then. Fine with me." He waited until Wyckoff and Hammond stalked out. Then, he grinned at Kim. "You're good."

***

As the senator was preparing to leave for his first major event of the evening, Cates rushed in and closed the door. "Ricky met with Hammond and his lawyer to offer him a deal if he ratted out Prinz. He blew up."

"Meaning what?"

"He got pissed at Kim Brady and she challenged him to a fight."

He burst out laughing. "She did what?"

"Honest. Nolan had to hold her back. Ricky said if he hadn't, she'd have kicked Hammond's ass."

"Good for her."

"Yeah, but Hammond didn't roll on Prinz, and it sounds like the feds don't have enough to hold him."

"Did Conti advise the NYPD?"

"First thing after Hammond left."

They might get some riot footage, after all.

CHAPTER EIGHTY-FIVE

Monday, June 4, 3:57 PM

Bob didn't say a word all the way back, not even when she checked the text.

She'd never lost it with a prisoner before. And she'd dealt with worse characters than Wesley Hammond. But he wasn't the reason she'd lost her cool, although she despised his entitled little ass.

It had been knowing that the text was waiting. Knowing it wasn't from Joanna or Cord or Vera. Because it was Triscari, taunting her yet again.

And she'd been right. *Let me guess. Of the three of them, you like the colored boy best. Am I truly a chameleon?*

Bob pulled into the parking lot and turned off the engine. "You okay?"

"He saw us."

"Yeah, on the street."

"No, Bob. He saw the four of us together. He noticed Cord. Heard what he said. He was in the lobby with us."

"So, he's staying there?"

Exactly what she'd been thinking. "It's possible. Or he followed us and got lucky." She paused to think. "I have to change it up on him." Vera had reported no activity or tower pings since Triscari's last text from the area of the Marriott.

Best to do nothing and let him tip his hand.

***

The turnout was damned good at the Brooklyn Council of Young Voters. He regarded Millennials with disdain, but this group gave him a warm round of applause even as he stepped up to the podium. "When Sabrina Dunn's predecessor took office a year ago, didn't he promise to bring in companies offering good jobs for young folks like yourselves?" It was a rhetorical question.

They yelled back, "Yes."

It stunned him, but he saw his opportunity. "Did he deliver on that promise?"

"No."

This was excellent. "And didn't he promise a city where everyone could walk where they pleased?"

"Yes!"

"And did he keep that promise?"

"No!"

"Has Sabrina Dunn made you feel safe on the city streets?"

"No!"

"On the subways?"

"No!"

"Do you want a mayor who will keep this city safe?"

"Yes!"

"And who is that mayor?" Come on, Justin. You and your guys, do your stuff.

"Brandt! Brandt! Brandt! Brandt!"

***

A text. *No response? Oh, of course. You have better things to do. But you don't. You're too obsessed.*

At least Jake was in the shower, so he wouldn't see her furiously texting Vera.

He'd pinged the same tower as her cell. He was right nearby. It had to be by chance. He couldn't know.

She slipped into the hallway and peered out the peephole of the front door of the building.

Two college age girls walked by the front of their brownstone. A neighbor came out, got into his car, and drove away. Nothing else.

She slipped back into the apartment.

Jake was waiting. "What's up?"

"I thought I heard someone at the front door. But it was nothing."

"No, I mean, what's up with you? You're wound tight as a watch spring. You've been like that for over a week, but it's getting worse."

No one could read her as well as Jake. "It's just work. This case is driving me nuts."

"Is it Brandt?"

Where did that come from? She laughed, a genuine laugh, grateful for the release. "Why would you ask that?"

"Because he has a thing for you. And, given his position, he could make things difficult for you if he wanted to do something about it."

She'd caught the momentary look of hunger in Brandt's eye at the restaurant. So had Jake. "He knows better than to try anything. He's got other issues."

"Like what?"

Good. A little gossip would take Jake's mind and hers off her brooding. "Rick Conti, the ADA, is gay. His partner is one of Brandt's staffers."

"Ha. I guess that does complicate things for him. I'm surprised the senator approves."

"He's probably grateful for the information it provides, but I imagine he worries what happens when it becomes public."

"How did you hear this?"

"The staffer is Cates, the guy who was shadowing me for a while. He's not a bad…"

A text. She had already reached for her cell when she caught herself.

"See," Jake said, "that's what I meant. I'm worried, Kim."

No sense in denying anything. She checked the text. *You're obsessed, whether or not you admit it. But an obsession rewarded is a revelation.*

"What…?"

She held up her hand and waited Vera's tracking information. Different cell tower. This one was at One Metro-Tech, a block away from the Marriott.

"Who's texting you? What's this all about?"

"I'm not sure, yet."

He didn't believe her. But she had to leave it at that.

CHAPTER EIGHTY-SIX

Tuesday, June 5, 6:22 AM

Kim hadn't slept, and she slipped out of the apartment before Jake was up. As she walked over to Cadman Plaza, she scanned in every direction several times, unable to shake the sense that Triscari was watching her every move. Every time she tried to get a better hold on him, he got a better hold on her. He was getting inside her head.

A bus was waiting at Tillary Street, and once she was aboard, she relaxed a little. Time for a little misdirection. He'd sent her the second text last night less than a half hour after the first. That was a first. He could have been pushing her. Or perhaps he just expected an immediate response. There had been no new text this morning.

Time to take the initiative. *Is that what you told your cousin, Angelina?*

She stepped off the bus outside the Castle and, after it pulled away, did another three-sixty scan. No Triscari and no Justin Cates. The thought of Cates made her smile. Learning of his relationship with Rick had made him more human in her eyes.

Sergeant Dhillon was still on duty when she signed in. "Early for you, Kim."

"It's that kind of case, Marshal." The TV was on, and Prinz was on the screen. "What's this?"

"A federal judge ordered him released yesterday. Said the FBI didn't have probable cause when they arrested him."

300

"Can you turn up the sound?" She stepped closer to the screen to listen.

Joanna appeared on screen, microphone in hand, in front of Prinz. "Considering recent events, do you intend to de-escalate your activities to reduce the incidence of street violence?"

Prinz pulled himself up, erect. "CHE will continue to press for human rights in this city. We do not seek violence. That results from forceful repression by a fascist, militaristic police force at the behest of politicians bought and owned by rich capitalists. If they leave us in peace, we will protest in peace. If they attack us, we will fight back. And you can tell that to your bosses." He pushed past her before she could say anything else.

"Now," Dhillon said, "there's a reasonable man. I can't believe they let him out. The department is on full alert for today and tonight."

***

He hadn't slept well. Two texts, and no response. There should have been something.

She was doing this on purpose, breaking the rhythm, trying to aggravate him, like Angelina had done, deliberately ignoring him. And then bringing that Irish boy close to home, flaunting him. Letting him kiss her.

His Angelina.

He started pacing. This wasn't good. He needed to satisfy himself again. It was only four days since, but Erica hadn't satisfied him. And she'd paid the price.

He took a shower. This was no time to be rash. He had laid a trap. The detective was prowling around it. He had to be patient. Calm. Rational. She would fall into it.

Once out of the shower, he shaved his face and head. Ordered room service breakfast and had the server leave it outside the door. No direct contact. The bitch detective had already been here and might very well come back.

After retrieving the breakfast tray from the hallway, he picked up Lotus Blossom's cell. Perhaps one more prod from the same number would jolt her.

And then he saw her text about Angelina.

He raised the offending cell to smash it. "Bitch!" How dare she?

But he caught himself. Using his victim's cell was part of his fight plan.

He started pacing. Back and forth. Working off the anger. The nerve. The gall.

But how could she have known?

Gina. The bitch detective had taken Gina away. So, Gina must have told everything she'd promised never to tell.

He called Gina's cell. Directly to voicemail.

How did they find Gina? How did they discover Angelina was his cousin, his forbidden love?

He tried Gina again. Same result.

This had to end, now. He couldn't run, as he'd done so many times before. This was unfinished business. *Your grandpa tried to find out what I told Angelina. I sent him to join her. I could tell you, but then…*

* * *

Kim nodded with satisfaction. The needle had sunk home. Vera reported two calls, both trying to reach Gina before his last text. All three pinging off the tower at One Metro-Tech.

The motherfucker had been there all along.

As with all the other texts, she kept this one to herself as the team met to discuss the latest.

Judge Vickers had revoked Wesley Hammond's bail, knowing he had no choice. The Prinz news wasn't so good. Following his brief encounter with Joanna on the courthouse steps, he'd broken away from his attorney and an unknown woman had whisked him into a dingy gray Toyota Camry that had sped away before the FBI could tail it.

"The commissioner," Bostwick said, "has the entire department on alert and SRG units all over the city are ready to respond."

"Think protesters will interfere with the voting today?" Cord asked.

When Bostwick didn't answer, Kim stepped up. "I doubt it. Prinz is trying to paint himself as a man of the people. Keeping them from voting doesn't do much for that image. More likely, it will be tonight. They prefer to work after dark, anyway."

"SRG agrees with you," Bostwick said. "Brandt's campaign is having a big thing at the Marriott tonight. He's got to be a prime target for CHE."

"Where we were yesterday?" Tim asked. "Where Triscari saw us?"

"Yes," Kim replied, "but he's likely left there by now."

Bostwick scowled. "It'll make things dicey if he hasn't. Have you heard from him, yet, today?"

"No." Dark and deep. If he wasn't at the Marriott, he was close by. And the other guys in the unit couldn't help her where she needed to go.

Time to respond. *But you can't always do what you want to do. Can you?*

CHAPTER EIGHTY-SEVEN

Tuesday, June 5, Noon

"Voters are turning out in large numbers for today's special mayoral election. Brooklyn District Attorney Bryce Mitchell shocked political observers and party insiders last night with his declaration of support for State Senator Raymond Brandt, a move that is being widely viewed as a sign that the party leadership has lost confidence in the progressive wing of the party. Joanna Dunbar reporting for ITN."

***

He had to get out of his room. This was going to be resolved tonight, and he needed to finalize his plan. He donned his sunglasses and herringbone snap-billed cap, shut off the TV, and headed out.

The lobby was a bevy of activity, and several news vans were parked outside.

"What's up?" he asked the concierge.

"Big election night party here tonight."

That could be quite useful.

He waited until he was out in the park to respond. The warmth of sunshine helped take the edge off his anger. He was still in control. And he'd prove it.

I can. You've already bent to my will. Before today is over, I will own you.

***

"Joanna, do you have a minute?" Mr. Lyons gestured for her to join him in his office. "I just wanted to say you're doing a fine job. Your reporting is top notch."

"Thank you."

"For tonight, we'll have reporters at both parties. I want you at Brandt's, but I want to talk to you first. Historically, you'd been critical of him, and even dug out his source of funding."

She had never been allowed to report it, but Joanna wasn't surprised he'd smoked it out. Such things always got out. "That's true. I was doing my job as a reporter."

"And yet he recommended you for this job. Why?"

When in doubt, tell the truth. "Because I asked through a mutual friend. I was afraid I'd never be able to work again."

"So, you made a deal with the devil?"

"I wouldn't say that. You saw my interview with him. Did I toss him puffballs?"

"No. His call surprised me. There's always a subtext in this business, the stuff you don't see that drives people. He was quite energetic in his recommendation. I just want to be sure there wasn't more to it than meets the eye."

"No, not with me."

"Good. Then please be at the Marriott by seven and be ready to give us updates. Interview as many pols as you can. Campaign workers, too. But be careful out there. I understand there may be trouble tonight with Prinz out."

***

Triscari had left his cell on. Judging by the tower pings, he was meandering between downtown and Brooklyn Heights.

305

She paused from marking each tower ping on her map to send a new text. *It must gall you to keep hiding. And yet you don't run, as you did for so long. Why is that?*

"You've been holding out on us." Bob's voice startled her. "Sorry. You can't do this alone." He closed the conference room door. "Cord's worried about you. He says he's never seen you like this."

"Triscari's going to strike again, soon."

He nodded toward her cell. "Did he say that?"

"Not in so many words. But his cooling-off periods have been getting shorter. And he's trying to fence with me."

"Trying to?"

She had to grin at that. "Okay, he's doing it. But this is the one way I can throw him off his game."

The buzz of her cell stopped him. "Better check that."

Because I chose to stop. New York is a target-rich city.

She didn't mind Bob reading over her shoulder. He stared at it. "He's threatening more attacks."

"Yes. And check these last several tower pings. Up Cadman Plaza, one hit on Pierrepont, a couple along Henry, over to Middagh and Hicks Streets, down to Joralemon, two pings to Sidney Place, where he was when he sent this last text."

"The bell isn't ringing, Kim."

"Check the map. I've been making notes as I go."

He stared at her markings. "PS 8, St. Ann's, Mary McDowell... all schools. Shit, he's scouting targets."

"That's what he wants us to think. But he's never attacked during the day except at Jones Beach, which had to be deserted, and he'd be a fool to try it in that neighborhood. He can hide in plain sight, but he can't kill in it."

"So, what's next? We go back out and search the streets?"

"No. We track him and wait. And I fence with him."

"The lieu won't like it, Kim."

"Then the lieu better not find out about it." She reached for her cell. *What use are targets when you're out of ammunition?*

CHAPTER EIGHTY-EIGHT

Tuesday, June 5, 1:41 PM

He uttered a low growl upon reading this latest insolence.

"Hey," a woman in her fifties called out. "You okay?"

He had no choice but to swallow his anger. "Yes, thank you. Allergies."

She backed away. "That didn't sound like no sneeze." She moved off before he could answer.

He grabbed a table in the plaza in front of Borough Hall. *When we meet, you will see how much ammunition I have.*

Sending it soothed his anger. After she replied, he would lay the bait.

***

Kim read it and smirked. Let him simmer a while.

"Lily's phone?" Bob asked.

Good. He was thinking along with her. "Lily's phone."

"He's too pissed to remember to turn it off."

"Correct. And he said, 'When we meet', which means he has something in mind. And he wouldn't mention that unless he was certain we were close to that point."

"If you keep him occupied with texts, we can track him. We could collar him right now."

"He's too slippery, and that area gives him way too many avenues of escape. Even the subway stations provide connections." Another text from Vera. *He's moving. Tower ping on Joralemon Street.* "Looks like he's moving west."

"Back to one of the schools?"

She checked the map. "Not likely. What else is over there?"

"Brooklyn Bridge Park? Pier 5 where the sports fields are? How about lunch at Estuary One?"

"I have a better idea." It only took a moment. *When we meet? Are you coming to see me?*

No response. She waited for ten minutes before it finally came in. *I thought you were bright. But you're not even as bright as the man who was stupid enough to let me shoot him in his own car.*

After a few minutes, she got an update from Vera. It looked like he was heading back toward Borough Hall.

She replied to his text. *You're right. I'm not at all bright. When can I expect you to arrive?*

***

He needed to keep moving. He found a bench by the Korean War Veteran's Plaza. It took him time to compose himself. *Let me explain how this works. I don't come to you. You come to me.*

He waited. Maybe she wouldn't reply. No matter. He wanted her to know where he was.

I suppose you expect me to wear a pleated skirt and saddle shoes.

"That would be quite nice," he said aloud, then quickly glanced around to be sure no one had heard him.

But he couldn't give her an inch.

What you wear won't matter. Only what I want of you.

***

"This is getting sick," Bob said.

"He's a serial offender. There are no rules." *Was that all that mattered when you killed Angelina?*

308

"You going to mention any of the others?" Bob asked.

"Only at the right time."

***

He leaped off the bench, startling a woman walking past him pushing a stroller. Walk. Keep walking.

How dare she mention… her. And she'd done it twice.

Calm. He needed calm.

As he walked, his mind drifted back to that night at the funeral home… lovely Angelina, in the casket, at peace… wearing the same yellow dress she'd worn at Easter that year. No one else would ever have her.

He could almost smell the flowers. And hear the sobs, the wailing of grieving aunts and cousins and grandmothers. Her mother, sick with grief. Young Gina, cowering and bewildered. And her brothers, quaking with a rage they couldn't slake.

They'd all suffered. And they'd all deserved it for standing in the way of true love.

Every victim since had brought the same satisfaction. Each one a sacrifice at the altar of Angelina.

He stopped at the light at Joralemon and Hicks. He'd been walking on autopilot, stopping at lights without knowing it. How interesting that his instincts would have taken him this way. The light changed, and he crossed, continuing on Joralemon Street. Almost to the following corner, but not all the way.

Don't linger, only long enough to appear to be admiring a lovely old brownstone, not staring at the blacked-out windows or the strange red standpipe just inside the wrought-iron fence.

Yes, he'd made a wise choice.

CHAPTER EIGHTY-NINE

Tuesday, June 5, 6:01 PM

"With three hours to go before the polls close, the Board of Elections reports a strong turnout across the city, resulting in long lines. Some voters reported waiting two hours to vote. Exit polls showed that the leading concern for voters is crime. We'll have full coverage throughout the evening, with on-site reporting from the New York Hilton in Manhattan where Sabrina Dunn will receive election returns, and from the Marriott at Brooklyn Bridge, Senator Brandt's headquarters for the evening."

***

He made his way through the packed lobby to the elevator. He had already pushed the button for his floor when two young men who looked like college students got on, each carrying a shopping bag.

"Hey," a security guard called after them. "Where are you guys going?"

"Our room," one said. A tall, skinny blond kid with the beginnings of a scraggly beard. "1203."

The guard nodded and waved them on.

The door closed and the same kid pushed the button for the ballroom floor.

Help from an unexpected source. How nice. "Push twelve as well. If the guard is watching the board, he'll notice if this car doesn't stop there."

The blond kid said nothing, but he pushed twelve.

Back in his room, he fired his next shot. *You have no right to speak of her. None.* Then, he added, *Tonight, I will teach you your lesson.*

***

Kim got off the phone and walked into Bostwick's office. "I just got a call from Ken Taylor. They assume CHE is targeting the Marriott tonight. They've already alerted the department, but he wanted to give us a heads-up."

"You're convinced Triscari is there?"

"Yes. But the department will certainly deploy the SRG, and once that happens, we lose control. He could slip away, especially if they use the Kettle."

Bostwick paused, rubbing his temples. "We can't dictate what tactics the SRG uses. As it is, they'll have limits because of everyone there for Brandt's party."

"At least, we should have their plan so we can work around it."

"What makes you so certain you have to collar him tonight?"

Telling him about the most recent text would lead to the other texts. No way. "Let's just say I am and let it go at that."

Bostwick gave her the same look her other lieutenants had given her at points like these in her investigations. "I'll call the SRG."

She returned to her desk, where she'd been updating her map with the latest Triscari tower pings. He'd gone west on Joralemon, and that had been the last ping. It was the second time she'd tracked him out that way, the only leg of his movements he'd repeated.

She and Jake had walked that way once, going to dinner at Estuary One. He'd laughed when she'd corrected him for referring to the roadway along Joralemon as "cobblestone", because it was Belgian block.

He'd felt the need to show her something he knew about that she didn't. Something about a brownstone they'd passed along the way. She'd teased him about needing to have the last word.

She texted him. *Wasn't there a house on Joralemon that you pointed out to me? Something about it not being a house?*

***

"Hi, Joanna."

She greeted Justin Cates with a wry smile. "I assume this is not a coincidence."

"No, I've been waiting for you. If you and your crew will follow me, I'll take you right up. Where's the van?"

"On the sidewalk just off Jay Street. Why?"

"Good choice. Things might get hot out on Adams Street. Or hadn't you heard?"

"I've heard." She introduced Justin to Tony, the cameraman. "Is it true the SRG is being deployed?"

Cates appeared stunned. "How should I know?"

But she flashed a disarming grin. "Because you usually do."

He blushed. "Yeah, it's true. The scent of Prinz is in the air."

CHAPTER NINETY

Tuesday, June 5, 7:36 PM

A captain in a spotless uniform entered the Castle as Kim was reading Jake's response to her earlier text. Marshal Dhillon, working a double shift, directed him back to Bostwick's office. A moment later, Bostwick waved the team into the conference room. The captain was from the SRG.

"I understand you have an operation planned for the Marriott tonight," the captain said.

Bostwick responded. "Yes. We've been tracking a serial rapist and murderer. He's eluded us so far, but there's a good chance we'll be able to collar him tonight."

"Why tonight?"

Kim took over. "He targets adolescent girls. His last murder was Friday. He has been attacking with increasing frequency, and we have surveilled him lurking near schools. We believe another attack is imminent, and we want to prevent it."

"How do you plan to proceed?" the captain asked.

"We're still working on that. But if you can tell us how you'll be deploying around the hotel, we can craft our plan accordingly."

He glared at her. "That information is on an as-needed basis, Detective."

"And we have the need. It goes no further than this room."

He held the glare. "You'll forgive me for saying so, but that's not your reputation. You have friends in the media."

"One friend, to whom I have revealed nothing that could jeopardize an operation. And she's told me far more than I've told her. But, if it helps, I assure you I will not be speaking to her tonight."

"I can vouch for Detective Brady's integrity," Bob said.

"So can we all," Bostwick added. "We're asking as much out of concern for your people as ours. We don't want either operation to fail."

After a moment, the captain opened his briefcase and extracted a folded map. "Very well." He hung the map on two hooks suspended above the marker board with the details of their hunt for Triscari. The map showed downtown Brooklyn from Cadman Plaza East to Lawrence Street, and from Tillary to Livingston. The hotel was highlighted in yellow, with exits marked in red. "As you can see, this is a difficult location to secure. We are already deploying to seal off Adams and Jay Streets between Johnson Street and Willoughby Plaza."

"What about Brandt's event?"

"We will have four checkpoints through which people can enter or exit the perimeter."

She stared at the map. "So, once inside, a person is free to go anywhere within the perimeter?"

"Everywhere except the hotel. We'll have checkpoints at all three entrances—Adams Street, and the two side walkways."

She gestured to the sketch on the board. "Is there any way we can get this to your people at the checkpoints to hold him if he tries to leave?"

He handed her his card. "If you send a digital version to my e-mail address, I'll forward it to the operation commander and ask him to forward it to all units. But our people will be much more interested in anyone trying to get in than getting out."

"Can we at least have one of our guys at each inner checkpoint?" she asked.

"Sure. I'll inform the commander. But be prepared to show ID."

***

The senator poured a Wild Turkey, his favorite bourbon, neat, while his wife changed for the evening in the suite's bedroom. He offered it to his campaign manager, who declined. He sipped alone. "I don't understand. The exit polls showed the big issue is crime."

"True. But the media isn't saying which way. Our own polling suggests there are still lots of folks in the city who buy Dunn's rant about police being the bad guys."

"You're saying we should have embraced reform earlier in the campaign?"

His manager shrugged. "I never second-guess myself, and I never analyze an election strategy until the votes are in. I'm not worried, but it's going to be a long night."

***

After the SRG captain left, Bostwick kept them in the conference room. "Kim, if three of you are sticking to checkpoints, how the hell will you deal with Triscari if he slips out?"

"I'm working on it. But thanks for vouching for me."

"Don't mention it. You need to tell me your plan, even if you don't tell the SRG. What am I sending you guys into?"

"I've been fencing with Triscari via texting. He knows I'm Dan Brady's granddaughter, and he wants a confrontation with me."

"You mean," Bostwick said, "he wants to kill you."

"Yes. Just as he wanted to kill his cousin, Gina, and killed the doorman to her building when she'd gone. If you consider the tenor of his texts, he's reached the end of his cooling-off period, gone beyond it, and that's affecting his judgment." She nodded at Bob, Cord, and Tim. "He knows what you all look like. When he sees you at the checkpoints, he will find the one with the most activity and leave that way. Probably Adams Street, because that's the most difficult to secure. Bob, I want you there."

"Thanks a lot."

"I have two good reasons. One is that you have a sharp eye, even when the shit comes down hard. You're the most likely to spot him, and you can tell me where he's going. If I'm wrong and he tries one of the other exits, Tim and Cord have a decent shot at catching him."

Marshal Dhillon, doing a double shift once again, called to Bostwick. "Phone call for you, Lieutenant."

"And where will you be, Detective Brady?" Bob asked after Bostwick had gone.

She pointed to the map the captain had left behind. "At the south end of the courthouse building."

Bob closed the conference room door. "Why there?"

She glanced from face to face. From the beginning, she'd known she'd have to tell them at some point. Now, here they were. She pointed at the SRG map. "In his wanderings around the neighborhood, he's only repeated one stretch—west on Joralemon to the river. The house at 58 Joralemon appears to be an ordinary brownstone until you look closely. The windows are blacked out. There are no basement apartment windows, just heavy black sheets of metal on the same angle as the front steps. And inside a low wrought-iron fence is a red sprinkler head for the Joralemon Street subway tunnel. It's not a house at all. It's a vent and an emergency exit for the line that runs nine stories below. At some point tonight, Triscari will run from the hotel, intending me to follow." She showed them the long exchange of texts.

Cord was the first to react. "You gone crazy?"

Bob pointed to the map. "And you plan to give chase?"

"Yes." She pointed at the map. "The shortest direct line from the hotel to the subway station is across the courthouse parking lot and past Borough Hall to the stairway. He'll go down to the tracks. The longest gap between trains is just around midnight, so he'll look to make his break shortly before."

Cord was dumbfounded. "You plan to chase him down to the tracks? What then?"

"He'll run along the westbound line until he reaches the emergency exit, then he'll climb part way up and wait for me. He thinks he's going to ambush me the way he did my grandfather."

"And if you follow him with no backup," Bob said, "he'll succeed." He turned to Cord. "You and I will switch posts tonight. I want you at the Adams Street exit. Once Kim gives chase, you're to follow as quickly as possible."

"Got it," Cord said.

It wasn't how she'd planned it, but she had to admit it made sense.

"Kim," Bob continued, "as soon as you spot Triscari going the direction you expect, you alert Cord. Cord will send me a pre-written text and I'll call for backup on Joralemon."

CHAPTER NINETY-ONE

Tuesday, June 5, 9:29 PM

"Joanna Dunbar here at Brandt campaign at the Marriott in Downtown Brooklyn. As you can see, there's a good crowd here and they've been having a good time, but with polls now having closed, all eyes are on the big board waiting for the numbers to come in. With me is one of the senator's team leaders. How do you feel about how things are going?"

"We're totally optimistic. My people got lots of positive feedback today, and our get-out-the-vote campaign was a gigantic success."

"That was your team's job, wasn't it?"

"Sure was. Before that, we did phone banking."

"When do you expect to have the result?"

"Probably not for a while. This is a diverse city, and huge. You don't fully appreciate just how big it is until you work on something like this."

"Thank you. This is Joanna Dunbar for the Independent Television Network."

***

Perfect. They wouldn't proclaim a winner for a long time. Whatever those kids had planned probably wouldn't occur until the party got rolling. Unless Brandt lost, which could still happen. But either way, events just might play into his hands.

Time for a text. *I'll bet you're getting impatient. They always do.*

He'd never baited a target like this. But then, he'd never picked a target like this. With luck, she'd give up where Gina was hiding before she got the full measure of what she had coming.

***

His campaign manager poured a cup of coffee from the pot just delivered. "First returns from Manhattan. Upper west side."

Senator Brandt snorted. "The People's Republic."

"Pretty much. Eighty percent for Dunn. That's a little better than I expected. So, we'll count that as good news."

"You going to post it on the big board?"

"In the old days, I wouldn't. Wouldn't want to discourage the troops. But they'll see it on the local news shows."

***

When Kim got the text from Triscari, she checked with Vera, still working from her cubicle at One Police Plaza. A couple of minutes later, she got Vera's response. *He's in the hotel or immediately outside.*

She texted the info to her three colleagues. All three checked back. SRG was tolerant of their presence, if not enthusiastic.

***

"We've just passed the ten o'clock mark, and results are coming in more heavily, now. With ten percent of all precincts reporting, Senator Brandt now has a slight lead with 50.2% of the votes. Our Joanna Dunbar is standing by at Brandt headquarters."

"As you can see, the mood here has picked up in the past half hour. Especially encouraging has been news from some areas of Brooklyn that pollsters had expected to go for Sabrina Dunn but who voted for Senator Brandt, instead. No one is calling the election, yet, because there are still too many 'swing' districts yet to report. And turnout in all districts has been higher than expected. Joanna Dunbar, ITN."

***

Kim was about to prod Triscari with another text when she got one from Bob. *Protestors pushing back SRG on Jay Street. Could get rough.*

***

"What the hell's going on, now?" Senator Brandt asked his campaign manager.

"A few demonstrators broke through the barricades on Jay Street. They'll be dealt with."

CHAPTER NINETY-TWO

Tuesday, June 5, 11:27 PM

"With eighty-two percent of precincts reporting, we at ITN are now calling the special mayoral election for State Senator Raymond Brandt, who now leads Sabrina Dunn by a margin of fifty-five percent to forty-five percent. Our Joanna Dunbar is at Brandt headquarters. Joanna, how's the mood, there?"

"What? Are we live? Oh. Thank you. The atmosphere here is electric as the news has already spread that two networks have called this election for Raymond Brandt. The band is playing, and everyone is dancing and enjoying themselves. I have the senator's campaign manager here. Sir, how did the results compare with your expectations coming into this morning?"

"We wanted a victory, and we got one. With only eighteen percent of precincts still to be counted, it's not possible for the acting mayor to reverse this result. The people of New York City have spoken."

***

It wouldn't be long, now. He slipped the Baretta into the pouch of his hoodie—another psychological weapon against his opponent. She'd be sure to think he'd discarded them. And the metal detectors the cops had set up at each entrance wouldn't scan those leaving, only those entering.

He rechecked the text he'd gotten over an hour ago from the bitch detective. *Coward.*

Is that so? We'll just see about that.

He made one last check around the room. He'd accumulated a few more items of clothing than he'd have preferred, but if he never saw them again, that would be fine. After tonight, he'd be leaving town, anyway.

The elevator going down was empty. No surprise. The bulk of traffic now would be between the lobby and the ballroom.

As it passed the ballroom floor, he wrinkled his nose. Was that smoke?

If so, it was another stroke of luck.

He was halfway to the front door in the lobby when the fire alarm sounded. Yes, that was smoke. Oh, those naughty boys.

He walked toward the door but stopped a few feet inside. Not long to wait, now.

***

Joanna pulled back from the security guard grabbing her arm. "What... Wait. I'm sorry, there's an alarm going off and... what? I can't, I'm in the middle of a live... just a moment. There is a smoke condition here, and they're telling us to evac..."

CHAPTER NINETY-THREE

Tuesday, June 5, 11:43 PM

The wail of sirens broke Kim's concentration. Fire engine sirens.

Multiples. And getting closer. If their objective was the hotel, that would remove at least one checkpoint.

Oh, shit.

Two engines approached on Adams Street from the north, while reflections from flashing red lights bounced off the hotel from Jay Street. The first group had to be from the firehouse on Middagh Street, while the second had to be from Tillary.

More sirens from behind her.

Shouts from further up Adams.

Her cell rang. "Cord, what the fuck happened?"

"An alarm in the hotel. SRG opened the checkpoints to let the fire engines through and..."

A lone figure darted down Adams across the street wearing a hoodie.

That fucking bastard.

"I see him. Go!"

She shoved the cell into her hip pocket and took off after Triscari all in one motion. He hurdled the low fence and cut through the parking lot next to the courthouse. He had a twenty- or thirty-yard lead. Moving quickly for an older guy.

He turned to look.

Never look, motherfucker. Shocked to see me so close behind?

He picked up a little more speed. This would not be easy. But it helped that she knew where he was going and why.

***

He reached the subway steps leading down to the Borough Hall Station. Empty. Excellent. She was closer than he'd expected. It would burnish his legend.

As he reached the platform, a Four train had just pulled out. Right on time. He now had seventeen minutes. They'd both have to go slow in the tunnel.

No one on the platform. The cameras had caught him on the way in, but regardless of how this played out, it wouldn't matter after tonight.

***

"Don't tell me I can't go out there, especially if there's a fire in here," Joanna yelled at the burley cop in riot gear holding her back. A group of firefighters rushed past her.

"The smoke condition is upstairs," the manager on duty said. "You're quite safe here in the lobby."

"There's a riot outside, lady," the cop said. "Just take it easy."

She stared out the glass door. The so-called rioters were standing in befuddled groups, staring at the activity that had overtaken them all. "I don't see any riot, officer. I see a bunch of confused kids."

She could see some signs they'd brought.

"Heil Brandt."

"NY lost to fascism."

"Police brutality—the new normal."

"Dear Mom, if I don't come home tonight, I'm in jail."

"Abolish police."

"Seize the means of production."

"Tell you what," she said to the cop. "Let me go out there, and if they kill me, my family won't sue the department."

"I'd let her go if I were you." Justin Cates. Now, there was help from an unexpected source.

CHAPTER NINETY-FOUR

Tuesday, June 5, 11:54 PM

Kim caught sight of him just as he disappeared down onto the tracks at the end of the platform.

The glare of the lights had hurt when she entered the station, so the dark of the tunnel was a relief. The electronic sign that signaled the next train showed nothing for another fifteen minutes. It was three tenths of a mile to the emergency exit leading upstairs to 58 Joralemon Street.

Where he planned to ambush her.

Three tenths in fifteen minutes. Fifteen hundred, eighty-four feet. Even with the need to go carefully, she could make that.

Footsteps echoed from the concrete path in the tunnel. He was ahead of her, but she couldn't gauge how far. The bright green of the first signal light shone like a beacon.

Jake had told her subway signals were approximately a thousand feet apart. She passed the green signal light. Two thirds there.

Up ahead, she caught a brief glint of light. Triscari's head. His lead was now about fifteen yards.

***

326

Breathing was harder than he'd expected. He should have been working out, doing some aerobic work. He'd considered using the hotel's fitness center but decided against it for fear of being recognized.

There it was, just ahead, well-lit on both sides—Emergency Exit.

He hesitated for a moment as a rat scurried away.

Climbed a ladder leading to the stairs.

It was nine stories up to the street, and he was already breathing hard. But he didn't need to climb all nine. Just enough to find a good vantage point from which to shoot.

CHAPTER NINETY-FIVE

Wednesday, June 6, 12:03 AM

For a moment, the lights at the exit lit him up like a Christmas display on a front lawn. When he hesitated, she reached for her piece but thought better of it.

His lead had shrunk further since her momentary glimpse on the track. You're getting too old for this, aren't you, Triscari?

She pulled herself up to the stairs and stopped to listen. Footsteps echoed in the tunnel behind her. Cord. No telling how far behind her he was.

Now, the game grew tricky. If she climbed the stairway without caution, he might have her sighted and shoot.

She strained to hear.

Steps on metal stairs.

Triscari couldn't climb and shoot at the same time.

She entered the stairwell as the sound of steps on metal stairs continued to echo.

***

He'd climbed three stories and was gasping. He had to rest.

Lying down on the landing, he pulled out the Baretta and drew a bead on the entrance to the stairwell below. He braced his arm on the lower part of the railing to lessen the shaking in his hand.

He should have been working out.

No sign of her.

***

The steps stopped as she reached the landing one story up. It was impossible to tell how far above her he was. But it couldn't be far because his panting echoed in the stairwell.

She could wait him out, and then Bob and the backup could come in from the street level.

But with a major demonstration and a fire in the hotel, backup would be scarce.

No sign of Cord, either. She hoped he was okay.

She was alone. Only one option. "You come here often, Paul?"

***

Shit. She was part way up the stairs. Not at the entrance. No chance at a clean shot.

Not yet.

He'd have to fence with her.

"Just as I planned." His voice was shaky. He took a deep breath to steady it. "Did you keep your promise? Skirt and saddle shoes?"

No response.

"At a loss for words already?"

"Gee," she called, "you sound a little shaky. I guess the exertion is too much for you."

"I'm just fine, thank you."

A laugh. "You don't sound fine. More like things are spinning out of control and you can't get a grip."

"I've got a grip on you, Detective."

***

She waited. Let him think he's stumped her.

"Detective?"

He was growing impatient. Good. Time to take it up a notch.

"If you expected me to play Angelina for you…"

"Shut up." His scream was so loud the echoes might have reached Joralemon Street.

"Isn't that what you wanted? Isn't that what you always want? To re-enact raping and killing your cousin Angelina?"

"Listen, you bitch, you don't mention her name."

"Stop me."

"What?"

"You heard me. Come out and stop me, old man."

A pause. "What am I, stupid? I'll just step out so you can shoot me?"

"You're not stupid. You're a coward, just as you were a coward at seventeen, afraid to kiss any girl but your cousin, and you're a coward now."

"I'm warning you…"

"Did they laugh at you? Your classmates?"

"Shut the fuck up!"

"Ha. Come on, then. Stop me. You're afraid I'll shoot you? Here." She pulled her Glock, put the safety on, and tossed it to the landing a half flight below. The clattering of it hitting the metal echoed and faded away. "Now, show me your courage. Toss yours away."

She waited. Nothing.

"Just as I expected. A coward."

CHAPTER NINETY-SIX

Wednesday, June 6, 12:08 AM
Now, he had her. He started down the steps. Halfway to the landing, he caught his first glimpse of her and fired.

Sparks flew as the slug hit metal and ricocheted off several surfaces.

He froze.

***

It seemed unlikely that he was still using the same pistol half a century after he killed Granddad. But perhaps she could goad him enough to find out. "I was wrong about you. You are stupid. Grotesquely stupid."

He laughed. "Yeah? Then how is it I'm the one with the gun?"

The Chief's Special remained nestled against her lower back, but he didn't need to know that. "Because a fired bullet travels either until it's buried in something or until it loses all kinetic energy. With the concrete walls in here and the steel staircase, a fired bullet will ricochet off everything it hits. You have a better chance of shooting yourself in here than shooting me."

Silence.

"So, that makes you a grotesquely stupid coward." She shifted position and stuck out her leg for the briefest moment.

He fired.

She pressed her back against the steel steps until the chorus of ricochets faded away.

"Two misses, genius. That leaves six rounds."

A pause. "What makes you say that?"

"You killed my grandfather with a Baretta M1935, which holds eight rounds. You're a traditional guy, so it makes sense you still have the same weapon."

Silence.

"That's not the only ammunition that's running low, is it?"

No response.

"And that's what's got you worried, now."

Still nothing.

"Cat got your tongue?"

"Shut your mouth."

"Ooh, that was mean. It must really bug you. Most guys freak out when it goes limp."

"Cut the shit." Louder this time.

"I've seen all the coroners' reports, including the results of the rape kit for each victim. You've been trending down."

She let it sink in.

"Down, as opposed to up, if you get my drift. You left less of a deposit with Martha Perez than you did with Lourdes Ramirez. And much less with sweet little Lily Ng. I mean hardly any."

"Shut the fuck up." It was a scream.

Followed by another shot.

CHAPTER NINETY-SEVEN

Wednesday, June 6, 12:10 AM

The slug ricocheted off the step pressing against her back, a jolt that took her breath away for a moment.

No backup yet. Perhaps there wouldn't be.

Cord should have been here by now.

She pulled the Chief's Special.

"That's three. Five left. But the ultimate was Erica Caruso, the girl at Jones Beach. Guess what the coroner found when he examined her. Go on, tell me. What did he find?"

"How the fuck should I know?"

"She was a virgin. Her hymen was intact. You weren't even able to…"

Clattering on the steps.

He thinks he's coming to finish me.

CHAPTER NINETY-EIGHT

Wednesday, June 6, 12:11 AM

She backed up on the landing in a two-handed stance, waiting for him.

He glimpsed her, stopped, and charged back up the steps.

She took off after him, careful not to give him a clear line of fire.

As he rounded the steps at the third story landing, he fired a wild shot. It hit the wall and ricocheted down toward the bottom of the stairwell. She resumed the chase. "Four rounds left."

Fourth story landing.

Then the fifth. His pace was slowing. She slowed to stay sheltered. "You couldn't get it up. That's why you beat Erica so badly."

Another shot. Another series of clatters down the stairwell.

"Three rounds left. No way out, Triscari."

"Fuck... you."

He resumed his climb. Sixth story landing. His steps were agonizingly slow.

"It's over, Triscari. Give it up." She rounded the turn on the landing and ducked back as he fired. "Two rounds."

He tried to fire again, but the Baretta slipped out of his hands. He rushed down the steps to retrieve it.

She slipped the Chief's Special back into her waistband.

The Baretta was resting one step from the bottom.

She rounded the steps a second time, grabbing him as he reached for the weapon.

She pulled him down, slamming his head against the steel banister support. He lunged at her, arms outstretched, reaching for her throat. As they grappled with one another, she caught him off-balance and shoved him with all her strength against the railing. He flipped over the side, hurtling to the bottom.

Six stories.

"That's for Dan Brady."

CHAPTER NINETY-NINE

Wednesday, June 6, 12:16 AM

"Kim, you okay?"

Cord. Calling up from the bottom of the stairwell. "I'm okay. Triscari's dead."

"Yeah. He landed a few feet from me."

No sound of steps on the stairs. "You coming up?"

"Can't. Lost my footing running along the tracks. Sprained my fucking ankle. If there's an ambulance outside when you get there, please send some paramedics down."

"Sure." With the adrenaline rush dissipated, she had to drag herself to the top. Nine stories down, a train rumbled by.

It took all her strength to open the heavy steel door onto Joralemon Street.

Flashing red and blue lights momentarily blinded her.

Bob and Tim rushed to her. Behind them, an ambulance crew, an Emergency Services Unit van, and several patrol cars.

Bob spoke first, grinning at her. "You look like shit." Then the grin vanished. "Where's Cord?"

"Bottom of the stairwell. Hurt his ankle in the tunnel. Triscari's down there, too."

"Dead?"

She nodded. "My Glock is down there somewhere, as well as his Baretta."

A team of paramedics rushed down the stairs.

Bostwick appeared. "You okay, Kim?"

"I'll live. He was a lousy shot." She handed over her Chief's Special.

Bostwick handled it with care. "This isn't standard department issue."

"It was in 1950, when my grandfather acquired it. I'm surrendering it to you because Internal Affairs will investigate this incident. The crime lab will find that no shot was fired from it or the Glock, and the only slugs in the stairwell are from the Baretta."

"No one suspects you of any wrongdoing," Bostwick said.

"A man died while being pursued by a Member of Service. IAB is duty-bound to investigate. I will co-operate in full."

"That's fine, Kim," Bostwick said. "Let's let the paramedics have a look at you."

"I'm okay."

The lieutenant laughed. "No, not even close."

***

Jake was waiting up when Kim got back to the apartment around two in the morning. The paramedics had found nothing more serious than a few bruises and abrasions, and one cut in her scalp, most likely from a bullet fragment from a ricochet. But they couldn't see what was inside.

She was certain Jake could see it as he held her. To her relief, the only thing he said was, "Brandt won, and the fire trucks rushing in broke up the riot before it could get started."

She couldn't focus. "I need a shower."

Time faded as hot water cascaded over her, washing away the sweat, the filth of the subway tunnel and the grime of the stairwell. It eased the grip of her vengeance, leaving only a quiet satisfaction. She texted Cousin Jim before she slipped into bed. *Granddad's killer is dead.*

Jake was still awake, and he pulled her close. "I love you."

"I love you, too."

When Internal Affairs interviewed her, she would recite the facts of everything that had occurred in the chase and inside the stairwell. They would also have all the physical evidence. IAB would clear her of any wrongdoing. She hoped Bostwick wouldn't put her in for a medal, but if he did, she'd accept it with good grace.

Tomorrow, she'd tell Jake everything. But for now, "This case has left me utterly exhausted. I'm taking extended leave after IAB clears me. I need time with you, uninterrupted. If you can get away from work, perhaps we can go back to St Thomas or maybe Bermuda. We can just be us, no outside pressures, and talk—really talk—about the future."

ACKNOWLEDGEMENTS

In June 2018, I attended the Algonkian Pitch Conference in New York, hoping to catch interest for the first Kim Brady novel, *Past Grief*. I was at lunch one afternoon with some of the other writers, and Kim Brady's backstory fascinated them. When I mentioned I wanted a future book to introduce Kim's grandfather, one member of the group, Dr. Denise Howard, said, "Maybe Kim could catch a cold case her grandfather couldn't solve." I agreed that was a great idea. The only problem was that I had already painted myself into a corner by setting Dan Brady's death a quarter century before Kim was born.

And then I researched the oldest cold case solved using DNA evidence: 55 years. Problem solved.

I was about halfway through the manuscript of *Proving a Villain* when an old friend of mine thanked me for naming my protagonist after him. His name is Jim Brady. I didn't tell him I hadn't named her for him. And when he suggested, as a joke, that Kim should have a middle-aged cousin named Jim who still played goalie in a Gentlemen's Hockey League, as Jim had, I took him up on it. Anyone who would like to have their name considered as a character in a future novel of mine can e-mail me at EJL.author@gmail.com. Please include if you would prefer to be a good or evil character.

As always, I thank my intrepid beta readers, Jan Foley, Ray Lodato, and Sydney Young, who continue to review my work with a sharp eye. I also thank Kim Howe, Elena Taylor, AJ McCarthy, Debbie Babitt, Sandy Manning and Nola Nash for their support. Thanks also to the

International Thriller Writers and Mystery Writers of America, both of which do great work supporting new writers.

None of the Kim Brady novels would have seen the light of day without the support of the crew at Black Rose Writing. Reagan Rothe's team, with David King in Production (including cover design), Justin Weeks in Sales, Chris Martin in Publicity, and Minna Rothe in marketing, are first class.

Most of all, I thank Cindy Leahy, my wife of 46 years, beta-reader, critic, researcher, devotee of true crime stories, fellow fan of baseball, hockey, basketball, soccer, and opera, and rabid Uno (card game) player. Life with her has been and continues to be an adventure.

ABOUT THE AUTHOR

Edward J. Leahy is the author of the *Kim Brady Detective Mystery* series. He was a finalist for the 2018 Freddie Award for Excellence. He is a member of the Mystery Writers of America and the International Thriller Writers and has been published by New York Teacher Magazine. He's a retired International Issue Specialist for the IRS with investigative experience and holds a B.A. and M.A. from St. John's University in Government & Politics. He serves on the Board of Directors of AHRC-NYC. Born and raised in the New York City Borough of Queens, he lives in Jackson Heights with his wife, Cindy.

NOTE FROM THE AUTHOR

Word-of-mouth is crucial for any author to succeed. If you enjoyed *Proving a Villain*, please leave a review online—anywhere you are able. Even if it's just a sentence or two. It would make all the difference and would be very much appreciated.

Thanks!
Edward J. Leahy

We hope you enjoyed reading this title from:

www.blackrosewriting.com

Subscribe to our mailing list – *The Rosevine* – and receive **FREE** books, daily deals, and stay current with news about upcoming releases and our hottest authors.
Scan the QR code below to sign up.

Already a subscriber? Please accept a sincere thank you for being a fan of Black Rose Writing authors.

View other Black Rose Writing titles at
www.blackrosewriting.com/books and use promo code
PRINT to receive a **20% discount** when purchasing.

www.ingramcontent.com/pod-product-compliance
Lightning Source LLC
Chambersburg PA
CBHW010727100726
47899CB00009B/2953